HOTEL MEGALODON

A DEEP SEA THRILLER

RICK CHESLER

Prologue

Fiji Islands

Five old men, natives to this island all, sat on a jungle-covered mountaintop overlooking a turquoise lagoon studded with coral formations. The dark blue Pacific lie beyond, powerful beyond measure, and deeper than most can comprehend. A white line of thundering surf demarcated the shallow lagoon from the great sea beyond. The men were intimately attuned to their natural surroundings, knew every bird responsible for the calls they heard, every insect buzzing about, every animal responsible for a set of tracks left behind. Even though it was daylight, a lit torch spewed scented smoke into the air.

They gathered around a large wooden bowl, intricately carved with tribal designs passed down for generations. Into this bowl they dipped coconut husks, and filled them with a muddy brown liquid called *kava*, a traditional South Pacific drink made from the roots of a plant known to have mild sedative properties. They drank in rounds, and before each round one man played a *lali* drum, a wooden percussive instrument made from a hollowed-out log. *Rap-rap-raprapraprap*...the rhythm began slowly, but soon increased in tempo until the men drank from their coconut husks, relaxing themselves with the earthen drink.

They did not usually venture so far from their village to conduct a kava ceremony, but today they met to discuss something of concern to the entire village. The tribal leader, a man with long, white dreadlocked hair, set his drinking cup down and stared down on the lagoon, where a floating armada of heavy machinery was visible even from this high vantage point. Barges with dredging equipment piled high with construction materials. Worse, the sounds of explosions occasionally rent the air as passages were blasted through the underwater coral reef to make way for the new

1

project. The villagers were grave-faced as they looked down upon the lagoon upon which they depended for much of their sustenance in the form of fishing, as had their fathers before them, and their grandfathers before them.

While much of Fiji had succumbed long ago to the international draw of tourism, their little island was far off the beaten path, far from the "mainland" as Fiji's main island of Viti Levu was known, even though it, too, was but another island in the South Pacific far from any continent. Now, it seemed that the modern world had caught up with them, and in most spectacular fashion, for under construction in the lagoon below was a luxury hotel. Not just any hotel, however, for this one even the villagers understood to be most special, even by Western standards.

It was to be an underwater hotel. Built on top of the living coral reef, it would be like an aquarium in reverse, where humans stayed in a clear plastic air bubble surrounded by water. The natives found it strange. You can see the reef any time you want to! Dive down and look at it, the village Chief always gives permission. But technically, the land fronting the lagoon was owned by the Fiji government, and they seized an opportunity to profit by offering a long-term lease to an Australian property developer.

Now, the cacophony of industrial scale activity was heard all day long as the builders carved out the reef and sculpted the land to their liking. The men looked at one another across the smoke from their torch. The tribal leader spoke first.

"It is bad for the sea."

The other four men nodded in agreement, but one had a response. "It brings work to our villagers and the neighboring villages."

"We cannot stop it," another said, staring down at the flurry of activity on the water.

The tribal leader nodded sagely. "We cannot stop it, but we must adapt our ways to it. We must respect the sea more than ever before."

Another of the tribe's elders spoke up. "The fishing has been different of late."

"Bad?" the drummer asked, taking up the *lali* sticks. It was time for another round.

The elder shrugged, along with a confused look. "Not bad, really. Just...*different*. What we used to catch here, we catch there. What we used to catch less of, we catch more of; what we used to catch more of, now we catch less. Fish I have not seen in many moons, now return. Fish we saw every day, now gone."

The men nodded, and the drummer brought the sticks to the drum. *Rap-rap-rapraprapraprap*...Again they dipped their coconut cups into the kava bowl, and drank. Very relaxed now, they allowed their thoughts to drift silently while they observed the goings-on far below. One of the men, a lifelong fisherman who supported the tribe with his catches, reminisced on the many outings he'd taken with his father in an outrigger canoe. After a spell, he felt like voicing his thoughts to the group.

"The balance may be upset," is how he summed up his thoughts. The others nodded, still sipping from their cups, aware that he referred to an ecological balance between sea and man. He then proceeded to tell a story about a particular fishing trip he had taken as a young boy.

He had seen it as a child, a living animal so disproportionately large, so enormous, that he would not have believed it had he not witnessed it with his very own eyes. He knew that scientists would never believe it without documentation. They would accuse him of telling spirit stories after drinking too much *kava*. Even some of the neighboring villagers seemed not to believe his account. But he had seen it, his father, too, bless his departed soul, and he spoke of it now. An animal that size likely lived a very long time. It could still be alive, he thought, down there somewhere, upset by the unnatural disturbances wrought by the foreigners tinkering with the reef.

"Should we warn the others?" one of them wanted know upon hearing the fisherman's tale.

The chief set down his cup, and looked at his peers in turn as he spoke. "There is good with this. There is bad. We take the good with the bad, and hope it is great enough. We need say nothing, but we pray. We pray every day."

Chapter 1

Six months later

Coco Keahi grinned at her distorted reflection in the mini-sub's acrylic dome. Her nose looked much broader and flatter than it really was, exaggerating her Polynesian ancestry. The curve of her long, flowing black hair was distorted as well. Of Hawaiian blood, that rare lineage had helped her to earn a full scholarship to the University of Hawaii to study marine biology. She had excelled in her studies, particularly in coursework having to do with coral reef ecology. Upon graduation, she did what most recent graduates do—look for a job. A poor market in Hawaii led her to pursue a family connection who had found employment in faraway Fiji, an island nation in the South Pacific a six hour flight away from her home island in the aloha state.

Something exciting was happening there, though, that made the distance seem trivial. A distant cousin working in Suva told her about an incredible new project being financed by an Australian property developer—an underwater hotel. As amazing as that sounded to Coco, at first she saw it as somewhere she'd like to go on vacation, not as a potential place to work. She was a marine biologist, not a maid or a bartender or something. At least she hoped so. She knew that before too long she'd have to take whatever kind of work she could get. But then her cousin had told her how they were hiring a staff marine biologist to give eco-tours to the hotel's guests and help design the interpretative signage peppered throughout the property that would explain the sea life.

She had looked into it as a long shot, might as well try that kind of thing. Every marine biologist along the entire Pacific Rim must want that job. After submitting the application online, she never thought she'd hear back. One day, though, she'd been surprised with a phone call requesting an interview. Before she knew it, she was flying to Fiji—one of the few places even more

4

exotic than Hawaii—all expenses paid. "Fiji is Hawaii fifty years ago!" she'd heard one of her aunties say.

Once there, before a panel of the hotel's stern-faced managers, Coco had been asked a series of questions that at first seemed liked they had nothing to do with the job. Situational questions like, "Can you tell us about a time when you were asked to do something you didn't want to do?" Or, "What would you do if you thought the work of a supervisor was not up to par?"

So on and so forth for over an hour, half a dozen people taking turns delivering the questions while the others took notes, and all the while she tried not to be distracted by the magnificent view through the floor-to-ceiling windows of the pristine, palm-studded lagoon outside. Later there were the questions she had expected and was more than prepared for—fish identification quizzes, name this type of coral, walk us through this underwater video of the reef, please, and narrate a virtual tour for us. What are some of the issues affecting manmade underwater structures over time?

She hadn't realized it at the time, but it was her responses to the first set of questions which had set her apart from her competition. Her psychological makeup was perfect for the job, which was important, because of the way in which she was to conduct eco-tours for the hotel's wealthy clientele: in a mini-sub. She was a certified SCUBA instructor already, sure, but when they told her upon offering her the job that her employment was contingent upon passing a submersible pilot training course, she'd been ecstatic.

She could picture her new business cards in her head: *Coco Keahi, Marine Biologist/ Submarine Pilot.* Wow! She had done it, she had landed her dream job at the tender age of twenty-three as the official marine biologist for the Triton Undersea Resort.

Now, as she refocused her eyes and looked through her reflection to the watery world outside her small craft, the view outside her dome window forced her to reign in her giddy thoughts. To her left was the newly constructed underwater hotel. A series of pod-like structures connected to a long central tube were situated a few feet above the lush and thriving coral reef. She knew by now that there were fifteen pods on each side of the tube. Inside each one was a luxury suite consisting of three rooms. Each suite had an acrylic viewing area, the material not unlike the dome her submersible was made from, that offered sweeping underwater views. Spaced only a few feet apart, the sides of the pods were the only sections built from opaque material in order to afford privacy to those in adjacent rooms.

Right now the suites were unoccupied, awaiting the grand opening of the resort scheduled for tomorrow. Coco was ready, but wanted to take the sub out to the far side of the lagoon to practice the drop-off view. She planned to take her passengers to the very edge of the lagoon where there was a cut in the circular atoll that lead directly into a deep submarine canyon. A narrow undersea trench, basically, that led into a miles-deep abyss. She wouldn't descend into it, of course. Her little sub wasn't rated for those kind of depths, and the average hotel guest would find it too frightening. It was dark down there, with not as much life to see compared to the vibrant colors of the lagoon's coral reef.

But she could take them right to the edge of the drop-off. Give them a look down into the real ocean for a few seconds, down into the yawning throat of the deep while she dispensed fun factoids about the deep sea being less explored than the moon, despite occupying the largest percentage of our planet of any habitat type, and stuff like that. Super-fun stuff for a marine biologist.

Coco banked the sub into a lazy turn until she headed away from the hotel across the reef, which occupied most of a shallow lagoon ringed by the coral atoll. Inside waters that were protected from the fury of the open ocean, the undersea complex sat at a depth of forty feet. This meant that during the day it was always well lit, the aquatic rooms flooded with seductive, cerulean light. Even at night, if the moon was full, its silver beams could be seen playing across the undersea garden from inside the suites. Coco was a little jealous that she didn't get to stay in one herself. She'd been inside them, of course, on a tour so that she would understand the experience for the guests, but the staff quarters were a much more simple set of bungalows, or *bures,* as they were known in Fiji, and on land, along with the rest of the support buildings for the underwater hotel.

She deftly navigated the craft beneath an overhang of branching corals, emerging on a flat, sandy patch which soon gave way to a rocky slope. She lined up the sub between the coral shelves on either side, and then hit the thruster button while moving the joystick to propel the craft forward and down.

She followed the slope down about ten feet until it gave way to an abrupt drop-off, the opening of the submarine canyon. Grains of sand spilled over into the tunnel-like gorge, a waterfall of sparkling flecks.

Right here...perfect!

She glanced over at the two empty seats next to her, which before long would be occupied by paying passengers. *So exciting!* This was the exact perfect spot from which to offer her "glimpse into the abyss," as she thought of it. She practiced the little spiel she would give, her voice echoing somewhat in the mostly empty sub cabin.

"Here we have a unique look into..." She paused, thought about her choice of words, and then continued while hovering the sub in place, poised above the canyon drop-off. "Here we can see down into the submarine canyon that leads straight into the deepest part of the ocean. Down there where it's thousands of feet deep, in the cold and perpetual darkness, exists a whole other world completely different from the coral reef on which our hotel sits..."

Yeah, that's pretty good! Just a little bit more, and that should do it for the canyon...

"Don't worry, we won't be going down there today! So just sit back, relax and—"

Suddenly the sand grains in front of her sub began to swirl up off the bottom as if set into motion by a tornado. *Sit back, relax and...*

At first Coco thought it was just some temporary upwelling, a current blasting up out of the deep to sweep through the canyon, and up onto the shallow reef. But as the seconds went on, the swirling sand intensified until it actually clouded the water, making it difficult for Coco to see outside the sub. *What's happening?*

She wasn't sure, but when she heard—and felt—the side of the sub bump against the coral shelf on her right side, she knew it was time to go. *Not so far down the slope next time!*

For this time, though, it was too late. She was at the edge of the sandy slope that dropped off into the canyon proper, spinning in place in the powerful current. To get back up onto the reef she'd have to break out of the spin, and get control of her machine. She tilted the joystick to the left and held it there, applying the left thruster only to counteract the rotation.

It worked. The sub shot off the slope out into the water above the canyon, the reef just behind her, the canyon dropping away beneath her. She looked around, taking her bearings, and then arced the submersible up and to the right, slanting up toward the reef. She decided not to try and channel back through the slot with all the turbulence there, but instead to rise in open water until she was above the level of the reef, and then shoot straight across until she was back over it.

Then she saw it. Down below, out of the corner of her vision. Her sub's dome was clear on the bottom as well, to allow 360-degree visibility. Looking between her feet, she gazed into the dark waters of the submarine canyon.

She could swear something just passed beneath her. But there was nothing there. Odd, she thought, still peering into the gloom, *the last time I came to the edge here, when I got the idea to add the Glimpse Into the Abyss as a stop, I thought I saw something, too. That shadowy shape...now here it is again?*

A sense came over her, something that made her quickly crane her neck to look up.

This time what she saw was not just a shadow. It was very real. Whatever it was, it was so large she couldn't really put it in perspective, but it was big, and moving fast—right at her sub. Even as she fought to control the sub, her mind tried to provide an explanation for what something so massive could be. Not a shark. There were plenty of reef sharks around here, sure. Blacktips and the like, but whatever this thing was, it was way larger than her sub, and none of those sharks were anywhere near that size.

A whale? She supposed it was possible that a rogue Humpback had ventured too close to the reef chasing a school of baitfish. Or maybe...a chunk of the reef itself separated from the shelf and fell away? She didn't think seismic events were common in this part of the world. In fact, geological stability of this very reef formation was listed as one of the selling points for the hotel out of all the places in the world they could have gone—Dubai, various Caribbean spots...Hawaii was out precisely because of the volcanic instability.

Coco had just completed the turn to point the sub back toward the reef, when she saw it again, rolling into her sub. A wall of...*something*...something dark...slammed into the left side of the submersible. She only had a split second for it to register, but something shiny, black and round passed briefly in front of her field of vision.

Was that an eye?

She didn't know, and right now she didn't really have time to care. Her sub slammed hard into the right lip of the reef shelf—a solid wall of coral. The impact jolted her in her bucket seat, accompanied by a loud *thud* that was followed by a sickening screech as the sub's starboard thruster assembly—a propeller in a circular caged mount—was dragged across the coral.

Then she saw something inexplicable. The gigantic thing slid down over the front of the viewing dome. Coco was distracted by the flashing array of instrument lights and braying systems alarms that indicated problems with the submersible, but she saw something white. Triangular. She heard a *nick* as whatever it was impacted the acrylic surface, and then, just like that, it was gone.

Shaken, she activated the controls she knew would put the submersible into reverse. Instead of moving straight back, though, as the craft should have, she veered backwards to the right, bringing the sub's rear into contact with the coral wall yet again.

Damn!

She tried the full reverse maneuver again with the same results: the craft went backwards, but to the right, into the wall. Coco cursed softly under her breath. This was not good. Not good at all. *Left thruster's toast.*

Then, for the first time since she began piloting subs, which wasn't all that long ago, she felt the sensation of fear. *What if I can't get this thing to the surface?* There was no way to simply open the dome hatch while at depth—the water pressure was too great. She did have a radio link to Topside operations in the hotel and on the island compound, but *Jesus*. She was supposed to start taking guests on rides in this thing *tomorrow*!

Something darker played on her fears as well. *What was that thing that caused this? What if it comes back for me?*

Coco forced herself to slow her breathing before attempting to maneuver the sub again. She looked back through the rear of the dome, but couldn't see anything in the suspended sand cloud. Activating the right thruster only, she brought the craft away from the coral wall and into open water. She looked over toward the reef, but it was too cloudy to make anything out. She eyed the dash-mounted compass. *West, good.* She knew the hotel lie in that direction.

With one thruster out, she had to propel the sub forward in a zigzag pattern, first left, then right, then left again. It worked, though, and before too long she was meandering through the familiar coral formations of the hotel's reef. She looked back through the dome over the seat backs, but saw nothing pursuing her. Then the outline of the sub's floating dock structure came into view, and she forgot about whatever she had seen, and focused on maneuvering her craft. Docking the sub with only one thruster would not be easy. She took it slow, guiding the vehicle through the underwater gate that indicated she would surface in the middle of the floating dock.

She raised the sub vertically until water sheeted off the top of the dome, and brilliant sunlight flooded the cabin. As usual, Mick Wright's grinning face was there to greet her, framed by a head of shaggy hair as he secured the sub in place with ropes, unlatched the dome hatch, and flipped it back. Coco breathed in the fresh air she always found so refreshing after the stale, dry, recycled air of the sub.

"Hey, what happened? Left thruster's bent to Hell! Big ding on the body, too!"

Coco climbed out of the sub and gave him a sheepish grin. She started to respond but Mick held a hand up.

"Save it. Here comes the big cheese. You're going to have to explain it him, anyway."

Coco cringed as she looked over to see a man striding purposefully out along the pier. He wasn't just their boss. He was everyone's boss, the owner of Triton Undersea Resort, L.L.C.

"Wonderful. How long you think this will take to fix?"

Mick looked at the ruined thruster and shook his head. "Not by tomorrow."

The hotel's owner walked up to his two employees, beaming.

"So how are we looking for tomorrow?"

Chapter 2

Coco Keahi smiled at James White, the Australian property developer who had designed the Triton Undersea Resort and had it built. The big cheese, as Mick called him. No reason not to be polite. She had considered not mentioning the damage to the sub unless Mr. White called attention to it, but Mick's estimate of time to repair had put an end to that little fantasy. Guests would be arriving tomorrow, the sub would not be in operational condition, and it was her fault. *Great. Gonna lose my job already.*

James White's hair was gray, but whenever he was outside, he kept it covered by a wide-brimmed white hat. He wore a casual Tommy Bahama outfit of shorts, sandals, and a button-down aloha-style shirt that featured the hotel's logo: TUR, with the "T" in the shape of a trident. He removed his designer sunglasses to address Coco, a sign he wanted to be taken seriously.

"Coco? Tomorrow? Are we ready? Need I remind you that a good chunk of Hollywood's A-list is flying in as we speak, not to mention heads of state, sports stars, sports team owners...people we need to impress? How are we doing?" He glanced down at the sub, and his expression brightened. "They're going to *love* going for rides in this thing!"

She'd been glancing over at the sub, and then Mick, to see if he might have any last-minute respite for her, like *Oh, got a small thruster problem, but no worries, mate, it'll be fixed in a jiffy, couple hours tops.* But Mick only shrugged a little as he returned her stare.

Coco cleared her throat while Mick pretended to be busy tethering the sub to the dock cleats. "*I'm* ready, Mr., White, but unfortunately, the submersible requires repairs to one of the thrusters. Mick tells me—"

White's expression darkened. "What? Can't that wait? This is not the time to be performing maintenance. We need our best foot forward starting tomorrow!"

Coco took a deep breath. "I realize that, Mr. White, but unfortunately, this is not routine maintenance, it's a serious repair that Mick estimates will take..." She turned her head in his direction as she trailed off.

"I think I can have it working tip-top by this time tomorrow." His voice and demeanor didn't exactly exude confidence.

White's face reddened. "This time tomorrow!"

He glanced at his Rolex, and then scowled at Coco. "We are supposed to be *fully operational* starting tomorrow morning! That includes all of our vehicles, especially the submarine, of which we only have one. What the hell happened?"

Coco relayed to him the events of her dive. As she spoke, White's face became even redder, his eyes narrowing. "Sounds like pilot error to me. So this is your fault!"

Coco was taken aback at such a direct accusation from someone whom she had known only a short period of time. *But it's true, isn't it?* Still...

"Like I said, sir, there was something down there that interfered with the sub."

"What, the bottom of the reef? I guess so! Smash up the thruster, did you?" He eyed the damaged propeller assembly. Then he added, "You were up late at the staff party last night, weren't you? Have a little too much to drink?"

"No, sir. I did not hit the bottom of the reef, and I didn't have too much to drink last night." The sound of her voice came out sharper than she had intended. White glared at her while she continued.

"I *saw* something, something that hit the sub."

For a moment there was only the sound of sea birds cawing and faraway voices as White and Mick looked at the sub pilot.

"Saw what?" their boss asked.

The image of the...*eye—was that really what it was?*—flashed inside her skull. "I—I'm not sure."

"Oh, Christ!" Clearly White was unsympathetic.

"No, really, I...I saw something big, moving."

13

"Well, you're the marine biologist. What the hell was it?"

There was an awkward hesitation during which White crossed his arms.

"I'm not sure."

"What do you mean, you're not sure?"

Coco blocked out the stares of the two men on her, and closed her eyes while she replayed a mental image of her sub dive. The black orb...the massive slab of a body...the speed and agility...Suddenly her memories were replaced with an image from years ago, during her studies. A biology textbook showing illustrations of extinct sea creatures. A prehistoric shark. Of course, that's not what she had seen. But then she eyed the nick on the sub's dome left by the thing's...*tooth?* She didn't want to call attention to any more damage on the sub, but she felt like she'd rather be believed than dismissed as an incompetent pilot.

"I'm not sure exactly what kind of shark it was, sir. But I do think it was a shark." *Maybe he'll just believe me, and I won't have to show him the dome damage.*

"What kind of damage can these little reef sharks we have here do to that three-ton submarine?" He glanced at the underwater craft. Coco moved closer to it.

"Here, let me show you." She stepped onto one of the sub's pontoons, and knelt in front of the dome bubble. White appeared irritated, checking his cell phone while he glanced up at her, but he remained standing on the dock. She traced her finger along the smooth acrylic surface until she found the indentation created by the impact during her encounter.

"Here, take a close look at this."

White frowned, but stepped onto the bobbing craft and knelt beside Coco, squinting at the clear dome, while Mick looked on from the dock. A triangular dent marred the otherwise smooth surface.

"Oh, come *on!*" White bellowed. "Smack dab in the middle of the viewing area! The whole dome will have to be replaced—but not until after opening weekend," he added, shooting Mick a stern glance. He nodded in return.

"Look." Coco placed a manicured fingernail next to the gouge. "See that bit of white in it?"

Her boss craned his neck in for a closer look. "What of it?"

"It's a tooth fragment."

"The hell it is!"

"Seriously."

White looked over at Mick. "So a little reef shark had enough force to bury that fragment in a quarter inch of acrylic? Really?" He guffawed as if expecting Mick to do the same. The marine mechanic gave a smile, but remained silent.

"That's only a small piece of the tooth, sir." Coco dug a fingernail into the crevice and extracted the bone-white chip. "See, just the very tip."

White leaned in to examine the extracted object, and then quickly withdrew. "That's ridiculous. If that's only the very tip then the tooth would be like six inches long. You take me for some kind of fool?"

Coco blushed with the acerbity of his retort. "Not at all, sir. I'm just—"

"I'll tell you what you're just doing," White cut her off. "You're just making damn sure that something like this never happens again with my sub, or you're fired. You got that?"

"Yes, sir."

"I'm docking your pay every day this sub isn't in service. And you—"he pointed a finger at Mick. "You had better have this thing fully operational by tomorrow. If you need to pay to have parts same-day air freighted in here, then do it. Hear me?"

"Loud and clear, sir. Don't worry, I'll patch her up."

White chuckled to himself as he huffed off down the dock. "Don't worry, right. Whole damn world's going to be watching this place starting tomorrow, but don't worry." He raised his voice as he stepped off the dock onto the beach, turned around, and called out, "You better worry! That's what I'm paying you to do!" Then he strode toward the complex of support buildings.

Coco exhaled a heavy sigh. "That went well."

Mick smiled. "Sorry I couldn't back you up more, but really, I have no idea how I'm going to fix this up by the end of the day tomorrow, much less by the morning." He eyed the sub dubiously. "I better go see about ordering those parts. See you tonight for dinner?"

"Yeah, sounds good," Coco said absent-mindedly while Mick trotted off the dock toward the office buildings.

She stood there turning over the small tooth tip in her fingers, her mind once again recalling the pages of that textbook and the drawing of the extinct shark, the name of which slowly surfaced in her mind as if rising from the deep like the beast itself, rising through the vast sea of geological time, great eras of time so vast they were incomprehensible to any human. The letters took shape in her consciousness, washing a chill across her body like water pushed ahead of something very large...

Carcharadon megalodon.

Coco pressed her pointer finger into the tooth to test the sharpness, and a small bead of blood appeared on the pad of her fingertip.

Chapter 3

James White gritted his teeth as he strode down the palm-studded footpath that wound along his resort's powdery white beach. The translucent pods of the underwater hotel beckoned beneath the surface of the calm lagoon. The tranquil scene did little to calm his nerves, however, as he stared out at what he had created. The most luxurious underwater hotel on the planet. Not merely a tank or habitat on the sea bottom that one had to scuba dive in and out of like some kind of inner space astronaut, but a full-scale hospitality operation with multiple suites and common areas including a lobby, gym, restaurant, even a night club, all accessible via submerged train tunnel without the guests ever feeling so much as a drop of water on their bodies.

For well over a decade, detractors had berated him as little more than a reckless dreamer, gambling other people's funds on his own personal pipedream. But tomorrow morning, in just a few hours, the first guests would arrive! The seemingly endless years of planning and red tape to see the project to completion were about to finally come to fruition. The nonstop rounds of pitch sessions to wealthy investors, all of whom were skeptical that White could really make such an outlandish architectural project work. Eventually he had convinced them all to invest staggering sums of money, the likes of which White himself would never have access to without them.

Now, it all came down to this grand opening weekend. If the list of high profile guests left raving about their new experience, White would be on the road to profitability, and to paying back his angel investors. His reputation as one of the world's premiere developers would be cemented.

To that end, everything should be ready. The grounds on the island were immaculate. Transport from the airport was arranged, the pier was ready for those arriving via mega-yacht, and the hotel itself was ready to go. All supplies fully stocked, staff prepped. Sure, the submersible was out of commission for a little while, but that was an extra perk, not the kind of thing most guests would want to avail themselves of the first thing upon arrival. They'd want to take in the sheer splendor of it all, the uniqueness. Nevertheless, something gnawed at his consciousness.

He began to stroll again as he considered it. He'd always done his best thinking while walking. At the end of the beach a winding footpath transitioned into a lush garden area that was meant to look like a wild rain forest but, of course it, was carefully manicured. He wound his way past breadfruit trees, ferns, and a colorful riot of flowering plants while Coco's words nagged at him.

I saw something big, moving.

He'd brushed her off, but what if she was right? A handcrafted wooden sign with arrows indicated the resort's Dolphin Lagoon was straight ahead, while the Main Lodge was off somewhere to the right. He continued straight. *Dolphins...* What was the problem there? Oh right, he thought, brushing a bird of paradise flower out of his face, one was missing. He'd asked them to inspect the lagoon gates and the fencing. Better stop in and check on that now. Swimming with the dolphins was a favorite guest activity, even more so than the submarine rides. He kept walking until he emerged on a calm, natural lagoon fronting a rocky section of coastline.

A lithe female trainer in a one-piece swimsuit with a whistle around her neck knelt on a floating dock. Before her, four dolphins were lined up, heads sticking out of the water like soldiers at attention. The trainer stood when she saw White approach. She gave the dolphins a hand signal, and instantly they dispersed, racing off into the lagoon for free play. James walked out on to the dock as the trainer brushed long stands of blond hair from her face.

"Good afternoon, Clarissa. Tomorrow's the big day! How're we doing?"

He could tell the smile she offered was forced. "The show is ready, and the dolphins we have are ready, but that's just it..."

"Still have one missing?"

"Calusa's still missing, but now so are two more—CJ and Max!"

White glanced over at the fencing on the lagoon's perimeter that kept other ocean creatures out. He knew it didn't really keep the dolphins in—they could jump over it if they really wanted, but their family was here, their easy meal ticket was here, so they stayed. In fact, during severe weather such as a cyclone, the plan was to let the dolphins out so that they wouldn't be trapped in the lagoon when the storm surge hit. Then, after the storm, they would swim back home. They'd always come back before.

"How long have they been gone?"

"Calusa going on three days now, CJ and Max, one day."

"Any guess as to why? Something happen?"

Clarissa shook her head, a look of embarrassment taking shape on her delicate features. It was her responsibility to know these dolphins. They were her charges, her *friends*, even. She felt terrible. "Not yet. My staff is aware of it, Tommy and Matt are out in the Zodiac looking for them right now."

"But what's causing it, Clarissa? We can't keep having the dolphins escaping. You know how those animal rights groups are, they'll say they don't like it here, they're meant to be out there..." He waved an arm out at the open ocean.

"I don't know, I..." She trailed off, gazing out at the sea.

"What is it?"

"I really have no idea why they left, but I did notice that all of the dolphins, not just those three, have been acting a little skittish lately. Oh..." Clarissa looked over at the far corner of the lagoon. "There was a rip in the fence over there, but the guys fixed it this afternoon."

"You think the missing ones took advantage of the opening, and decided to take a vacation?"

She appeared doubtful. "They can jump over any time they want."

White eyeballed his Rolex. "You can still put on the shows though, right, and do the swims with the animals you have?"

Clarissa twinged a bit at the use of the word "animals," as though her precious dolphins were nothing special. "I can, yes, but—"

"All I need to know!" He turned on a heel to walk away, but then spun back around as though suddenly remembering something. "Do me a favor, would you?" He continued without waiting for her response. "Make no mention of the missing animals to the guests. No public announcements during the shows about how many dolphins we usually have or anything like that, okay?" He raised his eyebrows for emphasis.

"Of course."

White left Clarissa on the docks and walked toward the building that housed his office. He moved slowly as he contemplated what he had just learned. Not just one dolphin escaped, but three. Not good, not good at all. And when coupled with Coco's sub incident...He stopped walking, gripped by a powerful thought that he tried to shake off without success.

What if she had been telling the truth, that she wasn't hung-over or stoned or whatever the hell it is the kids are into these days, and she really did meet up with a large shark down there? That would make the dolphins skittish, wouldn't it? He started walking again.

There was little he could do about any of it unless he was willing to delay the hotel's opening until the sub was fixed and the dolphins found, along with the reason for why they're so spooked in the first place. He was not willing to delay the launch, though. This place was open to the public tomorrow, and it better all go off without a hitch. It would be an international embarrassment of the highest magnitude should these well-heeled guests do anything but come away gushing about what an incredible and one-of-a-kind experience they'd just had. Anything less than that, including a last-minute cancellation due to facility issues, would not please his investors, and he could not afford to pay them back if the hotel didn't turn out to be profitable.

Coco and Mick would have to get their act together with the sub, and Clarissa would need to figure out those dolphins. He had more important things to do, like welcome the celebrity guests.

Chapter 4

The next morning

James White beamed as he stood, arms outstretched, on the veranda of a huge *bure* style lodge as an island taxi drove up carrying the hotel's first guests. There were two of them in this vehicle, travel weary after a long flight from the US mainland to Fiji's main island of Viti Levu and Nandi International Airport. From there they'd taken a chartered "puddle jumper" plane to White's private outer island resort haven, and the cab had delivered them here after a short ride from its small airport.

While a pair of native Fijian porters stepped up to carry the luggage, the driver opened the rear door, and a tall American man stepped out, one James recognized from a recent cover of Sports Illustrated magazine. John Rudd, star quarterback for the New England Patriots. And the shapely pair of legs pouring out of the car on the other side belonged to none other than his tabloid-hunted girlfriend, action sportswear model Staci Lincoln. She wore a Patriots ball cap over stylishly cropped blond hair, and oversized designer sunglasses. James walked down to greet them enthusiastically.

"Mr. Rudd, Ms. Lincoln: Welcome to the Triton Undersea Resort! You're our very first guests to arrive. Please, won't you come with me to our reception *bure* for a little refreshment before we take you down to your suite?"

The football player and his girlfriend headed up into the open-air, thatched roof structure where staff waited with drinks in cut coconuts, and a small musical ensemble played island music.

As soon as the couple had walked inside, another cab drove up and deposited six more guests. Saudi head of state, Abdullah bin Antoun, emerged from the vehicle first, followed by his wife. Both of them wore traditional Arabic robes and headgear. They smiled, and looked around slowly at their new surroundings, while their nanny wrangled their three young children from the cab. A bevy of porters descended on them and took their things. Again, James White was there to personally extend a hand.

So it went for the next hour or so, vehicles driving up, depositing well-heeled guests—an NBA franchise owner, an Internet company billionaire, a US senator, a supermodel...After they had been given a suitable amount of time to congregate in the reception *bure* with refreshments and to acclimate to their new environment, White stood at the entrance to the building and clapped his hands, ever conscious of the bevy of international reporters flitting about the property, shooting video, taking pictures and notes.

They'd been instructed not to disturb the guests, but selected staff, including White himself, were available to answer questions. The reporters were a hassle, to be sure; it was like having to be on your absolute best behavior at all times in your own house, but he knew that the payoff for putting up with the inconvenience was big-time exposure—basically free advertising. Not to mention the fact that the entire staff *should* be on their best behavior, White reflected. This was it. Opening weekend. Go big or go home. He would not get another chance at this. Indeed, he thought, watching a rock star accept two Fiji Bitter beers from a passing server and hand one to his Japanese girlfriend, it was a miracle he'd gotten this far.

So far at least, everyone seemed to be having a good time. The weather was cooperating, the brilliant South Pacific sun pouring into the open *bure*, no heavy rain forecasted, and light trade winds. It was perfect. The rest was up to him and his people. White consulted his Rolex Submariner, given to him as a token of appreciation for allowing the watchmaker to be the "official timekeeper for the world's first underwater luxury hotel." There would be more guests arriving today, but no more were due for at least a couple of hours. The baggage had been transported to the underwater rooms by now, and so it was time to deliver the guests to their suites. White moved to the center of the room, and addressed his guests.

"Ladies and gentlemen, as lovely as our topside accommodations are here at Triton, I know you can't wait to see your suites. So without further ado, if you'll follow me, I'll accompany you down to the hotel. Feel free to bring your food and beverages with you."

Excited chatter in multiple languages erupted as the guests followed White out of the reception *bure* onto a garden path that led toward the lagoon. White spoke quietly into a handheld two-way radio as he walked a little ahead of the guests. He put the hotel staff on alert that the first guests were coming down now.

White led the group past a quaint wooden sign reading Tunnel Entrance, and emerged onto the lagoon's beach in front of what was truly a marvel of marine engineering. What on first glance looked to be a dock of some sort, was actually an opening into a tunnel that led underwater. As the guests gathered on the beach in front of the opening, a voice issued from an unseen speaker.

ATTENTION...TRAIN ARRIVING IN 3...2...1...

Then a chime sounded, and with no noise at all, a tram-like vehicle glided to a stop in the tunnel's opening.

"So quiet!" a reporter who'd been allowed to make the trip into the hotel with the guests remarked.

White nodded. "Rubber wheels on a Plexiglas surface, plus it's a cable-and-pulley system, with the motor housed in a separate building, over there." He pointed a little ways behind them to a small structure where machinery churned within a soundproofed housing. "The motor's in there, not in the train, so there's no noise while it's in the tunnel. Nothing to detract from the undersea experience. This way, please!"

White led them with an outstretched arm to the tunnel entrance and the waiting train. "As you can see," he continued, "The tram itself is an open vehicle that rolls within a sealed, Plexiglas tube. You'll be able to look out underwater as we ride down to the hotel."

A chorus of appreciative murmurs followed as the guests boarded the tram. Soothing music played, over which a female voice welcomed them to Triton Undersea Resort, "the world's first and only luxury underwater hotel." Controlled remotely, the tram started to move shortly after the passengers had taken their seats. Seated next to the reporter, a young African American woman from the New York Times, White pointed to a camera mounted at the front of the train.

"Gives the operators a view of what's happening inside so they can wait for everyone to be seated." The reporter nodded, and jotted something down in her notepad.

The tram, with two identical ends, set into motion by rolling in the opposite direction from which it had come. The tube through which it was pulled slanted at an angle down toward the hotel. Immediately, it became a shade darker as the tram slid down into the deep. Outside the tube, the guests were excitedly pointing at small fish swimming by, their descent into the ocean made more real for having seen them.

The vehicle moved surprisingly fast through the cool, recycled air, and in about two minutes the first energized chatter from the guests broke out as the underwater hotel came into view. It appeared as two huge cylinders situated on the reef floor, and stretching to just beneath the lagoon's surface, with a long row of pods stemming from a central tube connecting the cylinders. The water was clear enough that from this distance they could see the entire complex. Dense schools of multi-colored fish swarmed around the structure. A squid shot between coral heads. A pair of lobster antennae twitched in the currents at the edge of their coral cave.

The seafloor. Even the guests seemed to know that it wasn't normal to have a hotel here. They had quieted as the tram drew nearer to their home for the next several days, the realization hitting them that they were *underwater,* and that this was no theme park attraction. This was the real deal. Mother Nature, modified to support humans where no humans should be. And in style, at that. Chandeliers and Persian rugs were visible through the mostly transparent structure.

The train tube disappeared into the cylindrical structure on the left, the lighting changing to soft LEDs and plasma screens beckoning everyone a warm welcome to Triton. Amazingly, the tube passed through the wall into the inside of the hotel such that not even an airlock was required. James White had battled with engineers over this for years. There would be no "wet room" or industrial type space requiring guests to wait in a damp, confined area while a suitable pressure was reached before the door could be opened. None of that. Just ride the train in, ride it back out, at will. The train tunnel extended from shore all the way down to the hotel, and right through the outer wall.

The tram slowed between two rows of potted palms, well lit with natural light from above, since the roof of the building was also clear Plexiglas or acrylic. The recorded voice informed passengers, "You have arrived at Triton Undersea Resort, your home on the ocean floor. We hope you enjoy your stay! Please exit to your right."

White added his own voice to the mix. "Welcome everyone! Hors d'oeuvres and champagne will be served now in the lobby. This way, please." He exited the train, and led the guests toward the sound of live piano music. The distance to walk was short, but it took time with the large group constantly stopping to look out the windows at the stunning reef view.

"It's like diving without getting wet!" one remarked.

"Like a Habitrail for people!" a child remarked. "This is how my hamster must feel, looking out at the world. Look, shark!" The boy put his hand on the glass as a small reef shark swam a few feet away.

Eventually, the group straggled into the lobby, where a Fijian man sat performing at a baby grand piano. Indian and Fijian servers circulated with trays of more food and drinks, the kind so-called foodies got all excited about. Beluga caviar. Starfruit. Ahi sushi. Free-flowing Moet White Star champagne. Shots of iced vodka. Bottled Fiji water. The food was trifling next to the view, though. The lobby had the largest uninterrupted expanse of windows in the entire hotel. With a three-story floor-to-ceiling height, the reef vista upon which they looked was unparalleled anywhere on the planet. It wasn't so much like they were looking at the reef. It was like they were a *part of* the reef.

Sea stars clung to the lower reaches of the windows. These would be scraped off by scuba-diving staff whose job it was to keep the glass clean should any type of marine growth start to impede the view. But for now, the viewing area was clean as could be, and the guests pointed here and there as they walked about, absolutely entranced. Overhead, White pointed out a school of manta rays appearing to fly over the transparent roof. He looked around at his clients. They were mixing with each other, enjoying the food, the setting having the desired effect. This would be a one-of-a-kind experience even for this been-there-done-that crowd.

He was in the process of explaining to the reporter where the kitchen was, when his two-way radio lit up. He wore an earpiece with it so that it wouldn't disturb the guests, but when he flipped his mic on he could talk softly, and still be heard on the other end.

"James here. Busy. What's up?"

"We've got a problem with the SWAC system. Need you to be briefed at earliest opportunity, over."

White couldn't suppress a look of irritation while stared down at the Italian marble floor. When he looked up again, he caught the NFL guy's girlfriend looking right at him, and he quickly slapped a smile back on his face. *Everything's great! Except apparently the SWAC system.* He knew that was the special air conditioning system the underwater hotel had, and that SWAC stood for Sea Water Air Conditioning.

"It's nice and cool down here, Al. Not sure what the problem is, but can you deal with it?" He smiled as he looked around the crowded lobby. Al's radio reply came, along with the noise of some kind of alarm that started braying in the background.

"It won't be nice and cool down there for long, James. Need you back up here to advise."

Chapter 5

James White rode the tram alone up out of the hotel. He scowled at a sea turtle gliding over his head. This had better be important, he thought, exiting the train tunnel onto the beach. Those guests down there were having a good time so far, though, and he felt comfortable enough to leave for a few minutes, maybe ride back down with the next influx of new arrivals.

He navigated the garden paths at a near trot whenever he was sure no one was looking until he reached a solid building—not a *bure*—on the edge of the topside complex. A sign in front of it proclaimed, Off Limits Area, Engineering Staff Only. White strode to the door, and unlocked it with one of the many keys on his key ring. He entered the single floor structure, and walked through a hallway to a room he knew the marine engineers who worked in here called "the situation room." He wasn't thrilled about having a situation on the hotel's opening day, but hopefully it was just these nerds being extra thorough, wanting to apprise him about some technical issue that could be bad if an improbable combination of events happened all at the same time.

As he passed through the completely empty building, though, room after room and the open cubicle area totally empty, he knew it must be serious. Even the break room was empty. Usually there were at least two guys in there playing Xbox games. They must all be in the Situation Room, which did not bode well. White turned down one more hallway, and was looking into the open door at his entire engineering staff seated around the conference table, arguing and pointing excitedly at their laptop screens.

There were eight men and two women in the room. James didn't recall the names of most of them, and he didn't care. He only needed to remember one, and that was Albert Johnson, his Engineering Manager. This was his circus. James breezed in, and stood at the head of the table, ignoring the empty chair delicately shoved at him by a shy, female Japanese electrical engineer.

"What have you got for me, Al?"

The room quieted as all eyes went to the marine engineer. "The hotel's air conditioning system stopped working about two hours ago."

"Two hours ago? So you could have let me know before we took the guests down there?"

Al shrugged. "At that time I thought it would be a minor problem we'd be able to get a handle on quickly. Wanted to run some diagnostics before sounding the alarm, so to speak."

"Yeah, I heard one over the radio. Literally."

"Right, that was the temperature alarm exceeding the upper threshold. It looks like the cold water intake pipe for the SWAC system either ruptured, or else has been completely obstructed by something."

In order to save money on air conditioning costs, which in the tropics are a necessary evil that accounts for a large percentage of all operational budgets, they decided to utilize a somewhat experimental system that would cool the hotel at a much lower cost than traditional air conditioning systems. This SWAC technology relied on sucking cold seawater found deep down in the ocean into a pipe to bring it up into the hotel on the reef, where it could be distributed throughout. The only electrical energy required was for the pumps to suck the water up the pipe. After it had been used for cooling via heat exchangers, the spent, warm seawater was expelled back into the ocean through a return pipe.

Both the intake and return pipes were located well away from the hotel's reef, both in order to hide the infrastructure so as not to spoil the natural views, as well as to prevent disturbance of sensitive reef ecology by the movement of water and altered temperatures associated with the pipes. The return pipe was placed on the outer reef slope at a depth of about sixty feet. Because of that shallow depth, it was easy to maintain, and Al informed James that his team had already determined that the problem wasn't with the return system.

"So you're not exactly sure yet what happened to the intake pipe, is that what I'm hearing?" White checked his Rolex, a not so subtle hint.

"Like I said, it's either a rupture—a puncture in one spot where the seawater is leaking out—or else the entire pipe structure has somehow been demolished."

"How could that happen?"

"I don't know, James. Rockslide? Subsea tsunami that never broke the surface? Instead of speculating, since you appear concerned about the time, what we should do is go down there and have a look."

White looked up at him sharply. Apparently Al did not like to be challenged in front of his team of super-nerds, even by his boss. "How deep is the intake, again? I thought you put it in with the help of an industrial sub rented from an oil company?"

Al nodded. "Yeah, that's right. It's only at 250 feet, though, which puts it well within the depth rating of our own mini-sub."

"It has a 1,000-foot rating," one of Al's engineers, a lanky bald American said while twirling his pen incessantly.

Al Jumped back in. "I know it doesn't have the tool-kit for actually making serious repairs the oil company sub has, but it would allow us to drop down there and have a look, see what the problem is. If we're lucky, it's just some stray flotsam clogging up the intake that can be removed with the mini-sub's grab arm," he finished, folding his arms as he looked at White.

The developer felt a knot take form in his stomach as he recalled his meeting with Coco and Mick yesterday at the sub dock. What'd he estimate? At least a day to fix that thruster? He glanced at his watch again. It hasn't even been twenty-four hours yet. *When it rains it fucking pours...*

"James? For a guy who seems worried about time you sure are taking long enough to answer."

"Our little sub is meant for eco-tours, not heavy equipment wrangling. Any chance we could get that oil sub or one like it over here in the next few hours?"

Al shot an inquisitive glance to a bespectacled Indian man who tapped some keys on a laptop, and then shook his head. "Three day wait at the earliest," he confirmed.

Al looked back to White, and raised his eyebrows. "We need to get a look at it, James. It's going to start getting warm down there."

White cursed under his breath. The thought of all those VIPs paying thousands of dollars per night to sweat their asses off was most unsavory indeed.

"I'll go tell Coco to get the sub ready." He'd have to leave it at that. He couldn't bring himself to break the news about their only submersible not being operational, the last he'd heard. He turned to leave, and whirled back around. "Do we have backup A/C, regular units? Something to cool the place off down there in the meantime?"

Al shook his head, but then looked around the table at his people, who also shook their heads. "Window units are obviously out." This elicited a round of chuckles from his crew of geeks, which irritated the crap out of White, so he hurried to continue. "If we take the chopper, we might be able to pick up a few wall units over in Suva, but even that would take a few hours plus install time."

White glared at him.

"We'll get on that, though, just in case as a backup. George, Rene, Alex—you three spec out the units, and make the run." He turned back to White.

"Hopefully, we won't need 'em after we go down in the sub, though, right?"

Chapter 6

"Look at this view, will you! Oh my God!" Staci Lincoln stood in the bedroom of their suite in the Triton Undersea Resort, bouncing up and down with excitement. Sunlight dappled across a vibrant coral reef, while a rainbow of brightly colored tropical fish darted about. Her pro-football player husband, John Rudd, seemed mildly interested at best in the ocean outside their room's floor-to-ceiling panoramic window. He stood behind his girlfriend, admiring her curvy form.

"It's a little hot in here, though, don't you think?" she said, still admiring the view.

"It sure is. I'm checking out the view, all right. Liking it!"

She reached back and swatted at him, a blow that he easily ducked. He caught her by the wrist, and led her to the king bed, done up with silk sheets and a down comforter emblazoned with the resort's logo.

"What are you doing?"

He pulled her onto the bed, and she protested weakly. "Hey, we're supposed to go to brunch. I'm hungry!"

"They said we're the first ones here. They can get things warmed up over there, while we get them warmed up in here." He pulled her on top of him.

"John..." Her objections became weaker and less frequent.

Staci gazed out the undersea window, watching the fishes. So many of them, she thought, like being miniaturized and immersed in an aquarium. *So beautiful...*

Then suddenly the school of fish she'd been watching organized into a tight ball, and swam quickly out of sight. Staci's hands explored John's body while she watched the reef, now devoid of fishes. *Where'd they go?*

Their room was cast a shade darker as a shadow overlay the reef. Staci figured it was clouds covering the sun far above, but then the gloom out the window seemed to grow larger, to move. John called out her name and she responded, but her heart wasn't in it.

What is that?

Then, for an instant, it materialized, clear as day, before departing just as quickly as it had come, leaving shifting rays of sunshine in its wake. Startled, she jumped up from the bed, and ran to the window.

"Babe, what's up!?" John looked confused, hurt.

"The fuck!"

"What about it?"

"I'm serious, John. What the fuck was that?"

"Was what?"

"A huge-ass shark just swam by our window!"

"C'mon. If you don't want to do it, just—"

"John, I'm not making this up. This thing was so big it took up the whole window!"

He took a deep breath, resigning himself to the fact that the moment had been killed. "It's probably just something the hotel cooked up for entertainment. I'm sure we'll hear about it at brunch."

Staci stood in front of the window, unconvinced. The reef that moments ago had been so lively was now still.

"All the fish are gone."

Chapter 7

"What do you think, Mick? Am I screwed or what?" Coco shielded her eyes from the sun, while Mick looked up from attaching a makeshift propeller assembly.

"Maybe not totally. I've got the proper part on order, but this should hold until that gets here. Pulled it from my trusty box of spares."

Coco eyed the new thruster. It was gray in color instead of black, and appeared to be slightly smaller in diameter. "What kind of sub was it on?"

He shrugged. "Some tourist mini-sub from when I worked in the Cayman Islands. It was in the junkyard. Scavengers got most of the good parts before I got there, but I rescued this."

"Does it work?"

"Let's find out." Mick moved toward the sub's cabin to test the new thruster, when they heard footsteps creaking out onto the wooden dock. Mick cupped a hand over his mouth as he faced Coco.

"Shit! It's the big cheese already. Hasn't even been one day yet."

"He must have a lot of confidence in you. At least it looks like we're working. Or you are, anyway. I'm just sitting around on my ass after I banged up the sub."

"You're advising me. Don't worry, I can spin it so that some of the damage wasn't your fault."

She gave him a lingering stare just before White walked up.

"Good afternoon. How's the progress?" he looked directly at Mick.

"Good, Mr. White. An identical thruster assembly has been ordered, rush air shipment from China, probably be here in two days."

White shook his head.

"However," Mick continued, "in the meantime, I've cooked up a little replacement. Take a look." He pointed to the mismatched thruster.

"Looks different. Does it work?"

"Hasn't been on a sea trial yet, but take a look." Mick stepped into the sub's cabin, and pressed the thruster control button. They heard a soft, even hum as the new propeller spun inside its cage. Mick let go of the button, and the blur of the blades settled into visible objects once again.

"Good. It's time for that sea trial."

Coco and Mick traded glances. Mick tried to buy some more time.

"I was hoping to do a little more testing, because if—"

White held up a hand. "Enough. A situation has arisen that necessitates use of this vehicle ASAP." He turned, and pointed a finger at Coco. "I need you to get in, and test it out right away."

Coco looked dubiously at the new thruster, at Mick, and then at the lagoon. "I guess I could take her for a spin in the shallows here, see how she—"

White shook his head while interrupting. "No, I need you to take her down to the SWAC intake pipe, and have a look at it."

Coco's mouth dropped open before she forced it closed. Mick recovered first.

"That pipe's at 250 feet, isn't it, sir?"

"That's right. There's a problem with the air conditioning in the hotel. It's not working. Al says he needs to get a look at the intake pipe, see if it's clogged or broken or what."

Coco spoke up. "What about the—"

"The oil company sub isn't available to us now. We need you to do it, Coco. Just drop down the canyon until you reach the pipe, have a look at it, get some pictures. Possibly we might need you to use the grab arm to remove debris if there is any blocking the pipe."

She gazed vacuously at the sub, thinking of the deepest dive she'd done in the craft yet...One hundred feet? Seventy-five? Now he was asking her to go two-hundred fifty? Perhaps he read her unease, because his next words were, "You can take Mick with you for an extra pair of eyes on that pipe."

The sub mechanic beamed. Ironically, he didn't usually get to ride in the vehicles he serviced. "Okay!"

"Now get this thing in the water! Let me know what you found the second you get back." White eyed the new thruster again, and shook his head before stalking off back down the dock.

Chapter 8

"Seriously. What a jerk." Coco flipped a few switches on the sub's instrument panel, and looked over at Mick as he pulled down the dome hatch before sliding into the co-pilot seat.

"Don't worry, we'll be able to test the new thruster on the way across the reef. If we have any problems whatsoever before we get to the drop-off, then we don't go deep. I don't care what the big cheese says."

Coco nodded her agreement as she maneuvered the submersible on the surface away from the dock, like a regular boat. "First sign of trouble, we call the dive."

When she had backed the sub away from the dock, she vented the air in the buoyancy tubes, causing the sub to sink below the surface. They watched as water sheeted over the dome, and they were immersed in the underwater world, an exciting sensation she doubted she would ever grow tired of.

When the craft was a few feet above the coral reef in about twenty feet of water, Coco eyeballed the "landmarks" that were by now very familiar to her—the cluster of brain corals off to the left, the staghorn coral formation to the right—she took her bearings based on these recognizable sights, and then activated both thrusters.

The sub hummed into forward motion, gliding across the reef as expected. "So far so good." She patted the instrument console. "C'mon little sub, you can do it!"

Mick shook his head, laughing. "You're too funny, you know that?"

"It's working so far, Mick!"

"Was there ever any doubt? It is my nearly supernatural repair skills we're talking about here."

It was Coco's turn to laugh, and before she knew it they were passing the hotel on their right side, one of the cylindrical towers sparkling in the muted sunlight. "There it is."

"The hot house."

They both laughed again. "Half a billion bucks, and no A/C. Ain't that a bitch?"

Coco's eyes bugged out. "Is that what it cost to build this place?"

"That's what I heard. Was only supposed to be half that, though."

"*Only* a quarter of a billion, huh?" Coco smiled as she banked the sub, following the curvature of the hotel's tower. Inside, they could see a few guests standing there in conversation, drinks in hand. One of them saw the submersible and waved, a gesture that Coco and Mick returned. They left the hotel behind, and headed toward the edge of the reef. Coco navigated beneath the coral overhang she knew marked the gateway to the drop-off.

"How's it handling?" Mick looked over at her.

"Good. To be honest, I don't even notice much difference."

"So you feel up to the task?" They approached the entrance to the submarine canyon, and Coco eased up on the throttle so that they hovered there, peering down the sandy slope. The same place where yesterday she'd seen that...*thing*, she thought.

"Thruster's good."

Mick tore his eyes away from the view down into the abyss to look at his pilot. "That's not what I asked."

Coco's brown eyes bore into Mick's baby blues. "Yeah, I'm fine. 250 feet. Only 200 more to go," she said, referencing the fact that they were currently already fifty feet down.

"Let's have a look at this bloody pipe then."

Coco picked up the radio transmitter that would allow her to talk to Topside, which would be one of the engineering team. "*Triton-1* to Topside, *Triton-1* to Topside, we are a go for pipe inspection. Entering the canyon now, over."

A few seconds ticked by while the two inhabitants of the submersible silently contemplated the slope in front of them that led to their dive's objective. Then the radio crackled with a male voice.

"Copy that, *Triton-1*. We anxiously await your report, over."
Coco turned to Mick. "Ready, Micky?"
He grinned in return. "Rock 'n roll!"
Coco angled the sub so that its nose pointed down, and then gunned the thrusters, hyper-cautious of the canyon's walls closing around their fragile craft. She pointed at a spot on the wall.
"That's where I hit before."
Mick looked out the window. "Don't see any busted up sub parts out there." He turned around, and gave her a grin.
"Don't speak too soon. I can always add new ones."
Mick shook his head as Coco threaded the needle with the sub through the narrow geological formation.
"You thread the needle with this thing better than I could, no doubt about that."
Before long they reached a point Coco recognized: the near-vertical drop-off into the canyon proper. She checked the sub's instruments and wiped the sweat from her hands on the sweatshirt she wore to ward off the sub's chilly air.
"Here we go." She flipped on the sub's external floodlights, since the water would be dimly lit at 250 feet. No need to have to do that while she was down there. It was a simple task, but there would be enough to do once they reached their target. She didn't put the sub into a nose-first dive, but rather just let the craft sink in a horizontal position. Mick craned his neck and looked up at the receding surface, the silhouette of the reef shelf becoming smaller as they descended.
At around 100 feet they passed through a thermocline, where a warm surface layer of water overlay a much colder one. These sometimes resulted in unpredictable turbulence, and Coco felt the sub jolt as they passed through it. Soon after, though, their vehicle resumed its easy downward trajectory, falling only with the force of gravity, no power required.
"200 feet," Coco called out after a few more minutes. Mick took hold of a control that enabled him to aim the spotlight outside the sub. He angled it down, sweeping from left to right, searching for the intake pipe.

"They must have run it down this same canyon right?" Coco took her eyes off the controls for a second to scan the water off to her left.

"Yeah, but it's covered with growth by now, and hard to see. Ah, but there it is!" Mick pointed almost straight down beneath them at a section of large diameter pipe that had just enough white beneath a layer of marine encrustation to make it stand out.

"I see it." Coco made a fine adjustment to the controls. "Right in the middle, yeah?"

"Right. So it should flare out into an intake in another—"

"There it is! Another thirty feet down, right where it should be."

"Great. Whoa!" Mick leaned closer to the see-through hatch to reduce glare from the sub's control panel lights.

"What?" Coco needed to concentrate on driving the sub, and couldn't afford the luxury of a prolonged look at things outside the way Mick could. She continued her slow descent toward the end of the pipe.

"It's banged up something awful." Mick played the spotlight on it for a few seconds longer, and then picked up the video camera, activating it. Coco leveled out the sub at the 250-foot mark, noting how dark it was down here. Looking up, she could see a hazy gray layer of light, but looking down was only darkness, save for the sub's lights.

She brought the sub as close as she dared to the pipe's intake which she could now clearly see was damaged.

"Stay away from the front of it," Mick warned. "The suction might create strong currents."

"I'll swing around back." Coco gingerly tapped the thruster joystick, maneuvering the submersible behind the opening of the pipe. She held the craft in a hover while they appraised the wrecked equipment. Mick rolled the video camera for a couple of minutes before setting it down and looking at the pipe with his naked eye.

"No wonder this thing isn't bringing the water up. Look at that." The section of interest was L-shaped, with the intake opening on the short end of the L, the long end extending up all the way to the reef, and from there to the hotel. The portion of pipe just above the intake section was extensively crushed, with many gaping holes in it. Even if suction was applied, any water pumped into the pipe would be lost out the holes. But it was the pattern of tears that gripped Coco's attention.

"What do you think happened to it, Mick?"

The Aussie rubbed the stubble on his face while he thought about the question. There was no easy answer. The intake was well away from the walls of the canyon. The stretch of pipe above them had no obvious damage. The actual opening of the intake was clear.

"No clue. I don't see how falling debris that broke off the reef from above could account for this, do you?"

Coco slowly circled the sub around the back of the pipe, seeking answers. Just as she was about to reverse to avoid drifting in front of the intake, she hovered the sub in place.

"See something?" Mick picked up the camera again.

Coco squinted at the pipe, into one of the jagged tears in it. A gleam of white arrested her gaze.

"Yeah. Hey Mick, how are you with the grab-arm?" The submersible was outfitted with a single tool: a manipulator arm with a claw on the end that could be used for gripping and moving small objects. It wasn't necessary for the eco-tours the resort used the sub for, but it had come that way from the manufacturer, and it "looked cool," as Coco put it, so they had let it be. Now, though, she saw an actual use for it.

Mick eyed the mechanical appendage doubtfully. "That little arm's not going to be able to do squat to fix that mangled pipe." He called the shots the way he saw them, and by now Coco was used to his directness and even appreciated it, especially during situations like these.

"I know. But I think I see something in it. If we can grab it, maybe it'll give us a clue as to what happened."

Mick eyeballed the grab-arm controls. "I'm game if you are." He tested the joystick that moved the arm, extending it, rotating it left and right, pressing the button that pinched the claws together.

Coco edged the sub in closer to the pipe, aware of the deep chasm yawning below her. When she was about three feet away she gave the throttle a touch of reverse to counteract her forward momentum, then paused, her hands frozen over the controls while she watched the pipe to see if the sub was drifting relative to it.

"That's it, you got it." Mick swung the grab-arm out towards the pipe. The mini-sub held position while Coco glanced down and around at their surroundings.

"Grab the prize."

"This is a heck of a first date, trying to win you something in a claw-grabber game."

Coco cracked a huge smile. "You sure know how to make a girl happy. Hold on, little bit of a current." She adjusted the sub's position with a burst of throttle, and Mick started with the grab-arm again. The claw extended into the jagged rip in the pipe, and closed around the white object.

"Got it, pulling back in three...two...one..."

Suddenly the sub was yanked to the left, rotating about the grab arm's claw which was still pinched around the object.

"Let go, let go!" No sooner had she uttered the words than the sub's motion stopped as the manipulator claw wrenched the object free from the inside of the shredded pipe.

"Got it! Reeling it back in..." Mick hit the button on the grab-arm joystick that retracted the arm. As it drew nearer the sub Coco let out an involuntary gasp.

"My god!"

Mick hadn't yet taken the time to actually focus on the object he had extracted, so focused was he on working the manipulator.

"What's up?"

"It...it can't be!"

"*What* can't be?" The claw hung up again just inside the edge of the opening. Mick tried a different combination of button pushes, and freed the object from the wreckage of the pipe. Still clutched in the mechanical claw, he retracted the arm again, this time pulling the object through the rip in the pipe.

"Big shark tooth..." was all she could bring herself to mutter. But in her mind ran that other word, the one she'd thought of on her ill-fated dive yesterday: *megalodon.*

Mick brought the grab-arm all the way into the sub and folded it back in to its resting position, the tooth grasped firmly in the machine's grip. That done, he finally got the chance to get a good look at what he had retrieved.

"Holy crap! Look at that thing! It's got to be six inches long."

Coco said nothing, staring at the tooth as though it were a terrible omen, while Mick continued to marvel at it.

"It'll make one hell of a necklace, right? Hey, what kind do you think it's from anyway, White Pointer? Sorry, that's what we call them down under. Great White?"

Coco still stared entranced at the pointed tooth.

"Coco? You okay?"

"It's not from a White."

"Aren't they the biggest? This is the biggest shark tooth I've ever seen, that's for sure, except for those fossilized dinosaur ones..."

That triggered it for Coco. "The *megalodons*."

"What?" Mick stared out into the gloom while he waited for her reply.

"*Carcharadon megalodon*. It's one of those dinosaur sharks you're talking about."

"Oh, right. So what's this one from?"

Coco turned away from her view of the tooth to look at Mick. "As crazy as it sounds, it's the right size and shape for a *megalodon*."

Mick appeared confused, furrowing his brow and gnawing on his lower lip. "But it's not fossilized. It's white."

Coco turned to stare at the tooth again. "I know, Mick. That's what worries me."

"I don't get it."

"Hold on, let's make the radio call to Topside."

Mick picked up the transmitter. "*Triton-1* to Topside, you copy?"

The reply was near-instant. Mick didn't recognize the voice. "Copy that, *Triton-1*, go ahead, over."

"Intake pipe is mangled up good. It's got big tears in it."

A slight pause, followed by, "Tears from what?"

Mick looked at Coco, who shrugged. "We don't know, but we've got video to show you once we—"

Coco's shrill scream cut the conversation short.

42

Chapter 9

The colossal fish moved gracefully up from the dark depths of the submarine canyon.

Mick put a hand on Coco's shoulder. "Let's go, Coco. It's a Great White. We're done here, no reason to stick around."

She dumped some of the sub's ballast along with a burst of vertical thrusters to initiate a rapid ascent. Her movements were hyper-fast, almost panicked, and Mick glanced over at the ruined intake pipe as their craft rose past it, almost hitting it.

"Coco, it's okay. Relax. Whites don't—"

"It's not a White!'

Mick sat in the co-pilot seat in stunned silence. He looked down at the approaching animal, and was surprised to see it much closer now, swimming in lazy-looking circles that nonetheless took it ever higher very quickly. Still, Mick had seen Whites before, diving in Australia back home, and this sure looked like one. The pointed snout, the stiff dorsal and pectoral fins, the uniquely jagged line demarcating the white underbelly from the dark dorsal surface. How could it not be a White? He voiced this question to Coco as she pulled the sub out of a semi-spin she'd created with her frantic maneuvering.

"Look at our sonar, Mick! That shark is still one hundred fifty feet away."

Mick felt the blood drain from his face as he riveted his gaze to the instrument's display. She was reading it accurately. He turned his head back to the shark, and sucked in his breath. It was impossibly big for a shark so far away. A large Great White was about twenty feet long. One hundred fifty feet away...this thing had to be three times that size! He shuddered involuntarily at the realization before turning back to Coco, still raising the sub.

"You're right. You're also the marine biologist, so lay it out for me."

Coco was getting a little tired of being reminded about her occupation lately. It seemed like suddenly she'd gone from being a glorified tour guide, to the only one who knew anything at all about what was happening to this place.

"I know it sounds crazy, but..." She broke off as she piloted the submersible around a coral outcropping. Then she stared down at the shark, still rising lazily.

"But what?" Mick prompted.

"The only thing I've ever heard about that it could be is a *Carcharadon megalodon.*"

The sub mechanic glanced down at the gigantic shark. "A what?"

"A *megalodon.* It's an extinct, prehistoric shark from the dinosaur days."

"If it's extinct, how is it swimming up after us right now?"

Coco shook her head. "No idea."

"What else could it be then? Maybe you're wrong."

"It's either a freakishly large Great White, much huger than any previously seen, or else it's a *megalodon,* somehow still alive, still extant. There's nothing else it could be. Even supersized, it doesn't look like a tiger shark, or a mako, or a bull shark, am I right?"

Mick stared down at the creature again. "Nope, it doesn't. It looks exactly like a super-sized White."

"It's got the predation patterns of a White, too. Look at it circling like that. Classic white shark behavior. Hey—get some shots of it, will you!"

Mick scrambled for the video camera. In all the excitement, it hadn't even occurred to him to shoot some footage. He aimed the device's lens down through the transparent floor of the sub at the moving leviathan below. He began to narrate.

"Too bad there's nothing to give it some scale, but this is what our sub pilot Coco Keahi thinks may be a megalodon shark." He panned out to show the sonar reading, then went back to the shark.

"Sonar has it at 150 feet below us. As you can see, an ordinary Great White would not appear so large from this distance. We estimate this fish to be at least sixty feet in length."

He recorded for a few more seconds, and then shut the camera off. "Is that tooth we grabbed the right size for a megalodon?"

She looked away from the controls long enough to meet his gaze, and nod solemnly.

"No idea how I'm going to explain this to James."

#

James White was at the sub dock to greet them upon return. "Well?" he asked the second that Mick pushed up the dome hatch. "What's it look like?"

Mick shook his head, and jumped onto the dock, then reached a hand out to pull Coco up. "It's been pulverized by something. Several large tears in it for a few feet just above the intake. No wonder you're not getting any water pressure. Here, take a look." He handed White the camera with a shot of the damaged pipe on screen. The hotel developer narrowed his eyes as he took in the details of the disconcerting image.

"Doesn't look like you'd be able to fix that," he admitted.

Coco agreed. "Unfortunately, it's not just a simple obstruction."

White looked up from the camera at her. "What's your opinion on how this happened?"

Coco hesitated while she gauged the expression of her boss. He seemed irritated, sure, but not like he was totally shutting himself off to being open. She decided to tell him her wild theory.

"I think an animal did it, sir." Best to ease into it, though. The sound of sea birds calling rent the air as he seemed to judge her response.

"What kind of animal? The same mysterious one that supposedly wrecked the sub yesterday, I suppose?"

Coco nodded matter-of-factly. "I believe so, Mr. White. Come here, take a look at this." She turned, and walked alongside the sub's manipulator arm, the six-inch white tooth still clutched firmly in its claw. She knelt and released it from the grabber, then handed it point first to White, whose eyes widened as he took it, and turned it over in his hands.

"Is this some kind of joke?" He directed his angry stare in turn to Coco and Mick, both of whom shook their heads but said nothing. "Because if it is," White went on, "it's not funny at all. In fact, you may as well tell me now: is this a hoax?" He thrust the giant tooth out in front of him. "I'm telling you, if I find out later it is, then you're both fired, mark my words."

The aggressiveness triggered Coco to assert her own position more forcefully. "We extracted this tooth from inside the pipe, Mr. White. To the best of my knowledge, it's a shark tooth, specifically one that is much larger than any currently known living species."

"I don't have time for games. Just tell me what the hell you think it is," White spat.

"I think it's a living relative of *Carcharadon* or perhaps *Carcharacles megalodon*, an extinct prehistoric shark about three times larger than the modern day Great White." She paused to gauge White's reaction.

He handed the tooth back to her. "Maybe you can use this on one of your eco lectures. I've got to get back to fixing the damned pipe. We've got guests down there now who are not accustomed to five star tropical hotels without air conditioning."

He opened the camera and removed its memory card, then handed the camera back to Mick. "I'll take this to the engineers so we can figure out what to do about it." Mick nodded, and White walked away.

He called out over his shoulder, "Make sure that sub is ready for more dives!"

#

Inside his private Triton office, James White loaded the camera's memory card into his desktop computer. He called up the images and video on his jumbo monitor, scowling at a couple of faux-glamour shots Mick took of Coco goofing around on the pier before the sub dive. He was somewhat surprised those two clowns had been able to bring back footage of the pipe; he knew Coco wasn't trained for that deep of a dive. Probably not the most prudent thing in the world to send her down there, but they had a situation on their hands, and that was her job. The psych tests they did on her during the interview process indicated she was highly adaptive, after all. And let's face it, if it actually happened to be true that she did encounter some sort of humongous sea creature down there, and that's why the sub was damaged...well then, she wasn't such a bad sub pilot at all, now was she?

He opened the last video, the one of the shark, and watched it, his face souring further with each turn the great fish took toward the surface. He deleted the shark video and everything else except for the shots of the intake pipe.

Then he ejected the memory card, and headed over to the engineering building.

Chapter 10

"It's fucking hot in here, Stanley!"

Priscilla Doherty, wife of Stanley Doherty, owner of one of the NBA's most celebrated teams, fanned herself with a room service menu while she lay in bed.

"Relax, I'll see if I can find a thermostat control somewhere." He looked around their suite. "I guess it won't be on that wall," he joked, pointing to the floor-to-ceiling acrylic window looking out on the reef.

"Seriously, Stan! I wanted to go to Bora Bora, and the over-water bungalows. You said this place would be amazing. I guess it is if you're looking for an underwater sauna."

"Oh, c'mon, look at that! It's pretty damn amazing don't you think?" He swept an arm out the window, where a school of fish suddenly darted out of view.

"You want to know what I think? I think they're still working the kinks out of this place, Stan. I don't know why we had to be in the first group of guests. Let someone else be the guinea pigs, I say. All those accident liability waivers we had to sign..."

Stanley gave up looking around for a thermostat, and instead picked up the room phone. "All right, all right, I'll call the front desk." Priscilla sighed heavily while he held the receiver to his ear. She listened to the one-way conversation while fanning herself at an ever-increasing pace.

"Yes, hello, this is Stanley Doherty. My wife and I are in the Manta Ray Suite, and it's awfully hot in here. I wonder if you could be so kind as to tell me where the thermostat is, or if you can adjust it from your end."

"You're too damned polite, Stan," his wife heckled him from the bed. He swatted the air in her direction, and furrowed his brow.

He nodded and said "uh-huh," and "I see," "Okay..." a few times before hanging up.

"What'd they say?" Priscilla peered at him over the top of her makeshift fan.

He took a deep breath before answering. "She told me there's a problem with the hotel's air conditioning right now—the entire hotel, not just our suite—but that it should be fixed soon."

Priscilla let the menu drop to cover her naked breasts. "Oh, great! 'Soon'! How soon is 'soon'?"

"I didn't ask. They're working on it, that's all she meant."

"Well, you should ask, Stanley!"

"She said that it's a little cooler in the common areas of the hotel. Why don't we go out and try the restaurant, get some lunch?"

"Are you even hungry?"

"I could eat, yeah."

She glanced at part of the menu she'd been fanning herself with, and appeared less than enthusiastic. He added, "If it's still too hot when we go to the restaurant, we'll take the tram back up to the beach, and get something to eat up there, how's that? She said they have topside *bures* they could put us in if we don't want to stay here while they're fixing the problem."

She snapped her head up. "I thought you said she said it would be fixed *soon*?"

"That's what she said."

"Well, if she's offering alternative accommodations already, how confident could she be that they'll have it fixed anytime soon?"

"I really don't know, honey. I'm just telling you what she said. You want to go eat?"

Chapter 11

Al Johnson screwed up his features into a visage of extreme distaste as he viewed the video White played of the SWAC intake pipe. He wagged his head slowly from side to side.

"*Not* good, James. Not good at all."

The room of marine engineers was silent, a huddle of pen-twirling, tablet-pecking geeks who knew their work was more than cut out for them.

"Can you please elaborate?" White watched as Johnson backed up the video to a frame of interest and froze it there. He pointed with the tip of a pen to an area on screen.

"You see this here?"

White nodded.

"This is not fixable. Way too many holes; the whole thing is mangled beyond repair. The entire lower section of pipe—at least twenty feet of it—will have to be cut off and a new section welded on. Major job."

"You're positive that's the only solution?"

Al looked at White with the same expression he reserved for kids with learning disabilities. "Yes, I'm positive, James." Then he looked around the table, addressing his engineers. "Do any of you hold a different opinion?"

None of them said anything.

"All right!" White yelled. "I believe you. So tell me about this process. How long will it take?"

Again the room was silent. White glanced at his Rolex.

"Days to weeks, rather than hours to days," Al said flatly.

White's faced turned crimson. "*Weeks*! Am I hearing this right?"

Al nodded. "Unfortunately, you are, James. I understand the urgency of the situation, and I wish I could paint a rosier picture for you, but I'm just being realistic here."

White let out a long breath, resigning himself to the fact that Al was right. "What does the fix entail?"

Al gave his boss a hard stare. "Why don't we start with what happened to this thing in the first place?" He glanced over at the video before continuing. "Because we don't want it to happen again, that's for sure, and so maybe we can do something to prevent it during the restoration process."

White, who'd been standing up to this point, took a seat at the table and tented his hands.

"Our marine biologist is blaming it on a large sea creature of indeterminate type."

"Indeterminate type?"

"She didn't see it happen. She speculates it may be a large shark. I think it's wishful thinking on her part. You know how marine biologists are—all obsessed about Jaws—she's probably hoping this will be her personal Jaws moment for all I know. You see what you want to see, and all that."

A wave of chuckling passed around the table. Al shrugged. "If it is an animal of any kind, it was probably just a random encounter, and will never happen again. I don't see what we could do about it, anyway."

"Build a cage around it?" one of the engineers put forth.

White stood again. "Good idea. See about implementing that after you get it back to the way it was. So in the meantime, Al, how's the intermediate fix with the wall units going?"

Al checked his smartphone. "Latest update a few minutes ago had my people in the air en route to Suva. As soon as they get there, they're heading to our supplier, and they'll be in contact."

"Contact me when you hear. I'll be down in the hotel."

#

In Mick's "sub shack," as he called the maintenance hut that held the tools of his trade, Coco stood in front of a workbench on which sat her laptop computer. She held the oversized tooth extracted from the pipe up to her screen where a photo of a life-sized megalodon tooth was shown to scale. It was black after undergoing the fossilization process over the eons, but other than color, the two teeth could have been from the same mouth.

"Looks like a match, doesn't it?" Mick looked over her shoulder while he performed a routine check of the sub's carbon dioxide scrubber, a small cylinder containing material that absorbed the gas so that it wouldn't accumulate in the close confines of the craft. Coco smiled without taking her eyes off the monitor.

"It sure does. Look at these serrations." She moved the mouse cursor over the tiny saw-like indentations on the sides of the extinct shark's tooth. "They're highly characteristic of a megalodon. Mick..."

She turned to look into his eyes, and he held her gaze.

"This is a megalodon. I'm sure of it. I don't know how...but this tooth...the size of that shark down there..."

Mick set the scrubber down on the bench, and turned all of his attention to Coco and the tooth. "That canyon—it goes way down deep, right?"

Coco nodded. "To the abyss."

"So is it possible a giant prehistoric shark could have survived in the deep ocean all this time? What would it eat? And why would it come up now, after so long?"

"You're just full of questions aren't you? I like that."

Mick smiled sheepishly. Coco went on.

"First question first. Is it possible? Nobody knows for sure, but to me it's not *im*possible. Riddle me this: what happens to whales when they die?"

Mick looked at the ceiling while he made a show of pondering this. "Unless they wash up on a beach somewhere, I guess they usually sink to the bottom of the ocean."

"Exactly! That's a heck of a lot of calories raining down from above."

"But megalodons are like Great Whites—they're hunters, not scavengers."

Coco shrugged, staring at the tooth in her hand. "Maybe they've adapted, evolved over time to a new environment. Perhaps climate change rendered the shallow seas uninhabitable for them— too warm, too salty, too *something*—so they went deep."

"Okay, but again, if they did, why would they come to the surface now?"

Coco tugged at her lower lip while she thought. At length, she said, "I know that the construction of the underwater hotel had quite an impact on the local marine environment. A negative one, some say. Dynamiting the reef to blast channels and post holes to place the building supports, dredging to create deeper water passages for bigger boats, tons of SONAR surveys that ping down into the ocean..."

Mick's eyes widened. "All that commotion could have disturbed the megalodon way down there!"

Coco tilted her head while she stared at the laptop screen. "It's just a thought. I don't have any way of knowing for sure."

The knock on the wooden door of the shack came about two seconds before it opened. James White poked his head inside.

"Coco. Come with me, please. I'm going down to the hotel, and want you to come with me to do an eco-lecture. Just from inside the main lobby or maybe the restaurant. Something to keep the guests happy down there while we work on the air conditioning issue."

Coco flipped her laptop shut. She tried to shove the tooth into the pocket of her shorts but it wouldn't fit, and actually tore through the fabric. She looked up to see White frowning at her, and so she handed the tooth to Mick.

"Mick, make absolutely sure that sub's ready to go at a moment's notice, okay? Everything charged, air topped off, all that. Clear?"

"As a bell, sir."

Coco trailed after White as he left the shack. She turned around to close the door, and looked back at Mick, who made a comical stabbing motion in White's direction with the tooth.

Chapter 12

Coco stepped into the tram along with James White and four newly arrived guests—a couple of investment bankers from New York City and their wives. In the reception *bure* he started to tell them about the air conditioning problem, but then stopped when a reporter drew near. In front of him, when the new guests asked if they could be shown down to their suites right away, White said of course, and so now here they were, rolling down the tunnel through the sea to the hotel.

As expected, the bankers were loving the ride, marveling at the sheer novelty of it. The reporter had been denied entrance to the hotel, which White put down to "capacity issues," but he knew there was already one reporter in the hotel, and didn't want to add more with the developing situation. When the train entered the hotel, more people were waiting to be taken back to shore than there were seats on the tram. They feigned politeness as the new passengers disembarked, and they got on.

"How is it? Leaving so soon?" the bankers inquired.

"Too damn hot," someone said point blank. "Ready to lay on the beach and catch the breezes for a while," said another. They were cordial, but Coco could see that their smiles were forced, their civility strained. A minor scuffle even broke out as a child threaded his way through the crowd and sprawled across a row of seats to save for the rest of his family. White diffused the situation by handing the displaced family a voucher good for a free meal at the hotel's restaurant, while reminding them that the tram would be back in about ten minutes.

Even with that, the latest arrivals were suitably impressed with the spectacle of it all. Walking around the grand lobby lit by shifting rays of sunlight filtered through the sapphire-hued lagoon, they stared in awe at the incredible view out the hotel's acrylic walls. Uniformed servers offered the new guests complimentary beverages, while White chatted up the clients, introducing Coco as the marine biologist in residence. After about ten minutes of this, one of the hotel staff approached White and spoke softly to him for a few seconds, her expression serious. White turned to the guests he'd been speaking with and excused himself and Coco, imploring them to enjoy their stay.

"What is it?" Coco asked as she and White followed the Fijian woman out of the lobby.

White kept his voice low. "Train alarm. Apparently the tram stopped in the tunnel. We'll find out more up here."

He nodded to a small room at the end of a hallway marked Employees Only. The staff woman led them inside and then left, closing the door behind them. The room was smaller than the walk-in closets of many of the hotel's guests, and served as a "switching station" for the tram. The room's only occupant besides White and Coco, a diminutive Indian man seated at a stool in front of a computer terminal of sorts, did not turn around to greet the newcomers as he hit buttons on a control panel. A battery of red LEDs blinked while an alarm buzzed.

"Kamal, that alarm is not audible outside this room, correct?"

"That is correct, sir. Only the fire alarms and flood alarms are audible throughout the hotel, sir, and those have not been activated."

"So what's the problem with the train?"

"I'm afraid the news is not good, Sir. The tram has been decoupled from the cable which means it has stopped about halfway up the tunnel on its way back up to the beach. Worse, I'm detecting an air pressure change in the tunnel, which means we likely have a leak."

"How about a video feed?"

Kamal shook his head. "The project to set that up, sir, is still ongoing. As you recall in the last progress meeting, we were instructed not to fast track anything that wasn't absolutely require—"

"Okay, okay, I get it. So we can't see what's going on in there."

"We can send people on foot from Topside, sir." Then he looked at Coco. "Or from the water via scuba or submersible."

"We can communicate with them, though, right? They can hear us through the PA system?"

"Yes, that system is still functional. It's one way though, so they can hear us, but we can't hear them."

"Good enough. Let me say something."

He reached for a microphone on a stand and then spoke into it. "Attention guests in the train tunnel. This is James White speaking on behalf of everyone here at the Triton Undersea Resort. We are aware of your situation, and are sending people to you now in the tunnel. Please stay put until help arrives. It will be there momentarily." He set the microphone back down.

Kamal appeared concerned. "I would expect that at least some of them will try to walk out of the tunnel, sir. They were almost halfway to the beach."

White shrugged. "That's fine if they do, but I still want them to know help is coming. Do we know who is on that tram?"

"We have no way of tracking who boards the tram, sir, nor would we ordinarily be able to know how many riders are aboard. However, in this case, we know that the tram is at maximum capacity since there were more people waiting to get on than could board. So there are twenty people aboard, sir."

"I happened to see that one of them was that reporter from the New York Times," Coco said.

"Shit." White raised his radio to his lips. "Hotel to Topside: Al, this is James, do you copy?" He repeated the message once before they heard Al's voice emanate from the radio.

"Al here, James. Train situation, right?"

"Right. Tram stopped about halfway through en route from hotel to beach with twenty on board. We need to get somebody in there now, Al. Escort the guests out."

"Bobby and Taj should be just about there now."

"Good. What do you recommend for an external view?"

"Probably SCUBA would be the most expedient, and thorough enough."

"Thanks, Al, keep me informed. Out."

White turned to Coco. "I need you to scuba dive over the tunnel, and check it out."

Chapter 13

Coco entered the hotel's dive locker. Situated in the lower part of the cylindrical tower on the opposite side of the hotel from the lobby, it featured a full dive shop including tanks, an air compressor, and other equipment. Access to the water for scuba diving was via an airlock—a wet-dry room with a system of double doors that sealed the chamber off from the rest of the hotel so that it could be flooded with water, and then emptied again.

Coco put on her scuba gear—a single air tank and regulator, buoyancy vest, mask, and fins—and stepped from the gear room into the airlock. She pressed the button to seal the first door, the one that separated the airlock from the dive area and the rest of the hotel. Then she stepped across the airlock to the outer door—the one beyond which the ocean waited. She strapped on her fins, and put her breathing mouthpiece in place. This last step—opening the outer door—was always a little unnerving for her, and this was the first time she'd had to do it by herself. The thought of all that water out there waiting to come rushing in was scary, but she knew that the airlock was slightly pressurized to prevent a catastrophic rush of water that could breach the hotel itself. When returning to the airlock, the process would be reversed, with greater pressure activated in order to expel the water back outside.

She read the pressure gauge on the wall, taking comfort in the green LED that told her the airlock was properly pressurized. Then she hit the button to open the outer door, and waited while it slid up. Water pooled inside the airlock, quickly rising to her knees, waist, and then chest as she stood there. Through her mask, she stared at the control buttons on the wall until the door had risen all the way up, the entire airlock now flooded. She inhaled through her mouthpiece, taking comfort in the familiar rasp as air was delivered to her. She kicked off the floor, and swam outside of the hotel, pausing to press the button on the outside wall to close the outer airlock door.

Looking to her right, the bulk of the underwater hotel stretched across the coral reef, the tower on its far end nearly reaching the lagoon's surface. It was an odd sensation, swimming along while looking into a glass building, watching people walk around inside. So surreal; she still hadn't gotten used to it. She had a job to do now, though, and a serious one at that, so she kicked faster, and forced her mind to focus as she finned over the corals.

The train tunnel itself wasn't easy to see from far away simply because it was so clear that it blended with the water. Unless the tram happened to be rolling through it when she looked, she'd often been surprised at just how invisible it seemed. That was one of Triton's selling points: architecture that was a harmonious fit with the natural seascape. But right now it made it difficult to discern the structure, even though she knew where it was.

She angled away from the hotel when she neared the opposite end.

There! The train tunnel.

Coco spotted the glint of sunlight off the shiny surface. She headed toward it. She looked down and ahead at the reef as she went, and found herself questioning something. *What was different?* By now she'd logged hundreds of hours on this reef. She knew it like her own backyard in Hawaii, and right now something didn't seem quite the same. It hit her as she glided past a large coral head, one that usually teemed with activity.

The fish! Where were they? That was it. The entire reef was just so...*still*. Not normal at all. But there was no time to dwell on ecological matters. This was a safety dive. Potentially even a rescue dive, she reminded herself.

She neared the train tunnel not far from the hotel. She knew the tram was farther up, about halfway to shore. The structure was suspended a few feet up from the ocean floor—more so the farther it got away from the hotel as it angled up toward the island—and she had a choice to make: swim over or under the tunnel. She took the high road, looking down into the tram tunnel as she passed over. No tram.

She kicked along over the top of the tunnel as it angled up toward the beach. As she neared the middle of the tunnel, problems became apparent. Water pooled on the tunnel floor. A few of the light fixtures had shattered. They weren't needed in the daytime, but the tram was designed to run 24/7. How had that happened? she wondered, looking for the tram up ahead. Did the tram hit the walls, and shake them loose? She was definitely no expert in how the tunnel system was constructed, but it seemed unlikely.

A few fin strokes later, and the tram came into view. A sharp *hiss* came from her regulator mouthpiece as she sucked in her breath at the sight of it. From Kamal's description, she'd been expecting that the cable attached to the tram's flywheel system that pulled it along had separated from it, leaving the tramcar sitting there waiting for someone to reattach it.

That was far from the sight with which she was greeted.

The entire tram lay on its side. A significant crack raced along the top of the tunnel, and ran down along the side. Water dripped steadily into the tunnel. Coco had to swim away from the crack to get a clear view of the tram, and when she did, it was not a pleasant one.

She could see now that at least a couple of passengers had been pinned beneath the tram when it overturned, their arms crushed beneath them. Water sprayed into the tunnel from the crack, making it difficult to see clearly, but it looked as though a few of the passengers were rendering aid to those injured. She could see one woman, arm held beneath the tram, a puddle of blood seeping out from under it, shrieking at the top of her lungs while two men held her closely. To Coco the woman's screams were oddly silent. She could only watch, not hear. A couple of those in the tunnel saw her, and they pointed.

\#

In the tram tunnel, Stanley and Priscilla Doherty looked into each other's eyes, Stanley from a kneeling position on the acrylic floor, and Priscilla from inside the overturned tram with one arm crushed beneath the vehicle. Her face was very pale, and her eyes were open, but her breathing was shallow. Around them was chaos as their fellow passengers struggled up from their tram seats in a daze.

"Priscilla, stay with me, dear. Don't fall asleep. I want you to try to slide your arm out from under the tram when I lift up on it, okay? Can you do that?"

Just then a passenger from the row of seats behind them fell from the left side of the seat—the side of the tram that was in the air—and landed on the inside of the tram next to Stanley, adding to the pressure on his wife's arm.

"Watch it, asshole!" Stanley shoved the guy off the tram, and he went sprawling on the slick tunnel floor. The man got to his feet and lumbered at Stanley, saying nothing, but his intent was clear on his rage-addled face.

"My wife is trapped here!" Stanley tried appealing to the person's sense of mercy, but it apparently mattered little if at all to him, for he kept coming.

The big man threw himself on the sports franchise owner, and tackled him to the ground. It was clear that neither man was a trained fighter, nor were they experienced in how to prevent damage to themselves. An ungainly series of grappling, hair-pulling, and missed punches ensued. Stanley's foe lashed out with a foot, the kick finding only air. Both fighters heard those around them yelling to look up.

"What is that?" The dark shape that passed over the tunnel had something sinister about it beyond its sheer size. The way it moved, calculating yet almost aloof...whatever it was it looked to be in no hurry, yet it also seemed like it didn't need to be in a hurry because it could do whatever it wanted, whenever it wanted.

"Boat? Sinking boat?" someone suggested.

"I read on the website this place has a submarine. Maybe they're bringing it down to rescue us?" tried another.

"It's gone already," a woman declared, pointing up out of the leaking tunnel. "I think it was a whale."

"Who gives a fuck what it was?" said a well-known rock star. "Let's get the fuck out of here before this thing falls apart."

"How?" someone said.

"Just walk out." He grabbed his now disheveled girlfriend, a waif-like Japanese woman, by the hand, and started to tread up the artificial incline that led to the beach. At that moment, the man who had been fighting with Stanley pointed up through the tunnel.

"Look, a scuba diver!"

And then their world caved in on them.

Chapter 14

Coco floated above the tunnel, trying understand what went wrong here, and how she could be of most help to the people inside. She thought the damage to the tunnel must have been caused when the train car crashed, although if that was the case she found it odd that the tunnel leaked water from two places many yards apart. She was all too aware that she was no structural engineer. Which reminded her...Mr. White. What was he thinking? Sending a marine fricking biologist down to assess a tunnel collapse? Some of his engineers must be divers; where the hell were they?

Then she saw a shape so large, so pervasive, that it blotted out the sun. It was so all-encompassing that at first she assumed it was a cloud passing over the sun. But then she watched it sink lower in the water, still moving while the sun shined once again down to the reef, its light doing little to lift her spirits. For a moment she just floated there above the plagued tunnel, shivering in a void of uncertainty.

What was that?

But deep down she knew what it was. *That's your visitor from the sub.* Only now, she felt naked being in the presence of the monstrosity without even so much as her little submersible to shield her.

She forced herself into motion before she could think the word...

Megalodon...

She saw the people pointing at her, and instinctively she did what she could to protect them: she pointed up along the tunnel toward the beach. *Go that way. Don't wait for anyone to come and get you. Go now,* she implored them mentally, wishing she had some way to communicate with them. At least a couple of them did seem to be walking out, though, and she swam alongside the tunnel in the same direction that they went, gesturing with what she hoped looked like urgent pointing motions to head up to the beach.

Coco's head was on a swivel as she looked around for the megalodon, not quite believing that's what she was doing. *I'm checking over my shoulder for a* megalodon? *Whatever. For a really big shark. That's probably all it is. Maybe if I'm lucky, it's a whale shark or some other behemoth that only eats plankton and krill.* But then she flashed on that tooth taken from the pipe, and knew that was nothing more than wishful thinking. *If wishes were horses, she could hear her mother saying...*

What she saw next heading in her direction scared her, but it wasn't a fish.

Two people, both men, came running down the tunnel—from the beach side—to the wrecked tram. She was surprised to feel a pang of relief when she saw that neither was Mick. It was a terrible mixture of relief and foreboding; that something very bad was about to happen, but at least someone she cared for—*you do care about him, don't you?*—wouldn't be around to be hurt by it.

Suddenly the gloomy mass—so large that it appeared fish-like only with sufficient distance away from it—rose from the reef not far in front of her, perhaps adjacent to the two approaching men. Inside the tunnel she could see the tourists turning to face it, some patting those next to them on the arm to turn and look at it. The rapid shifting from light to dark was unsettling.

The gargantuan fish rose until it was atop the tunnel, its caudal fin slicing the surface of the lagoon as it angled its conical nose downward. Coco felt as though she were not even present in this moment, like she was watching a movie or in a dream (or nightmare, as the case may be). *You're not watching a megalodon, you're not watching a megalodon...*was the phrase she tried to force through her brain, but her mind refused to accept that false premise as it processed the reality in front of her: A sixty-foot-plus shark that looked a lot like a great white. *What else could it be?*

She was jarred from her thoughts at that moment as the megalodon gave a powerful burst of its tail, propelling it forward and down with shocking speed. Coco had absolutely no idea what she would do—what she *could* do—if the prehistoric beast decided to turn toward her. She was sitting in the middle of the water column with absolutely no cover of any kind except for the tunnel. Closer to the hotel, the bottom of it was nearer to the reef, but here it was elevated well above the seafloor.

Fortunately for Coco, she was not the fish's target. The megalodon did not let up speed as it neared the tunnel, nor did it veer away. Coco had no idea why, but the huge shark rammed its weighty snout into the acrylic structure. She cringed with the crunching sound that travelled through the water to her ears.

She watched, helpless and spellbound at the same time, as the two staff members just arriving were knocked off their feet just before the tunnel's roof imploded with the force of the mighty fish. She had to tear her gaze from those men, though, to watch the megalodon, which, unbelievably, even with its great size, was pulled into the now open tunnel as the incredible suction of incoming water took it into the air-filled space.

It wouldn't remain air-filled for long, though, Coco realized with a start. Like watching some kind of disaster movie in slow motion, she processed the unthinkable: the train tunnel was flooding with water. Everyone inside was about to perish. Those nearest to the opening—the two hotel staff— were simply crushed by the unimaginable onslaught of rushing seawater, while those further back by the tram found themselves in the unenviable position of watching the water rise around them until they were trapped in a water-filled tube.

Coco kicked toward the opening created by the megalodon. The beastly fish—yes, it was a fish, she was certain of that now— thrashed around inside the partially filled tunnel, breaking it apart even more. Its motions were slow, but immensely powerful, like an earth-moving machine capable of displacing many tons of material. When the inside of the tunnel was completely filled, the marine animal gained even more strength, and proceeded to bash the remaining Plexiglas material out of its way. Then the gigantic shark rolled free of the train tube on the side away from Coco, shaking its wide snout back and forth.

Coco dropped lower to the reef, and swam toward the tram, which she could now see wobbling with the surge of water in the tunnel. Coco's mind was awash with terror at the ghastly spectacle playing out before her. Many people were going to drown here, of this she had little doubt. Was there anything she could do to save even one of them? Trapped in that flooded train tube was a terrible situation to be sure, but one that was potentially survivable, Coco realized, provided that the person didn't panic, was at least an okay swimmer, and had the good fortune not to be hit in the head by a piece of heavy equipment on the way up—or be consumed by a rampaging prehistoric shark, she added to herself glumly.

Coco looked into the tunnel as she swam alongside. She saw two people float past her, already drowned, the woman's designer handbag still strapped to her drifting corpse. Then a glimmer of hope as she saw a group of four emerge from the gash in the top of the tunnel that had been ripped open by the megalodon. That glimmer faded as quickly as it appeared when the ginormous creature spun alarmingly fast for its size and barreled at what it no doubt considered to be prey. Coco finned up over the top of the tunnel, wanting a better view, wanting to help the people somehow, even though she had no idea what, if anything, she could do.

Distract the shark? She looked down, and saw that another section of tunnel had been ripped apart, one she hadn't noticed before. She would be able to fit through it, but the megalodon would not, at least not without stopping to bash it open first. She removed her scuba mouthpiece, and yelled as loudly as she could into the ocean. Still the shark was unwavering in its approach to the four struggling prey items. She yelled again until she thought her lungs would burst. No change. She removed her dive knife from a sheath on her calf, and banged the blunt end against her aluminum scuba tank, producing a piercing clanging noise.

Amazingly, the megalodon changed course. It didn't stop, but it whirled around, and with almost the same speed it had built up, proceeded to charge at her. Coco grinned for a split second in spite of the situation as she saw the four terrified swimmers stroke for the lagoon's shimmering surface. Then she darted inside the tunnel like a reef creature ducking into a crevice to avoid a predator.

It was completely flooded now, and the moment of elation she had felt at saving the foursome above was crushed into oblivion by what she encountered here. Bodies everywhere. The bodies of people who just minutes before were simply tourists looking for a unique and exciting—but not this exciting—experience, now dead, all of them.

Wait!

She almost missed it—the frantic motion of an arm waving from the floor of the tunnel. Up ahead by the tram, where the water had engulfed the tunnel only moments ago. Movement. She started to kick to move faster, but as soon as Coco was inside the tunnel it was like stepping into a raging river. She was swept along fast toward the tram, and realized she would not be able to stop. She saw two people who were way beyond terrified—a man and a woman. She remembered seeing them in the reception *bure* only hours ago. It was hard to believe this had happened to them.

The man was pulling on his wife, yanking her out from beneath the tram. Coco grabbed onto a handrail on the tram to hold herself in position. She knew the two victims wouldn't be able to see clearly, not having masks on, but she could tell the man was aware someone was here. He reached out to her. Coco took his hand, and pulled him to her. She could see him starting to panic, unable to communicate, and not knowing what he was supposed to do in order to be rescued.

Coco's scuba training kicked in. She knew that within seconds he'd start flailing around in a blind panic unless she got the situation under some kind of control. She felt for her "octopus," a spare regulator mouthpiece to be used in emergencies when a diver's primary regulator malfunctioned, or if another diver ran out of air. Rather than sharing a single mouthpiece, it enabled the diver performing the rescue to give the stricken diver their own breathing source. She cupped the mouthpiece end of the hose in her right hand while clutching the side of the tram with her left. She waved the regulator in front of the Stanley's face, knowing he couldn't see clearly, but wanting to let him know what was coming, then she shoved the regulator into his mouth.

She hoped he'd been scuba diving at some point in his life before, because then he'd know that you needed to blow out first before breathing in, to expel the water inside the outer part of the mouthpiece. She had no way to explain that to him now, though, and so had to hope that either he knew it already, or would be okay dealing with it on the fly.

She was pleased to see his hand situate the regulator in his mouth, and bubbles blow out of it immediately, meaning he had breathed out first. Good. Now to focus on the missus, who was in full-fledged panic mode. Coco grabbed her, and pulled her the rest of the way out from under the tram, wary of the fact that should she lose her grip on her she would drift away further into the tunnel, and they would not be able to find her in time.

Coco encircled Priscilla Doherty with one arm while she took her own primary regulator out of her mouth, and placed it in Priscilla's. Stanley's wife did not have the presence of mind to exhale first, and breathed in water. She started choking, arms flailing. Coco and Stanley gripped her hard while they fought not to be carried away by the torrent of water passing through the tunnel. Coco refused to let Priscilla spit the mouthpiece out or jerk her head away, knowing it'd be over for her if she did. She held her in place until she breathed in, and her eyes bugged out with the realization that she got air instead of water. Coco waited while she took a few breaths to calm herself down.

Coco needed to breathe, too, but recognized that Stanley was the less panic prone of the two of them, and so she reached out and made a grabbing motion in front of his face. She didn't know what she would do if he decided to fight her for the mouthpiece. To her great relief, he nodded, took one more breath, removed the regulator from his mouth, and handed it to Coco.

She placed it in her mouth, and took a couple of quick breaths while looking around. This was it. She had to get these people to the surface before they were separated, or one of them panicked too much. Coco identified a large rip in the side of the tunnel, but it went against the still-flowing current. They had to get to it in order to escape the tunnel. She decided to let Priscilla keep her mouthpiece, and buddy-breathe with Stanley while they moved.

She handed the mouthpiece back to Stanley, tapped him on the shoulder to get his undivided attention, and then pointed to her right. *Time to move.* The man nodded his understanding. He sure as hell didn't want to hang out here any longer, either, Coco thought. And he wasn't too scared to move. Good.

The tether to Priscilla was shorter, the primary regulator hose not designed with sharing in mind. This meant Coco would have to swim with Priscilla very close to her, which was probably a good idea anyway, Coco thought. Stanley, with the longer hose, could get as far as a couple of feet away from Coco's right side. In this manner, she set off to her right up the tunnel, bucking the torrential current.

Fortunately the tram was still there for them to hold onto, even though now it wobbled in the current. Her hands occupied grabbing the tram and prodding the Doherty's along, she relied on her fins to push forward along the train car. She felt bad for Stanley and Priscilla, pushing forward with one hand waving out in front of their faces, barely able to see, but somehow they kept on. A terrible moment transpired when a corpse drifted out of the tram right in front of them; Coco pushed it above their heads where it was caught in the fast-moving water, and carried away before her rescuees could bump into it.

At the end of the tram she looked up, searching for the smashed open section of tunnel roof.

There!

An opening large enough for them to fit through. Coco didn't have a free hand to check her pressure gauge to see how much air she had remaining in her tank, but with the three of them breathing off of it, she knew it wouldn't last long. At least once they got out of the tunnel they'd have an unobstructed path to the surface of the lagoon.

And to the megalodon...

She forced that thought from her mind as she pointed toward the roof of the destroyed tunnel, hoping that her two charges would catch her meaning in spite of the fact that they wouldn't be able to see any details. She couldn't see the shark, at least, not that she was looking as hard as she could have. But it wasn't lurking just outside the tunnel waiting for them. To stay here much longer was to invite death for them all, though, so it was time to move.

Coco let go of the tram and put one arm on the man, one on the woman and kicked off the bottom. The unlikely trio ascended the ten feet or so to the tunnel roof and Coco dragged them through the jagged aperture into open water.

Then the woman began to panic. Coco didn't know what the problem was. She had air, she could see her blowing a frenetic curtain of bubbles, rapidly consuming their remaining breathing gas. But for whatever reason, she had had enough.

But so had Coco. Still kicking, she glanced up at the surface. At the sun. She wanted to push them away now, but was worried they wouldn't know not to hold their breath, which could cause a serious diving injury called an air embolism, a bursting of the lungs due to expanding air as the pressure decreased. Coco resigned herself to dragging her two victims the rest of the way to surface so that she could keep an eye on them.

The last few feet up scared Coco the most, for she knew that was where they were most vulnerable to the apex predator in their midst. To a megalodon, three humans splashing around on top of the water was like ringing a dinner bell. She hauled them the last few feet, the sunlight growing more intense, until their heads burst through the water into the world of air. She could read the stunned expressions of the married couple as they spit the mouthpieces out, not believing they were actually breathing natural air once again. There was not time to let them rejoice in the moment.

"Swim for the beach. Go!"

She assumed they knew how to swim. They damn well better, she though, sticking her mask back underwater, scanning back and forth for signs of the—

Megalodon! There it was, down by the tunnel, but now swerving their way.

"Get out of the water now! Shark is coming!"

They made for a clumsy pair of swimmers, dogpaddling their way toward the beach, but at least they were making progress. The megalodon was too, though, and it was ridiculously fast. Coco watched as the gargantuan animal passed beneath her, the sheer girth of its body halfway to the surface. It was angling up now, homing in on the splashy swimmers who still had a good ways to go to reach the beach.

"Swim faster! Keep going!" Coco spurred them on one last time before she vented the air from her scuba vest, and sank below the surface. She knew she stood a far better chance against the finned marauder on scuba at the bottom than did the pair of swimmers up top. By the looks of it, the megalodon could simply swallow both of them whole.

Coco banged on her tank with her dive knife, and again the giant shark changed direction. She had bought them a little time. She kept banging on the tank while she swam to the bottom. When she reached it, she spotted a good-sized outcropping of hard coral, and wedged herself into it, hoping against hope that it was enough.

Chapter 15

The megalodon seemed to fly over Coco's stony sanctuary, gliding past the coral formation with a dip of its left pectoral fin. Its snout was far too big to penetrate deep enough to get at Coco. Yet, as she consulted her pressure gauge, she knew that she didn't have much air remaining, and so wouldn't be able to hunker down here for long.

She had two choices: reach the beach, or swim back into the hotel's airlock. She wasn't going to lie to herself. Dry land sounded great right about now. She could scuba toward the beach along the bottom rather than on the surface as the couple had been forced to do, and once the water grew shallow enough—perhaps ten feet—the dino-shark would be too big to go any further; so she didn't really even have to make it all the way to the beach to be safe. Still, it was the farther of the two options. The hotel was a short underwater swim away, with some cover provided by the coral formations in which she could hide.

She made up her mind to go for the hotel. She looked out at the airlock from inside the maze of corals, a couple of parrotfish darting about her, also seeking sanctuary. When she saw the oversized shark start into a wide turn to its right, some distance from the hotel, Coco made her move. She pushed out of the coral, and shot toward the underwater building.

Almost as soon as she was free of her cover, the wary predator accelerated its turn, whipping its massive body around in a surprising show of agility. So much for an easy dash to safety, she thought, eyeing the next clump of corals up ahead that might offer shelter from the beast.

She shot across the reef, just high enough to avoid the main bottom structure. She kicked and used her arms, feeling the drag of the scuba tank on her back as she sought every iota of speed from her muscles. Out of her peripheral vision she saw something roughly the size of an eighteen-wheeler barreling towards her. She reached the next large clump of corals, and nestled amongst them. This one was not as substantial as the last, and she felt terribly exposed, her entire scuba tank sticking up into the water. Again, a population of fish displaced by her body flitted about, also seeking refuge.

This time the megalodon took a low-speed but more direct approach, ramming its snout into the base of the coral formation in which Coco hid. Like a slow motion train wreck, Coco watched clouds of silt and debris flake up into the water with the shark's impact. She heard a crunching sound as its body impacted with the reef, and lowered her head until her mask touched the coral and she was eye to eye with a small decorator shrimp twiddling its antennae.

Then the big shark backed up and shook its monolithic head like a dog getting out of a pool, showering bits of reef debris in every direction. What happened next chilled Coco beyond words. Her next breath from the regulator was hard to pull. She knew from experience that this meant she was only a few breaths from a completely empty tank. She glanced at her pressure gauge and saw it redlined on zero. The mad dash across the reef evading the monster had taken its toll on her air consumption, the heavy exertion depleting what remained in her tank after the rescue breathing. She drew her dive knife, aware of what a pathetic weapon it was against so gigantic a foe.

She was in the process of debating the lesser of two evils—make a mad dash for the airlock, and hope the megalodon didn't pluck her off in the process, or sticking around here in the corals just long enough to stab it (hopefully in the eye) which might discourage it enough to leave. Because no animal, no matter how large or ferocious, liked to be stabbed in the eye.

But in the end her decision was made for her. At that moment she—and the shark—heard splashing from above. Raising her head enough to look up at the surface, she saw the unmistakable outline of a swimmer. Looking a little closer, she could see that this particular swimmer wore full clothing. It wasn't one of the two she had just rescued, that much she could tell. For that she was grateful. Her rescue of those people could represent the last positive act of her short life, after all. The person was definitely a tunnel survivor, though, she was sure of that. Someone who had managed to somehow swim up and out of the flooded tunnel on their own, only to unknowingly swim over the largest predator ever to roam the seas.

The megalodon moved.

It whirled around, its imposing tail swishing in short, powerful strokes as it propelled itself along the reef floor until it was beneath the target of its sensory investigation.

Coco shivered despite the tropical water. The predator's behavior telegraphed its intentions. Like most sharks, it preferred to attack its prey from below and behind, in a single, incapacitating rush that stunned the fight out of its victim while they bled to death from the first debilitating bite. As Coco's lungs worked hard to pull the next breath—possibly the last breath—from the tank, she knew that there was nothing she could do for the swimmer. Nothing at all. Best not to let the person's death be for nothing, and use it to make her escape.

Coco pulled out of her protective coral fortress with her arms, shooting across the reef once more, this time straight for the cylindrical tower that housed the airlock. Halfway there, she looked up, and saw the unthinkable: the megalodon lunging at the swimmer, most of its form disappearing from view as it catapulted itself into the air along with its prey—"air jaws"—before landing back with a bloody splash.

The marine biologist forced her limbs to stay in motion as she continued crossing the reef. She didn't know what would happen next with the shark. Would it go after the two people she'd rescued if they haven't made it to the beach yet? They should have by now, she thought, even at their slow pace.

Or would the shark single her out now that the easier prey was gone?

Just as this unpleasant thought compelled her to move even faster, she started to take a deep breath. But nothing came out of the regulator. It was like it was sealed shut. She sucked harder but still nothing was released.

She was completely out of air.

Normally an ascent from this depth, pushing off the reef to reach the surface, would be easily doable for the experienced diver. But with a megalodon lurking above? Not an option.

Coco eyed the remaining distance to the airlock door. Maybe thirty feet. She didn't know if the shark was bearing down on her, and didn't care. When you had to breathe you had to breathe.

Even so, Coco willed herself not to swim spastically in an attempt to gain more speed, but to keep her strokes efficient, to glide gracefully through the water. Panic was the enemy of all divers. Stay calm, she told herself. *Stay calm.* She mentally envisioned herself swimming with the dolphins off her home beach in Waimanalo, Hawaii, early in the morning before school, a rainbow in the sky after a light, warm rain. Before she knew it she was gliding up to the outer airlock door, not even feeling a terrible urge to breathe yet.

She knew that wouldn't last, though, so wasted no time reaching out for the button that would open the outer door. She slapped it and waited.

Nothing happened.

A dark, dark chill began to entomb Coco's very soul. As calm as she was, she would not make it to the surface, even without the megalodon. She had been telling herself all she needed to do was to reach the airlock, and everything was okay. *Now what?*

Finally, she heard a faint mechanical hum, and then the door raised up. She didn't wait for it to lift all the way. Coco lowered herself to the seafloor and slid under the door into the still flooded airlock.

Shit!

She hadn't taken into account that she'd have to close the outer door, then hit the inner door button, and wait for the chamber to drain. She didn't know how long that was altogether—normally it didn't seem like much—but it was a frighteningly long time from where she was sitting. She forced the panic back, and did what she knew had to be done if she wanted to live. Inside the airlock, she swam to the inner door, and hit the button on the wall there.

She heard another mechanical whir, and then the outer door started to close, lowering. It was maddening to have to simply wait while her lungs burned and glowing spots began to cloud her vision. Then, with two feet remaining before the door contacted the bottom of its frame, she saw the eye of the monster rush up to the airlock.

Chapter 16

As Coco watched the megalodon wedge the tip of its snout beneath the outer airlock door, preventing it from closing, she realized with an odd sense of detachment that she no longer felt the irrepressible urge to breathe. She also knew that was a perilous situation to be in.

Coco was intimately familiar with the dangers of shallow water blackout. Her first love, her high school sweetheart from Hawaii, had drowned while freediving to spear fish off Oahu. He and his friends had practiced an aggressive form of snorkeling known as "freediving," where they would hyperventilate—take multiple deep breaths in rapid succession before holding the final one—to saturate their lungs with oxygen in order to stay down longer on a single breath. The problem with doing this too many times in a row is that it overrides the body's natural alarm system—the urge to breathe—and one can simply black out without warning.

Coco's cells had now been without oxygen for so long that her body could no longer give her a warning. It had already done that, and she had still done nothing about it as far as her lungs were concerned. The next step was to pass out. And that would spell death for the marine biologist, shark, or no shark.

Deciding to make the utmost use of whatever seconds she had remaining, Coco drew her dive knife, and swam to the megalodon. Crouching low, she thrust the blade to the hilt in the megalodon's nose. The animal withdrew immediately in a flurry of head-shaking, taking the knife, still embedded in its snout, with it.

The door dropped the rest of the way shut, and Coco kicked off of it, pushing herself back over to the inner door. She waited. She heard the mechanical sucking noise as the water was vacuumed from the space. She looked up toward the ceiling while she waited for the water level to drop. *C'mon, C'mon, C'mon...*

After what seemed an eternity, but in reality was only a few seconds, Coco saw the ceiling of the airlock vanish from view as the water level dropped. She swam up to greet the layer of air that materialized as the water level lowered. She raised her upturned face, and greedily gulped air, air that was sweeter than any she had ever breathed in her life. She tore off her mask, and stood there taking rushed breaths as the water dropped to her shoulders, her waist, her knees...When her feet were dry, she heard a humming noise as the inner airlock door slid upward.

A smile formed on her lips as she looked into the hotel's dive locker. She had made it. Coco took off her fins, and walked into hotel. She then closed the inner airlock door behind her. Walking into the dive shop, she found it totally empty. She had thought maybe the systems guys would have sent someone to greet her when they noticed the airlock activation, but no.

Good to know I'm on my own, she thought, walking through the shop out into the hotel's thoroughfare area, a large hallway that led to several different areas. She knew White would disapprove of her walking around the hotel dripping wet in only a one-piece swimsuit, but she didn't care for his rules right about now. With the train tunnel destroyed, the airlock was now the only way to get in or out of the hotel. Here inside, they were cut off from land. It was not a comforting thought. People were dead, he needed to know, and she needed to know what he was doing about it.

She walked toward the train control room, the last place she had seen her boss. Amazingly, she passed a couple of guests who appeared oblivious to anything that was going on, standing there holding hands and gazing out across the reef in wonder. They smiled pleasantly at Coco as she walked by. She returned the smile, but said nothing.

The door to the control room was closed. Coco pushed on the lever handle to open it, but found it to be locked. She heard footsteps from within, and then White's voice: "Who is it?"

"Coco!"

She heard the latch click open from the inside, and then the door swung open. James White peered past Coco to the common area outside, checking for people. When he saw that she was alone, he turned around and walked back to the control console where Kamal was still seated, but now focused on Coco rather than the controls.

"Close the door behind you, please," White told Coco. She did so, then turned to look at the two men. They appeared shaken, White's face ghostly pale, and even Kalik's drained of most of its color.

"What happened?" White implored her.

She relayed the account of events from her scuba dive, how she saw most die in the tunnel, but distracted the shark from four swimmers, and then rescued Stanley and Priscilla before being chased across the reef by the...*megalodon*. She now called it what she thought it was, no longer caring if White doubted her. When she was done, he ran his fingers through his hair, and stared at the ceiling for a moment before coming back with, "You knew this monster shark was out there on the edge of the reef, and you didn't warn us about it?"

Coco's faced turned crimson with rage. Kamal appeared uncomfortable, looking away from her. "Now listen here, Mr. White! I *did* tell you about what I saw in the submarine canyon. I wasn't sure of what it was at that point, and you—"She was going to say, *you dismissed it as me being hung-over*, but he spoke over her.

"You weren't sure of what it was! Well guess what, Coco— you're the goddamn marine biologist around here! I'm paying you to be sure! Now people are dead because *you* weren't sure!"

Coco's mind seemed to be floating away from her. She could barely process what she was hearing after all she'd been through. Kamal said White's name in a low voice, as if to suggest that he should back off, but that was the extent of his intervention. She was so flabbergasted that she still had said nothing when a voice blared from the control station radio set.

"Topside to Train Control, you copy?" White tore his angry gaze from Coco, and moved to pick up the transmitter.

"Control here, Topside, go ahead."

"Control: our team sent two to investigate the tunnel, and neither have returned. Two men—Bobby and Taj. Any word?"

White hung his head in an uncomfortable mixture of shame and disgust. Coco was incredulous.

"You haven't told them what happened yet?"

"You just told us what happened—we just found out!"

The look on Kamal's face told Coco that wasn't entirely true. She appealed to him. "Kamal, the instruments must have told you—"

"Shut up!" White bellowed. "The instruments suggested a tunnel failure, but we couldn't say for sure it wasn't the indicators failing. That's why we sent you out there. Let me talk!"

He picked up the radio microphone again, and keyed it. "Topside, we sent a diver for a look at the tunnel, and she just returned. There has been a complete flooding of the tunnel. Multiple fatalities reported, your tunnel team among them." White's arm hung down to his side, letting the microphone dangle, as if too defeated to say more.

"Control: I heard 'multiple fatalities including my tunnel team' and 'tunnel flooded,' is that correct, over?"

Understandably, the topside employee wanted confirmation before spreading such horrendous news. Somehow making it seem like an irritated gesture, White raised the transmitter to his lips. "You heard it right."

"How did the tunnel flood?"

"We're not sure yet, but apparently some kind of impact—"

"It was a giant shark!" Coco yelled over him. "A *Carcharadon megalodon*! Why don't you listen to me, Mr. White? I'm the expert, remember?"

White spoke under his breath, and off-air to Coco. "Just because you *saw* a shark in the area doesn't mean that shark was responsible for collapsing the tunnel."

Coco started to tell him how she saw the shark ram into the tunnel when the Topside operator's voice crackled through the speaker.

"A *shark* flooded the tunnel?" The Topside engineer came back, voice brimming with incredulity. "Structurally impossible!"

White regained some measure of enthusiasm. "I concur with that assessment. However, Coco, here, insists that she saw a...large shark, shall we call it, in the area."

"Not just—'*in the area,*' but in the tunnel!" Coco was going to say, but she broke off as soon as she saw White's finger let go of the transmit button. All communication was going through him, and him alone. His face grew angry and beet red, eyes narrowing, his carotid bulging. He thrust a finger at Coco, and hissed at her.

"You listen to me: you are my employee, and you will do as I say, and right now I say do not talk to anyone but me about this incident. I sent you out there to see what happened and report back to *me*, not to anyone else, is that fucking clear, bitch?"

Coco's mouth dropped open in deep disbelief. Even Kamal looked stunned. White was losing it. Whatever this enterprise represented to him, she knew that for whatever reason, its failure was not something he knew how to deal with. She'd heard the staff rumors around the beach, that he'd over-extended himself financially, that although he was a rich guy by most people's standards, the majority of the funds to build this place had come from other people and businesses, solicited by him. Should the venture fail, he'd be deep in debt.

Her disbelief turned to anger that he thought he could treat her like that. "I'll say what I want. It's my professional opinion."

"If I want your opinion I'll ask for it. You work for me, remember?"

Coco looked down at the swimsuit she wore, wishing she had her regular uniform on, the one she normally stuck the Triton Undersea Resort pin on, so she could rip it off and throw it on the floor. The swimsuit bore the Triton logo, but she couldn't very well take that off right now. Coco's inner voice told her not to say what she was about to utter, that she would regret it, but she could not stop herself.

"Not anymore, asshole. I quit."

She took note of Kamal's eyes widening by the second, of White cocking his head as though he had to actually think about something instead of shooting his mouth off, and then she turned and walked to the door.

The Topside guy's voice came over the radio, and asked if White could still hear him. White ignored him, shouting after Coco.

"You signed a contract. You can't quit!"

"The hell I can't. I'm out of here."

But as soon as Coco opened the door and stepped out into the breezeway, she realized the absurdity of her statement, of her actions. *You're not out of here. There's no more tunnel, remember, dumbass? The only way out of here right now is to scuba through the airlock and swim to the beach, and with that living fossil out there, that's not exactly a bright move, is it?*

Chapter 17

Coco stood in the long, wide hallway of the underwater hotel in a daze. What to do now? The Arab family walked past her, glancing curiously at her wet swimsuit. She decided to go back to the dive locker, and change back into her clothes so that she would be more comfortable roaming the hotel and deciding her next move.

That done, she retraced the same route, past the train control room, the door to which was still shut. She could hear White and Kamal conversing inside with someone on the radio, and she considered going inside and trying to retract her resignation, but then she thought about what that jerk White had said to her. The feelings were dredged up inside her again, and she kept walking until she reached a fork in the hallway. To the right the sign read, *Neptune's Bounty Restaurant*, and she went that way.

The underwater eatery was supposed to be a gourmet dining establishment, and the food was good—mostly local fish and shellfish dishes with a curry flair—but in her opinion not any better than what one could get in the regular restaurants around Fiji. But the view, of course, was unparalleled. All that underwater panorama did for Coco now, though, was to rekindle the terror of her recent scuba dive...the ruined tunnel that now cut them off from land, the dead tourists, the megalodon...

Coco walked through a grandiose entrance, passing between twin two-story golden tridents to a lobby where a hostess decked out in a slinky cocktail dress actually stood waiting at a podium. *Do any of these people know anything about what's going on?* Coco wondered.

"*Hey* girl!" she said upon recognizing Coco as she walked up. She was also an American transplant, but from the mainland, brought here because of her good looks and native U.S. English skills, so as to add to the international resort's cosmopolitan appeal. She wore her blond hair up in a bun with a pair of chopsticks through it, and a sapphire twinkled on her pert, upturned nose in the sunlight that filtered through the clear domed roof.

"Hey Tricia." Coco could not muster the energy to fake a peppy greeting.

"You dining alone?"

"Actually, just want the bar." She looked past Tricia to an alcove of the restaurant that jutted out over the reef from the rest of the hotel. A sign reading *The Wet Bar* hung over a full-service horseshoe-shaped drink station, around which a good number of patrons were currently seated.

"You and everybody else! You waiting for the next tram out of here too? I heard there's some kind of problem with it."

Coco flashed on the bodies floating past her in the flooded tunnel, the tram knocking around inside. *Some kind of problem with it, yeah.* Yet she didn't have the fortitude right now to break the news to Tricia. She just wanted a drink.

"It's going to be down for a while."

Tricia frowned. "How about the A/C? Is that going yet? At least we have the fans in here." She tilted her head skyward, where a conveyor belt system pulled a series of thatched blade fans. No wonder so many people want to be in here, Coco thought. She hadn't noticed it when she walked in because her mind was spinning with the recent events, but it was noticeably cooler in here than in the rest of the hotel.

"No A/C yet, either. Time to hit the watering hole. Feel free to join me if you get the chance."

Coco headed to the bar, and found an empty seat facing the reef outside. Reflexively she scanned the coral for signs of the megalodon, but saw none. A few reef fish even darted about like normal. Then the bartender caught her eye, and flashed his best sexy smile while he mixed a drink. He must also be clueless as to the current reality of this place, she thought, watching him flip a glass in the air, and then catch it like a cheesy imitation of Tom Cruise in that movie Cocktail. Still, she returned the smile because she needed a drink bad.

He dispensed the drink to an older woman from Germany, and then sauntered over to Coco.

"Aloha, Coco! Lemme, guess...mai tai?"

"Hey Aiden." Like Tricia, Aiden was a young American brought from the mainland. Supposedly he'd been trained at one of the top mixology schools in the U.S., but although she wouldn't tell him, she didn't think his mai tai's were as good as the ones back home. Still, they reminded her of Hawaii, so it was what she usually ordered.

"Extra strong."

"Whoa, rough day with the fishes, eh?" He grinned at her while he began mixing the drink. *If you only knew*, she thought, but did not say. Apparently the restaurant and bar were a bubble for the uninformed. She knew that Aiden pictured her like some kind of mermaid, flitting about the reef with a rainbow of tropical fish trailing behind her. If only it were so, she thought, looking around at the other patrons while he moved off to finish her drink. *If only it were so.*

She could overhear the customers discussing when the tram would be operating again, and she was glad she was wearing personal clothes, and not a Triton uniform. The anonymity was short-lived, however, because when Aiden set her mai tai down in front of her he said, "A lot of my clients want to know when the train starts rolling again. You heard anything about that?"

Strangely, even with so much more to worry about, it still annoyed Coco to hear Aiden call them *clients*, as he always did, instead of customers or regulars or something less pretentious.

"Not my problem, Aiden," she said, sipping from the drink.

He smiled mischievously at her, watching her suck on the beverage. "I know, you're a biologist not a technical person or whatever, but I just thought you might know."

She looked up from the mai tai. "No, what I mean is, it's literally not my problem anymore." She gesticulated at the hotel with her hands. "This whole place. I no longer work here. I quit this afternoon."

Aiden's mouth dropped, and his eyes grew wide. "You *what*? Quit the best job in the world? Are you shitting me?"

"Nope. I quit." Coco bent her head to the straw. Aiden hustled behind the bar, got someone a beer, and then returned with a shot of rum that he set down in front of Coco.

"On the house. Wanna tell me what happened?"

Coco stared at a barracuda swimming past the picturesque wall window. "That guy White's a dick. That's basically what happened." She picked up the shot and knocked it back, handing the shot glass directly to Aiden, who shot her a disapproving stare.

"That's all you're going to say? What the hell *happened*, Coco? Everybody says you were a rising star of this place, driving the sub, setting up the eco-tours...and with everybody stuck down here now, I'd think they need you more than ever. "

"He won't listen to me, doesn't respect me." Coco went back to the mai tai, then looked back up at Aiden, and lowered her voice. "He's *dangerous*."

"How so?"

"Doesn't give a crap about anybody but himself. I think he's been cutting corners to save a buck, and he's worried he'll be found liable for everything that's gone wrong so far."

"What about the train? When will it be working again?"

Coco didn't care what White had to say about her telling people the truth, but she didn't want to start a full-on panic; if it took them this long to fix the A/C, then she guess that tunnel would probably never be fixed.

"Forget about the train. Put a fork in it. It's done. It's demolished," she summed up.

Aiden's hand stopped wiping the rag around the inside of the glass he was drying. "Say *what*?"

"I wouldn't repeat this unless you want a full-on panic on your hands, but the entire train tunnel is flooded and useless. People have died."

Aiden reared his head back, and resumed drying the glassware. "Coco, that's not funny. Rough day or not..."

"Of course it's not funny!" She raised her voice a little too loud, and caught one of the customers turning her head to look at her. She toned it down, and continued. "But it's true."

"Coco..." Aiden looked around the bar to make sure no one needed him, then held her gaze once more. He eyed her drink. "Hey, is this really about Mick?"

Coco looked puzzled. "Mick? No. Why?"

Aiden shrugged, looked a bit uncomfortable. "I know you and him hang out together, that's all. And the other night..." He paused while drying a glass.

"The other night what?"

"I saw Mick with Clarissa. Right here. In the bar." He patted the polished wood surface.

A hot flash burned through Coco as she pictured the dolphin trainer. She didn't need this right now, and told Aiden so.

"All right, I'm sorry. I know you've had a hell of a day." He looked around the bar again, then lowered his voice.

"Who died?"

"Almost everybody on the last tram out. I saved a couple of them...I think," she finished, realizing she wasn't sure if the swimmers had actually made it to the beach or not. They probably did, but she sure would like to find out. She eyed the bar behind Aiden, looking for a telephone. She knew that many areas of the hotel had landline connections or radio with Topside.

"So you're saying that we're all stuck in here, with no way to get back to the surface?"

Coco took another drag from her drink and shrugged. "Unless you can scuba dive."

Aiden reached up, and rang the ship's bell that hung over the bar. Everyone looked over and he shouted, "Next round on the house for everybody! Drink up!"

Coco covered her face with her hand. "What are you doing?"

Aiden was already busy taking orders. "Hey, I'm from Florida where we have hurricane parties. Now we're all trapped in an underwater hotel for who knows how long? Let's get everybody in a good mood before they find out how bad it really is."

Chapter 18

Stanley and Priscilla Doherty collapsed on the powdery white sand fringing the lagoon. Both of them heaved and choked, still clinging to one another in their sopping wet clothes.

"Priscilla...Dear! Are you okay?"

Stanley's wife only sobbed in response. But that was good enough for him. She was alive. They were alive. Thanks to that scuba diver. A woman, because he remembered looking into those brown eyes. Even through the dive mask, and even under the extreme duress of the moment, his brain had registered the fact that she was a beautiful young woman. If it wasn't for her, he had no doubt that he and Priscilla would have died down there in that god-awful tunnel with all of the others...*the others*.

Until now, self-preservation had kept him from really thinking about what he had seen down there. But now, his body idle for the first time since the tram crashed, a ghoulish kaleidoscope of macabre images flooded Stanley's brain. People he had had the most banal small talk with only minutes earlier had been drowned and crushed in front of his eyes. Swallowed by a sea creature. He tried, but failed to block the gurgling sounds from his memory of a man drowning, a man mere feet away that he had been helpless to aid. He and Priscilla being chased by that monstrosity...

Then it was all just too much, and he broke down in tears alongside his wife, commiserating at water's edge, at the very boundary beyond which a terror unlike any they had ever experienced must still be out there, waiting...

One didn't get to own an NBA team without a sense of drive, though, and after a few minutes Stanley convinced his wife to come with him to the reception *bure*. They had to let the hotel staff know about this. Had to let the world know. He recalled the tram tour guide voice saying that the tunnel was the main way in or out of the hotel. Now that it was decimated, did that mean everyone still down there was marooned in the hotel? He supposed they must have some type of communications with the facilities on land, but this was no time to speculate. He helped his wife to her feet.

"I am truly sorry, honey. Never again. You're right, we should have gone to Tahiti."

"Let's go home, Stan."

"I couldn't agree more, honey."

They followed paths that now seemed nauseatingly charming, to the main *bure*, seeing no one along the way.

"Where the hell is everybody?" Stanley wanted to know. His wife was still too distraught to speak, so he answered for her. "With this whole place falling to pieces, you'd think they'd have people crawling all over to fix it. I don't see anybody anywhere."

They reached the main building, and ascended its broad, gently inclined wooden steps.

"They must all be in here." This from Priscilla, her first full sentence since the ordeal.

The sound of chattering people and laughter made its way to their ears before they reached the top of the steps. Inside, Stanley was taken aback to see a near party-like atmosphere in full swing. A row of taxis was pulled up outside, still depositing tourists. Servers armed with trays of complimentary beverages dispensed their wares to travel-weary guests newly arrived to the tropics. Behind the front desk, a pair of young Indian women were busy checking in the new arrivals. Even more unbelievably to the Dohertys, a reporter and cameraman were shooting a live piece.

The reporter, an Australian woman in her early thirties on assignment from a Sydney TV station, flitted about from guest to guest, asking routine fluff questions like, *Where are you from? What do you think so far?* and one which seemed to be her favorite: *Does it scare you at all to stay in an underwater hotel?*

"It scares the shit out of us!" Stanley said, hijacking the reporter's interview from a middle-aged Japanese couple who had arrived minutes earlier. A couple of heads turned his way, and when Stanley saw he had a larger audience, he said, "We just almost died down there!" He swiveled his head to look over at the staff behind the front desk. "Don't you know about what happened? Why are you still checking people in?"

The reporter hastily thanked the Japanese people for their time, and approached her cameraman, speaking softly to him. Stanley saw the man nod, and then the reporter approached the Dohertys, microphone in hand, extended toward Stanley.

"Sir, may I get your name?"

"I'm Stanley Doherty, and this is my wife, Priscilla."

The reporter gave a hand signal to her cameraman for him to stop filming, while she flipped through a small notebook. She ran a manicured fingernail down one of its pages until her eyebrows raised.

"Mr. and Mrs. Doherty, owners of the Los Angeles Lakers?"

"Yes, yes, but listen, that's not important." Stanley almost choked up as he flashed on the weirdly gigantic shark, its blurry, indistinct form in the tunnel, and then its ungodly presence as its fins sliced through the lagoon's shallow water, hunting, prowling, pursuing...

Putting his arm around his wife and drawing her closer, he knew what was important now. Whatever time they had left together on this Earth, that's what was important. Not any basketball team, or any fancy vacations, and certainly not any underwater hotel.

If he could keep even one person safe by telling the world what happened to him and Priscilla, then by God that's what he would do. He was a businessman, a large employer himself, and he understood fully that owners of businesses responded swiftly to media accusations. If this...what was his name...White, that's it, this White fellow wanted to play cover-up in order to make a few bucks, well then, two could play at that game.

"What is important, Mr. Doherty? You and your wife appear to be soaking wet. Are you okay? Do you require medical attention?"

Stanley shook his head. "We're okay, thanks to one brave scuba diving woman. The important thing is that the people still down there get help. The hotel is isolated now. The train tunnel is gone. I don't know why they don't know—"He pointed to the front desk.

"Mr. Doherty, what is it that happened down there? Can you tell us?"

He related how the tram crashed in the tunnel, and then the tunnel itself cracked apart and flooded. He spoke of an enormous shark, at which point the reporter gave her cameraman the signal to cut filming. She lowered her head while still directing her eyes toward Stanley.

"Enormous shark? Look, I'm all for publicity, but I need to be sure. This isn't some kind of promotional stunt for the hotel, is it?"

Stanley retuned her gaze. "I wish it was."

Chapter 19

"I can't hold them off any longer. You have to talk to someone, Mr. White. Here, it's the Operations Manager." Kamal handed him a cordless phone that was currently online with the hotel's topside front desk. White snatched the phone from his hand, and stared at it as though it represented the devil come to take him to the fiery pits of Hell.

"James here."

"Jesus, James, I've been trying to get through to you for a half an hour. All hell's breaking loose up here. Have you seen the news?"

White felt a knot form in his stomach. "What news?"

"No, then. Okay, you might want to be sitting down for this. You know that NBA owner—Doherty?"

"Yes...Christ, was he on the tram?"

"He sure as fuck was. And his wife."

"That's terrible. Make sure his family—and the press—get my sincere condolences."

White's Operations Manager gave a wicked-sounding laugh. "You haven't heard jack shit down there, have you?"

"We're working on—"

"Shut up and listen, James!"

White averted his gaze from Kamal, uncomfortable with his people hearing another employee talking to the boss in such a manner. But that was the least of his concerns now.

"All right, what the hell is it?"

"The Doherty's aren't dead, Jim. They survived. They walked straight into the front desk, dripping fucking wet, and spoke to a Sydney TV reporter on camera about how they personally witnessed multiple hotel guests die in the train tunnel."

White was speechless.

"Oh, not going to run your big-ass mouth now, are you?" his manager goaded. Kamal looked away from White, and pretended to adjust some controls.

"They're...they're not dead? That's great! How—"

"Save the fake pity for the press, Jim. I don't give a fuck. How'd they make it, you ask? A little angel in scuba gear apparently quite literally lifted them from their watery grave to the surface, where they were able to swim to shore. I can't wait to see their review on TripAdvisor, Jimmy, old boy! Gonna be positively glowing, right?"

"So Coco saved them."

"Yeah, the marine biologist. Reporters are asking for her up here, too. You should send her up, Jim. We could use some positive press about now. Let them see a hotel hero, someone doing the best they can in the face of unforeseen circumstances, that kind of thing."

White exchanged an uncomfortable glance with Kamal as he flashed on Coco quitting not long ago. "Tunnel's out, no one can go topside from here right now. Engineering is working on an emergency tunnel fix."

"Fuck that, Jim. Emergency tunnel my ass. They'll say, yes sir, Mr. White, we'll get right on it, but they don't have any real skin in the game. They're a bunch of nerds getting paid to solve puzzles. That's all it is for them. If they can't do it, oh well. Tomorrow's another day on the job, and if they can't work here, they'll go work somewhere else. They haven't even got the A/C running again yet have they?"

"No."

"So think about it, Jim, how long will it take to get another tunnel in place? A long fucking time, that's how long! Longer than we have. You can't keep a Saudi fucking prince down there forever before he takes some kind of action. Send up the angel. We need her up here."

White opened his mouth to say she quit, but nothing came out. It was as if his throat was so parched that he could not form the words.

"No arguments, good."

"No, wait," White croaked. "Seriously. The tunnel. How's she supposed to get up there?"

"She's a scuba diver. She can dive out of there. *Oh!*" The manager shouted the word as though having some sort of epiphany.

"What?" White hated the feeling that he was losing control of the situation to someone else, but at the same time he couldn't deny that he needed help. Even on the most personal level, White had to admit that the idea of being trapped down here, even for a short while, didn't exactly sit well with him.

"Surely some of the guests down there now are also scuba certified. You can have Coco lead any of those who can scuba out of the hotel up to the beach, where we'll have a welcome party waiting to give them the royal treatment, set them up right away with topside bungalows, showers, meals, whatever they want. The media will see us evacuating guests to safety, the guests will be happy, it's a win-win."

"Okay, that sounds good."

"What about you, Jim—you certified?"

"What?"

"Are you a certified diver? You're *certifiable*, I know that, but my point is if you can dive, you should come up with Coco's group."

"I'm not."

There was silence on the other end of the line for a beat.

Then, "Not at all? You never took one of those little resort courses, like on a cruise ship or something? Anything?"

"No. I've never been diving at all. And besides," he added almost gleefully, glad to have an extra reason not to send anyone out there in case he asked him to dive anyway, even though he wasn't certified.

"Besides what?"

"Coco was worried about something in the water, some..." He hesitated, searching for the right word. *Mega—what's it?* wouldn't cut it.

"Some *what!*"

"Some creature or animal or something. Maybe a big shark. I don't know. She was all freaked out about it. Said it may have caused the tunnel failure."

They heard a spitting noise emanate from the phone's speaker. "Fuck that. Here's a thought for her on that: If an animal did that to the train tunnel, which is made of the same material the hotel is made of, then that animal can do the same thing to the hotel. That ought to make her feel better about getting the fuck out of there *pronto.*"

Kamal frowned as he surveyed an array of indicator lights.

"Thanks, that sure makes me feel better."

"Hey, we've got to start getting people out of there. Get creative, Jim. Do what you have to do."

"Okay. What about the sub?"

"What sub? Our sub!" The manager laughed.

"Yeah, I know it can only hold two passengers, but that'd be something. We could have Mick make several trips."

"No. The whole sub tour thing was designed to run from topside. Passengers board it from the floating dock, it dives the reef then returns to the dock. It can go down to the hotel, but has no way to go inside it. The scuba airlock is much too small."

"I thought we had plans for—"

"For a sub docking station in the hotel?"

"Yeah. What happened to that?"

"The key word there was *plans*, Jim. It was too expensive, we had enough on our hands with the hotel itself, and so it got pushed to the *maybe later* list. So listen—"

They heard a series of beeps interrupt the call. "Oh shit," the manager said.

"What is it?" White's mind was racing as he tried to estimate the probability that Al's team would be able to get another tunnel in place to the hotel anytime soon. *They knew to forget about the A/C for now, and focus on the tunnel, right?*

"The Board's patching in. They want to talk to you. I'm sorry pal, I did my best to buy you some more time, but they want an update from the horse's ass, I mean mouth."

"I've got to—"

"Clicking over now... Mr. Cimmaron, hi, I've got James on the line down in the hotel. Can you hear me, sir?"

The voice of an elderly man came back. "Hi Marty, I'm here in Singapore for the World Technology conference with Anne Hathaway and Pedro Simone. We're due to speak in about...ten minutes...but my advisors alerted me to a developing situation with the underwater hotel that may be cause for concern?"

"That's right, Mr. Cimmaron, I'm glad you called. James is going to update you on that situation. Go ahead, James." White could practically hear the glee dripping from the Ops Manager's voice, taking great pleasure in how he must be squirming right now.

Kamal raised his eyebrows as he watched the rest of the color drain from White's face while he brought the phone closer to his lips.

"Hello, Mr. Cimmaron, this is James. Thanks for calling in."

"Uh huh. So how bad is the situation there, James? People have died? Is that true?"

"Unfortunately, that is true, Mr. Cimmaron." He heard the man's breath suck in sharply across the line. "We don't yet know how many, but it does look like the danger has passed for now."

"How many people are in the hotel with you now?"

White looked to Kamal, who tapped some buttons on a keyboard built in to the console. He pointed to a number on the screen.

"Fortunately we stopped taking more guests down at the first hint of danger, Mr. Cimmaron, but there are still thirty-three people inside, including ten staff."

"Understood. Now listen. I need you to get every single one of those people—staff included— out of that hotel and onto dry land right now, James, is that clear?"

"Yes, sir, my team is working on a temporary evacuation tunnel right now, and—"

"I heard all about that. Forget that. Well, don't forget it—let them keep working on it, but we have another option I haven't heard discussed yet."

"And that is?"

"The escape pods."

Silence fell on both ends of the line. The gears in White's brain seemed to churn to a halt while he searched his mind for a reference. "Escape...Oh, *those*. Mr. Cimmaron, with all due respect, that system is far from tried and true. It's really more of a last resort when all other options have failed."

Cimmaron raised his voice a degree. "All other options *have* failed, James! People are dead! How bad do you want things to get! If I may be so bold as to remind you, this is mostly *my* money on the line here!"

Kamal's expression rapidly grew concerned, right along with White's. This was getting downright ugly. He furrowed his brow as he moved along the control panel, looking for anything having to do with the escape pod mechanism. White eyed him hopefully until Kamal looked up from the switchboard and shook his head. Wherever the emergency escape controls were, they weren't in here.

"I'm well aware of that, Mr. Cimmaraon," White said, "but once that system is activated—if we even know how to activate it—it's a major project to restore the hotel to operating condition. Basically, as I recall, some of the hotel's rooms are equipped with mechanisms that allow them to break away and float to the surface when the escape apparatus is put into play."

"Precisely! Just what the doctor ordered right now. No more discussion, make it happen!"

"That system has never been tested."

"That is unfortunate. Nevertheless, we need to use it now, so it's trial by fire, as they say."

"Mr. Cimmaron, if I may, if we wait just a few more hours we may have a new tunnel."

"We may, or we may not. I don't really care what we may or may not have. We need those people out of there now! What part of *get them out now* don't you understand?"

"Very well. I'll get in touch with our land-based team, sir, and I'll make it happen."

"Good. We can write this venture off now, James, chalk it up to experience, and there will be others. We can *learn* from this. But if we have any more deaths—forget it. At a certain point negative publicity becomes inescapable."

White started to say goodbye, but then heard the line click over, and his Ops Manager's voice came back on.

"You heard the man, Jim. Get everybody into the lobby, and turn that place into a big-ass escape pod. Oh, and get Coco up here, quick-like."

Chapter 20

White threw the phone down and turned to Kamal. "I'm going to go get Coco." He ignored the discouraging look on Kamal's face and continued. "There's nothing more to do with the train controls, so I need you to work on the escape pods. First find out how they work—if they even work—then once you've done that, let me know, and we'll talk about next steps. Got it?"

Kamal nodded. "I'll need to get in touch with the Engineering team for that, sir, but I will do that now, and figure it out."

White was already moving off toward the door. "Good. Keep me updated." He got to the doorway, and turned around. "And Kamal?"

"Sir?"

"Do not actually activate the escape pod system without notifying me first. I don't care who gives you clearance. Do I make myself clear?"

"Of course, sir."

White left, and strode down the big well-lit hallway, currently devoid of other people. He was not looking forward to asking Coco to come back to work for him, but at the same time he knew he had to suck it up. He had absolutely no choice in the matter. He'd have to apologize to that half-drunken waif, and ask her to take some people to the surface. As he walked, he wondered how many of the guests might be scuba certified. Probably at least a few. These were, after all, a clientele who were enamored enough of the ocean to spend big bucks on staying in an underwater hotel. Some of them will be scuba certified. And some of them, White reflected as he glanced out on the sun-dappled reef, might just say they're certified even though they're not to have a chance of getting out of this place. He'd have to warn Coco to check their certification cards, or she could run in to trouble with a bunch of panicky newbs who don't know what they're doing underwater.

Speaking of...where the Hell was Coco? A pang of adrenaline hit him as he considered that she might have already scuba dived back to shore on her own. She did quit, after all. Then he heard the chatter of multiple human voices coming from up ahead. The restaurant bar. Figures people would be gathered there at this point. She might be in there, or if not, someone might have seen her, or know where she is. The proposition of showing his face in front of a bunch of guests right now made him slightly queasy, though. They'd have lots of questions, and he had very few answers.

He stood at the junction of hallways, one leading off to the right to the restaurant, and the one he had been walking continuing straight to the grand lobby. There would probably be people there, too, but not as many. He took a deep breath, smoothed out his shirt, and walked off toward the restaurant. He had to man up, and deal with it.

He entered *Neptune's Bounty,* and was pleased to see two tables occupied with diners—a Japanese couple supposedly connected to the Kobe beef empire, and an American family of three whose background White was unsure of—and that fact alone had to mean they had to have serious power. The hostess greeted him with a pleasant smile. She'd better. He had been against going through so much trouble to bring someone all the way from the States to do such a simple job, but the business partners had insisted she'd be worth it. Presentation was everything, they'd told him.

"Hi, Mr. White! Come in for a bite?"

"Hi, uh..." *What is this girl's name again?* He was usually pretty good with names, employing a mnemonic device to associate some detail about them with their first or last name. He looked her up and down, admiring the supple curves. *Hot piece of tail...Tail—Tricia!*

"Hi there, Trish. Actually no, I'm not hungry yet. I'm actually looking for Coco. Is she over there?" He looked toward the crowded bar.

Tricia nodded enthusiastically. "She is! Would you like me to get her for you?"

Now that was considerate. She was offering him a way not to have to show his face over there. Points for that. But what if Coco simply said no, she didn't want to talk to him? If he went over there, he'd have the opportunity to turn on the charm in person.

"Thanks for the offer, but I'll just go over there myself."

"Sounds good, Mr. White! Let me know if you need anything."

She busied herself by pecking at the touch-screen reservation system while White made his way to the *Wet Bar*. He spotted Coco with her back to him, bare skin revealing a tattoo of a sea turtle, or *honu* as she called it. She sat at the end of the bar facing the window to the reef, where a grouper the size of a VW bug, nicknamed "Oliver" by the staff, hovered just outside, entertaining the guests who waved at it and posed for pictures. He caught the bartender giving Coco a heads up with a subtle nod in his direction. She didn't turn around. White slipped into a seat next to her, avoiding eye contact with the other patrons.

He wasn't pleased to see the empty shot glass in front of her, and a full one in her hand, especially given that he needed her to scuba dive, but there was nothing he could do about it except remind himself to be especially nice.

"Can I get you anything, Mr. White?" Aiden asked.

White looked at Coco and said, "Nothing for me, thanks, but I'll be happy to cover her tab."

The bartender nodded, and took the cue to walk away. White turned to Coco, who gave him a hard stare through slightly glassy eyes.

"Excuse me, Coco, but I came to apologize." He tested the waters. She said nothing, but didn't leave. "I'm sorry about the way I acted earlier. It was inappropriate, and I regret it. I was under a lot of stress, and extremely upset after hearing about those guests who died in the tunnel. I still am, but that doesn't excuse my behavior."

Coco looked him in the eyes and nodded, though still said nothing. She drained the last of her shot unapologetically, and said,

"Apology accepted, Mr. White." Then she raised a finger to gain Aiden's attention.

"Coco," White said, aware that with every drink she took she pushed back her window for being able to dive, "I'd like to hire you back. I made a mistake, and I admit it. Let's just get you back on the job, and pretend the whole thing never happened, shall we?"

Aiden came over, and Coco ordered a mai tai before addressing White. "Sorry, I'm not looking for a job right now."

White gave an awkward laugh. He knew it was pathetic, really, but that was his reaction. "Retired now, eh?"

"No, just on vacation. I'll probably roam around the South Pacific for a little while, and then go back to Hawaii, and get back to work there."

White sighed. "Coco, look. I said I'm sorry. We both know you're the best person for this job. That's why I hired you in the first place. Tell you what: I'll give you a raise if you go back to work right now."

Coco perked up at this. Marine biologists, especially young ones, were not highly paid. "How much?"

"Ten percent."

Coco took another drink, and said nothing.

"Okay, okay. Twenty-five percent. But seriously, the Board would never approve more—"

"Deal!"

She set the rest of her mai tai down on the bar with a *clack*, and extended her hand. White was surprised at how quickly she'd moved, given the alcohol. He gripped her hand, and pumped it. "Deal," he echoed. Then, after a beat, "Welcome back."

"Glad to be back. So when do I start?"

"I need you to start now."

Coco pushed the drink back, indicating she was done with it. "Okay, what do you need me to do?"

He explained how he needed her to scuba dive from the hotel to shore with any scuba certified guests or employees who wanted to go.

"Okay, but I can't dive drunk, Mr. White. No matter what. I don't know what your opinion of me really is, but there are two things in this world that I'll never do. I don't drive drunk, and I don't dive drunk. Megalodon or no megalodon."

White put on his best understanding expression. "Of course. I'm not asking you to do that, or to step out of your comfort zone. Go take a nap for a while in one of the staff rooms. You have to scuba to leave the hotel at some point anyway, right? So all I'm asking is that when you do, you take with you anybody who is certified who says they'd like to go."

White smiled, more to himself than outwardly. Coco's buzz was actually working to his advantage. He didn't mind slowing down the timetable. What a perfect excuse to tell Cimmaron! *She's drunk! Can't dive right now! Guess that means we'll just have to delay the dog and pony show with the reporters for a little while longer...*

Suddenly the bar patrons nearest the window began to scream.

Chapter 21

"What is it? What's wrong?" White asked.

Coco was worried some other part of the hotel's infrastructure was now in trouble, but then followed the gazes of those nearest the window.

Oliver's head drifted past the Wet Bar's main viewing window, trailing a cloud of dull red blood. A school of small fish nibbled and pecked at the grouper's open innards.

"Oliver's been cut in half," Coco said to White. Around them some of the patrons uttered words such as "disgusting" and "how morbid." A few began to walk away.

White leaned over the bar to Aiden, waving for his attention. It wasn't to order a drink.

"Do we have shades or shutters that can be pulled down?"

The bartender held his hands up in a gesture of helplessness. "None were ever installed. They talked about it once, because believe it or not it does get pretty sunny in here around three or four, but they were never put in."

White clasped a hand to his forehead. Another thing that was talked about, but never implemented. Figures. He turned to his marine biologist instead.

"Coco, now that you're back on staff, can you explain to the people that what we're seeing is just part of the food chain, the circle of life and all that shit you know about?"

She frowned at her boss. "You know damn well by now that it's almost certainly not a normal act of predation."

White's face lit up, seizing on a loophole in her words. "*Almost certainly*. So it could be. Big shark, but not one of the dinosaur ones, okay? People can't handle that. Just go with it. Please." He leaned in closer to her when he saw Aiden and a couple of patrons as well taking more interest in their conversation. "We've got to keep everybody calm."

Coco shrugged and stood. She reached up, and rang the brass bell over the bar. When she had everyone's attention, she addressed them with an authoritative demeanor.

"People, people, listen up, please! It looks like our friend Oliver the grouper has been eaten by a large shark. As you know, the Triton Undersea Resort is not an aquarium. This is the real ocean, true nature and wildlife on display 24/7 for those of us lucky enough to have the chance to stay down here."

Too late she realized the oversight in her choice of words, and she braced herself for the barrage of smartass remarks that weren't long in coming.

"Lucky enough to still be alive down here at any rate!" one man said, eliciting a round of nervous laughter.

"Dumb enough to stay down here," said another.

Coco glanced at White to see if he would use this as an opportunity to update on the hotel's emergency status, but he remained silent, so she went on. "That reminds me. I'll be leading a scuba group out of the hotel, and up to the beach. I'll be going around trying to round up those who are interested. Spread the word, please." Immediately hands went up with questions. Coco waved them down.

"This is for certified scuba divers only, who want to leave the hotel. All scuba gear will be provided so long as you show me the C-card. Meet me at the dive shop in..." She paused, wondering exactly how long it would take for the booze she'd already consumed to wear off. "...two hours."

A flurry of conversation broke out among the guests. "I'll be there," one man called out.

"Me too," said another. A man and wife argued, apparently over the fact that he was certified, but she was not. She urged him not to leave her down here without him, and he replied that he may be able to help fix the situation. The woman started to cry at that point, and Coco left White to placate her.

As she approached the woman, a dark shadow dampened the light in the underwater room. Most of the guests didn't notice or pay attention to it, but Coco and the other staff knew it wasn't a usual occurrence. Coco's blood ran cold as she looked up and out the window. Suddenly the underside of a fish so enormous it looked at first to be a large boat passed overhead. But no. As much as Coco wanted for that to be true, she knew what it was.

The megalodon had returned.

"What was that?" Coco was almost relieved to hear White ask the question. It would finally give her a chance to explain what she knew, to let him see her side of things. She looked away from the monstrous fish as it arced away from the Wet Bar and locked eyes with her boss.

"I've been telling you what I think it is, sir. I know you don't want me to scare anyone, so let's just say...it starts with an 'M'."

"More bullshit about a prehistoric shark?"

Coco gave him a look to kill.

"Don't say it," White pre-empted her. "Mega-what's' it?"

"Yes. *Carcharadon megalodon*. That thing out there is not a boat, a whale, a whale shark, or a submarine. It's a megalodon."

"Great white shark?" White practically begged.

Coco shook her head, and widened her eyes, as if to get across to him that he still wasn't getting it, or still wasn't playing ball, or both. "It's many times too large for that. It's the exact right size for an adult female megalodon according to the documented, peer reviewed fossil record."

White threw his hands up, aware people were looking at him, but unable to contain his frustration any longer. "How is that possible? Can you please tell me that? That an animal supposedly extinct for millions of years is now swimming roughshod over my hotel?"

It was Coco's turn to be frustrated. "I don't know! If I knew that I would be a superstar biologist. I'm not. I'm just reacting to what I observed. Everything I know tells me that's what it is. Maybe it survived all these eons living in the deep sea, eating giant squid and whale carcasses that rain down from above."

"So why come up now, then?" White's face was red, angry. Angry at a primal monstrosity that was rapidly destroying his career, something that was both a terrible threat, and a conundrum which he did not understand.

Coco tipped her head back and shrugged. "Of course, I can't possibly know that yet, Mr. White. But if I had to guess, maybe..." She stared out the window, where light passed freely to the bottom once again.

"Maybe what?"

"Maybe the construction of the hotel disturbed it somehow. Altered its natural patterns?"

"Oh Christ. There's nothing we can do about it then, if that's the case, isn't it?"

Behind her she heard Aiden tell a customer that he was sorry, but the bar was out of whiskey, would he like something else?

"Short of figuring out which of its patterns was disturbed and how, and then restoring the conditions that favored that behavior in the first place, no, I'm afraid not."

White gave her a hard stare. "You sound quite smug. Does it please you to see me in such a difficult position?"

She gave him a critical stare, one that let him know that perhaps she was rethinking her decision to rejoin the staff. "Of course not! What do you want me to do when you ask my opinion about what's out there, about what I saw with my own eyes? *Lie?*" She raised her voice on the last word of the sentence, drawing multiple stares from the clientele, including the man who had just been denied his drink of choice.

That man, a wealthy Texas oil investor, approached White and Coco, drawn in to the scent of conflict like a shark to chum.

"I say there, you two work here, don't you?" White bristled at being put on the same level as Coco, but handled it well, smiling and extending a hand. Right now he wished he did only work here instead of being in charge of running the place. What a clusterfuck. But he was deep in it now—quite literally—and so he'd have to play it by ear. He'd gotten himself into this mess, and he could get himself out of it.

"Yes, sir, Mr. Bradenton, is it?"

The man looked taken aback that White knew his name. Apparently he hadn't looked too closely at any of the promotional materials sent out. Too busy to care, probably.

"That's correct. Listen, can I ask you a question?" He went on without waiting for a response. "What in the Hell is going on down here?"

He was met with two blank stares. Others were looking on, eager to hear the answer. But his line of inquiry was not what it seemed.

"Running out of whiskey on the first day? Say what?"

White smiled sheepishly, and looked down at the floor—some kind of fancy marble with embedded fossils of fish and shells and sea stars—before looking back up at the Texan.

"On behalf of the bar, my good Sir, I apologize profusely. I'll have our staff double-check our inventory, and make sure to notify you as soon as some whiskey becomes available. You have my word on that."

The oilman beamed. "That's all a man can ask for. Meanwhile, let's hope you don't run out of beer..." He turned and raised a finger in Aiden's direction. "Barkeep!"

White pulled Coco off to one side. "Can you have some coffee or something and try to get some of these people out of here? I'm not asking you to do anything stupid, okay? Just do what you can to speed things up, that's all I ask. Have a Red Bull or something, can you?"

She leveled a stare at him, nodding slowly at the end of it.

"If we're not out of those, too."

A flurry of activity broke the awkward pause that followed. Chairs tipping over, feet stampeding. The room, darkening.

Coco looked over toward the window in time to see its full fury. The megalodon, barreling toward the Wet Bar like the world's largest torpedo, unadorned fury aimed at all of them.

Chapter 22

The impact took the form of a frightening crunching sound followed by extensive spider webbing of the acrylic that made up the Wet Bar's main viewing window.

"It's attacking us!" a woman yelled before turning and running.

James White was immediately transported back in time to the planning meetings for the hotel's developers, where the question of glass strength had been raised. A breach in the integrity of the acrylic was unheard of, they'd assured him. The engineers had promptly assuaged all fears with mind-numbing numerical responses about crush depth and thickness and pounds of pressure per square inch, the bottom line of which was this: nothing, not the water depth on the reef, not someone pounding on the acrylic from the outside with a hammer, not an earthquake—*nothing*—could affect the integrity of that miracle plastic glass.

A *Carcharadon megalodon* hadn't been part of that equation, however.

Now, only one thing was paramount: evacuate the room to avoid more deaths. And his marine biologist, as usual, was one step ahead of him. Coco jumped onto the bar, cupped her hands around her mouth, and yelled to the panicked crowd. "Everybody out of the bar! This way!" She pointed out through the restaurant into the main thoroughfare, then turned to White.

"I read that the different rooms of the hotel can be sealed off as a safety feature in the event of a pressure breach. Is that true?"

White nodded, still not quite believing he was living through this nightmare scenario. In a million years, he'd never have guessed that he'd be putting the emergency procedures to the test during opening weekend. It was unfathomable, and yet, as he took in the dribbles of water making their way down the *inside* of the bar window, he accepted that it was also very, very real.

"That's right, people, come this way, please!" White began ushering guests toward the exit. He yelled over to Tricia, urging her to assist the guests out into the hallway. Most of them did not need any additional encouragement. A couple had their smartphones aimed at the window, taking video. The shark had again disappeared from view, but Coco feared it was making another of its wide turns before coming back.

Aiden jumped over the bar, and assisted in guiding patrons toward the exit. One man took advantage of the unattended bar and jumped behind it, hurriedly pouring himself a drink before he too, evacuated. Then the room darkened again, sending up a chorus of screams from the people who now knew what it meant.

Coco reached the restaurant lobby first, asking Trish if there was a control panel to seal it off from the rest of the hotel. She received a blank look in return, asked her to assist the stampeding guests into the hallway and away from the restaurant, and then ran over to James White, eyeballing the radio clipped to his belt.

"I don't see a control panel here. How do we seal it off?"

"There's a Main Control Room, separate from the one for the train." He raised his walkie-talkie to his mouth. Numerous people approached him with questions, but Coco fended them off, answering their questions while directing them outside as White talked on the radio.

"Caesar, come in!" He repeated himself two more times before Caesar's voice blasted through the radio.

"No good news on the new tunnel yet, boss."

"This isn't about that. New problem. Need you to get to Main Controls and seal off the restaurant, over."

A beat went by, and then Caesar returned, "You mean activate the pressure seal to compartmentalize the restaurant, Sir?"

"Yes, that's exactly what I mean; do it now."

"Has there been a breach?"

Even Coco had to roll her eyes at the question. She was gaining a tiny bit of appreciation for what White had to deal with on a day-to-day basis, although she suspected that this situation was mostly his fault.

"Yes, Caesar, there has been a serious breach; water is coming into the Wet Bar after the shark rammed the main viewing window, *over*."

"I am on my way to the control room now, Sir. Standby, I need to confirm everyone is out of the restaurant before I seal it off, over."

"Copy that, waiting for your call." He glanced back toward the window, and saw water running across the floor now. "Please hurry, Caesar. If the window goes..."

Coco studied his face as she imagined what he must be thinking of: the thick rush of water that would invade the hotel if that window were to completely give way, sweeping all of them into the hallway. Those who weren't crushed by the sheer force of the seawater impacting their bodies or throwing them into hard objects would perish by drowning...

His eyes focused on hers, ejecting them from their mutual reverie. But what he said next was not what she expected.

"Coco, I know you think this is all my fault. I'm doing what I can to fix it. I need your help."

His directness blindsided her, but her reflexes were sharp, honed by her recent life-or-death scuba experience where she had made a series of successful split-second decisions that had saved her life and those of others.

"This is your place. Of course, it's your fault. If it had been successful you would have taken the credit for that, right?"

The question hung in the air with the shouts of the escaping patrons. It was a harsh barb, she knew that, but nothing compared to the way those people had died in that tunnel out there. He slitted his eyes as he looked at her, but said nothing. A man with a red scratch across his forehead walked up to White.

"Which way do we go?"

White herded him off to the right, then turned back to Coco. "Now is not the time to analyze how this happened, okay? Now is the time to get these people to safety. Can you do a last sweep of the restaurant, and make sure no one else is in there?" Coco gave him a hard stare, and wordlessly turned back into the restaurant, the floor of which was now slick with water.

No sooner had she gone back inside, when White's radio crackled again with Casesar's voice. He immediately reached for the volume knob and turned it down.

Chapter 23

Too late, Coco realized that she should have Aiden with her. He knew the bar better than anyone. Looking back toward the restaurant entrance, though, she could not see him. He was with most of the others who had been escorted out into the hall and to the right, toward the main lobby. She was on her own in here to do a sweep of the place, and make sure no one else was left behind before the entire restaurant area was sealed off...

Suddenly the ramifications of this decision struck her, and struck her hard. Once again, she had let White goad her into doing something incredibly stupid. She climbed up onto the bar, and jumped behind it. There was no one back here, passed out from too much liquor curled up in a ball somewhere. These weren't those kind of people. This wasn't some roadside trucker bar. More likely some baron of industry with zero situational awareness was conducting a transaction huddled over his smartphone at a corner table.

She called out, "Hey, anybody in here?" as she jumped back over the bar, and walked toward the compromised window. The spider web of cracks was more extensive now, whole sheets of water spilling down the inside of it, making the reef outside appear blurry. And there, off to the left, she saw it. A shadowy, blurred image. Moving. Big. There was absolutely nothing she could do about what was out there, though, so she concentrated on what she could control. She finished her sweep of the bar area, sidestepping knocked-over chairs and broken glass.

No one here. Then she heard a popping noise, and the tinkle of glass hitting the tile floor, followed quickly by the sound of softly splashing water, like from a small fountain. A small diameter chunk of the acrylic had come loose, forced inside by the water pressure outside. She didn't know how long it would hold on, but that window was severely compromised, and to be in here when it failed was to die.

She jogged toward the main restaurant, calling out as she went. "Anybody in here? Anybody here?"

No response.

And then she heard it. A humming sound. Faint, but down here one became attuned quickly to the self-contained environment. Every sound, every sight. It all meant something. This was out of the norm. Coco threaded her way through a group of dining tables until she reached the front of the restaurant, the reservation station Tricia had been standing at now vacant.

Then she heard a loud clack as a release mechanism disengaged and a solid metal door dropped from the ceiling. She called out, "Hey, I'm still in here!" in vain, feeling her own voice bounce back into the sealed off room. Panic gripped her as she looked around, but even as she did, she knew there was no other way out of here but the front entrance. She recalled with a shiver how Aiden had complained about having no service entrance, that if they needed anything it had to be brought right through the front entrance in full view of the guests. When he had complained to White he had been told to "plan ahead." As if White planned ahead; his lack of ability to do so was the reason they were all in this mess now.

She realized it, then, too late. He had planned ahead, now, though, hadn't he? She was in here, he was out there with all of the guests and other staff...was that an accident? In her mind's eye she replayed the series of events just before she had went back inside the restaurant. *Can you do a last sweep of the restaurant, and make sure no one else is in there?* But just before that he had told Caesar to let him know when he was ready to activate the pressure door, *so he could make sure no one was inside...except for me! He knows I blame him for this catastrophe unfolding, for the deaths of those people in the tunnel...*

No, she told herself, shaking it off. *That's ridiculous. You're just being paranoid. The guy's an asshole but he's not a killer.* She forced herself to get back to reality, and figure a way out of here before it was too late. She looked around. *Communicate.* She had to communicate. Her gaze lit on the bar. She pictured Aiden talking on the phone back there, and ran toward it. All she had to do was let someone know she was in here, Caesar would get the word to raise the door, she'd slink out, slightly embarrassed, but none the worse for wear, they'd seal the door again, and all's well that ends well. *Right?*

She jumped over the bar again and looked beneath the drink station for the phone. There it was. It was the same as the rest of the hotel phones, a modern conferencing style wired phone with multiple buttons, just dial an extension to talk within the hotel. She eyed Front Desk and was about to hit that when she paused. *That's a little like calling a friend to dial 911 for you when you could just dial it yourself, isn't it?*

From her right came another tinkle of a piece of acrylic hitting the floor with a constant stream of water thereafter. She glanced over at the window. Megalodon or no megalodon, when that window broke, the force of the water would crush her anywhere in here, not much different than being in an explosion. She would not even get the chance to hold her breath and swim for the surface. Her only hope was through that door. And since the door was lead-lined steel designed to keep out the tons and tons of pressure exerted by the ocean pouring in here, her only real hope was to open that door.

Coco looked again at the phone's extension buttons. Forget the front desk. She traced an index finger down the rest of the row of buttons...Maid service, Topside Front Desk, Dive Shop, (*that's me!*), Activities Coordinator, Train Control Room, *Main Control Room*...that's it!

As another section of the window exploded into the room, this one larger than the last, Coco hit the button to talk to Engineering. They'd be able to raise that door.

Chapter 24

James White deposited his flock of guests with an already stressed Front Desk employee, and quietly slipped away. Certain he was out of sight, he began running down one of the smaller hallways. He found the door he was looking for, marked Main Control Room, and pushed his way inside without knocking.

Caesar was inside, alone, seated at another control console, much larger than the one for the train controls. An African-American in his mid-thirties, Caesar was well liked by all staff due to his easy-going nature, and skill on the ukulele at parties. He looked up at White, surprised. "The door should be in place," he said, concerned that something else had gone wrong.

"It is. I just thought I would stop by and double check with you to make sure it's actually sealed—no pressure alarms, anything like that?"

Caesar furrowed his brow. "The door is sealed, but so far the window has held."

"How about the emergency pod system?"

Caesar nodded, and turned to a different portion of the control board. "Yes, so—"

The phone rang, a light blinking on its face. Caesar swiveled in his chair, but White raised a hand and moved for the phone. "I'll get it." He reached over, and hit the button to send the call directly to voicemail. Caesar gave him a quizzical look. "That wasn't Topside Engineering was it, because I'm waiting to hear about the tunnel, they—"

"No, it wasn't. Just Front Desk trying to track me down. It's not important. Not compared to this," he said, pointing at the console. "Now, you were saying about the emergency pod system?"

Caesar wheeled his chair over to the right, away from the phone, and pointed to a bank of controls. "Yes, sir. This panel here..."

#

Coco exhaled heavily as she clicked the button to disconnect from Engineering. No one there. *Guess I'll have to try Front Desk after all...* She was looking for the right button when the room darkened in shadow again. Unable to keep herself from looking away, she turned her head toward the window. There, gliding down from above, was the great fish. The megalodon soared over the reef, so massive its belly nearly scraped coral while the tip of its dorsal almost broke the surface.

Meanwhile, the Front Desk phone rang while the employee normally at the desk was busy taking care of the restaurant crowd dumped on her by White. The huge fish turned at that moment and came back toward the window, gathering speed and momentum. Coco froze like a deer in headlights, knowing that this was it. If the megalodon hit the window full force it was going to shatter. What could she do? *What can I do?* Every neuron of her mind screamed the question.

She glanced over at the entrance again, at the stout metal door protecting the rest of the hotel from the destructive forces she was about to take head on. Was there a release switch on the walls in here? Her gaze swept over the walls, even the ceiling, but came up empty. Desperate, she bent back down to the phone, and pressed the button for Topside Front Desk where there was more likely to be someone present.

She pressed the button at the same time the megalodon's great snout impacted with the Wet Bar's acrylic wall, caving it in.

Untold tons of water began to inundate the bar and restaurant, and Coco knew that she had seconds left to make what may very well be the last decision of her life. Where to be, what to do *right now*?

She saw the most unbelievable sight she had ever witnessed in her young life: a prehistoric fish being dumped inside a restaurant by a raging flood driven by the forces of physics to fill an engineered air bubble, a bubble that was keeping Coco alive, but not for long. Even in the face of the gargantuan predator, her fear was directed at the water itself. That frightful torrent.

Chairs and tables were splintered into pieces, and exploded about the room like matchsticks, their metal and glass and wood fragments becoming deadly shrapnel. Water rushed inside the entertainment space, and Coco took the only available shelter from the brunt of the oncoming force: she ducked behind the bar itself. Though confronted with hopelessness, Coco's mind grasped onto the only possible way to survive she could think of. A long shot, to be sure, but a shot nonetheless, and beggars couldn't be choosers, right?

She ducked beneath the bar, squatting on the floor while gazing up at the top of the window she could still see. If the bar structure was strong enough to hold up, it might shield her from the brunt of the rushing water's force long enough to attempt to swim out through the broken window to the surface once the space had flooded.

Coco hyperventilated as the water pounded into the bar, rapidly inhaling and exhaling to saturate her lungs with oxygen, thinking of her free diver ex-boyfriend in Hawaii as she did so. Things had not worked out between them, but he had taught her some things all the same, and this was one of them. Memories of better times soothed her a trifle, just enough to collect her nerves in order to perform the hyperventilation technique.

Then the ocean was cascading over her, pouring into the space behind the bar, her sanctuary against the onslaught. The sound of crashing water and objects hurled against each other assailed her ears, so loud it made it difficult to think straight. Then the back bar area began filling with water, so much faster than she had anticipated, immediately to her waist, then a few seconds later to her shoulders in a swirling maelstrom of furious seawater.

She looked up at the displaced window again, knowing that her vision was about to be severely limited. She wished she at least had her snorkel gear, but here she was without it, and there was absolutely nothing she could do except deal with it. Deal with it or die.

Coco did her best to time her hyperventilation so that her last breath—the full one—would be completed a moment before she was submerged and would need to move. For once, Coco thought as she filled her lungs full to the bursting point, something worked out as she had planned. She felt her lungs stretch with the fullest breath she'd ever taken in her life, and then the water rushed over her head. At least it felt warm, not much different than the stale air inside the bar without air conditioning.

She lined up her planned path from the bar to the open window as the sea closed over her. Then she kicked off of the floor, shooting up at a slant toward the gaping portal. A white, hazy light issued from beyond the broken window, and she propelled herself through the swirling water toward that. Making headway was difficult. She would travel forward a couple of feet and then be tossed sideways for ten, or pulled down onto some furniture.

She kept going, kicking with her feet, and keeping her hands out in front of her as much as she could. To her left she saw a mammoth, swishing shape, and guessed it was the megalodon, wedged deep into the restaurant with the sudden influx of water. Instinctively she veered away from the blurry form, only to be caught in an eddy and washed back towards it. Eyes open in the salty sting of the seawater, she saw its blurry tail swing at her. Then she felt something extremely rough, like sandpaper, brush against her arm, shredding her skin.

Thankfully, another bout of chaotic currents took her away from the trapped monster, sending her back toward the bar. Shark or no shark, though, Coco knew that lack of air was about to become a critical problem. She was exerting herself a lot in an attempt to fight the deluge, and she knew her time was very limited. Reaching the end of the bar, she kicked off of it straight across the floor, not attempting to angle up to the window as she had done before. The currents were slightly less for some reason when she took this path, and soon she found herself at the bottom of the ripped out viewing window.

Looking up to verify she was about to kick off in the right direction, she saw the glorious sun penetrating the depths to the hotel, the great ball of light that signified the realm of air and land where she belonged. She kicked off the floor of the Wet Bar, now truly living up to its name, and passed cleanly through the open window frame into the sea beyond.

As soon as she was outside the window she felt powerful forces buoying her upwards as the indoor space filled, and the water sloshed back against the sea, welling upwards. She tumbled head over heels as she spun off toward the surface. When at last she slowed she caught a glimpse of the megalodon inside the bar, turning, still swimming, seeking a way back outside.

Her fear of the hunter outweighed her need to breathe, even though her lungs had begun to burn. She swam over the top of the hotel as she was lifted higher, to remove herself from the beast's line of sight. Not that it needed sight to track her down. As a marine scientist, Coco knew the shark had a fantastic sense of smell, and that its electrical sensory organs, the Ampullae of Lorenzini, could likely detect her muscle contractions from some distance away. For the mighty megalodon, she was but another prey item to be sensed, tracked, and consumed.

Coco scissor kicked her way up, feeling the strength of the currents grow weaker as she neared the surface of the lagoon. White spots swam across her field of vision as she moved through the water, her body's oxygen reserves dangerously low. It grew lighter around her as she ascended, though, and that gave her hope, gave her the fortitude to continue, knowing that the surface was close by.

Then her head broke through into the air, bright sunlight dazzling her eyes. She didn't allow herself the luxury of gloating that she had made it out of the hotel, though. Not yet. Not when there was a sixty-foot shark only about thirty feet below her. She spun in the water, taking her bearings. She had to make the beach. There! The ribbon of white sand lined with tall coconut palms never looked so inviting as it did now.

She swam toward the island, careful to avoid splashy strokes that would excite the mega-predator lurking below. She moved forward with a modified breaststroke, keeping her hands and feet below the water's surface at all times, silent through the water. To keep her mind off the fear she knew was right there, lurking below the surface of her consciousness, she pictured James White's face, and how she would pulverize it when she caught up with the bastard.

He had tricked her into going back inside the restaurant just before the pressure door slammed shut, of this she had no doubt. There was no one in there who needed rescuing. He knew that! He only wanted her to go back inside so that he could trap her in there, and say it was an accident—oh, how terrible, the poor girl! Such an unfortunate string of events has befallen my perfect little hotel. But now *Coco Keahi won't be around to tell anyone the details of how James White let things slip out of control, how he wasn't as careful as he could have been...*

She lost herself in these thoughts as she propelled herself toward the beach, forgetting about the megalodon, forgetting about how lucky she was to have escaped the hotel with her life. She focused only on how she would exact revenge on White. Her thoughts were grim, yet an effective distraction, for when she next raised her head above water to check her progress, she was rewarded with a much closer view of that gorgeous, white sand. Something, she didn't know what, except some vague sense, compelled her to turn and look back toward the hotel. She wished she hadn't, but there it was: a sail-like dorsal fin breaking the lagoon's surface above the hotel...turning until it was perpendicular to the beach. Moving forward toward her...

Swim! Silence no longer mattered. She needed speed at all costs if she was going to make it to the beach in time. She broke into a rapid crawl stroke that at one time had earned her a spot on her high school swim team, before she had grown bored of pools, and dropped out to spend more time free diving with her boyfriend, and doing long distance solo ocean swims. But she was grateful for the focus on speed her competition days had given her, for she needed all the help she could get now.

Coco pushed and pushed toward the island until she felt the knuckles of her right hand bash the coral on a downstroke. The pain told her she had made it. Land! She crawled forward, knowing the megalodon wouldn't venture into such shallow waters, but terrified all the same of the imagery playing in her mind of big sharks skimming up onto wet sand in order to nab a seal. Was she one lunge away from being eaten?

She saw no one on shore, no one standing there and pointing to the giant shark that might at this very second be opening its jaws to ingest her entire body. She was alone. When she felt her knees bump the bottom she began crawling fast on her hands and knees until she felt the soft squishiness of the wet sand on the beach. She hauled herself out onto the dry sand like a seal, flopping there, exhausted.

She lolled her head to one side to look out on the lagoon. The megalodon's huge dorsal was there, but still out by the hotel. It hadn't followed her in to the beach. She supposed that it, too, had had enough excitement for the time being. But as she pushed herself up from the sand, she knew that there was much more in store for her today. White—that would-be murderer—was still down there in the hotel with all those people. Who knows who else he might decide to eliminate because he perceived them to be some sort of a threat?

She had to do something, but she wasn't sure what. Let people know what happened? Who? And what proof did she have? No one else heard White tell her to go back into the restaurant. It would be his word against hers, and who was she? Some recent college graduate, an entry-level worker, basically, while he was the boss, a seasoned professional.

She stopped walking when she reached the edge of the beach where the little foothpath wound its way back to the complex of buildings that supported the hotel. Who should she tell? Another thing, she thought to herself as she dripped seawater onto the vegetation, is *what could anybody do about it?* There was no way into the hotel now other than to scuba dive past a megalodon into the airlock. *No thanks.* What's more...who could she trust? Some of White's inner circle may be just as untrustworthy as he. She looked around. Another path ran along the top of the beach to the right, toward the sub dock. Mick would probably be out there.

The sub...it also couldn't directly access the hotel, but it could get a close look inside, and it could drop small supplies just outside the airlock. Not exactly sure of her next move, but desperately wanting to do something that would help save the people still trapped in the hotel, Coco took off at a trot along the beach path toward the submersible dock.

Chapter 25

Coco felt comforted when her bare feet hit the wooden planks of the pier that led out to the submersible dock. Mick would be out there. He was on her side, at least she could count on that. Maybe he had some new information on what was developing around here. She padded out along the pier, looking left toward the complex of support buildings on shore. Everything was eerily quiet. No one was visible walking around or anything.

She reached the sub dock where a single shed-style outbuilding squatted in the sun. The sub itself bobbed peacefully at the dock. She didn't see Mick so she walked around to the end of the sub shack. He must be inside working on some parts, probably still fixing the damage she did to the thruster. She rounded the corner, and saw that the door was open.

She was about to call out Mick's name when she saw movement inside the shack, in the corner. A hand moving over a slender back that was partially covered by long, blonde hair... There were two people in there, not just one. Mick's face was buried in the neck of...a woman...locked in embrace...Coco felt a welling of embarrassment and...something else...*jealousy*? She turned to leave, but the one of the boards creaked, and Mick's head raised.

"Coco!"

The woman snapped around, and Coco recognized the face of Clarissa, the dolphin trainer.

"I...I'm sorry. I'll go." Coco turned to leave.

"Coco, wait!" Mick broke free from Clarissa, and moved toward the door. Coco turned around.

"What?"

"It's nothing. I didn't realize you two were..."

Clarissa appraised Coco coolly while she composed herself, brushing her hair out of her face, straightening her clothes. "Well, that's one way to find out, I suppose." She shot Mick a disapproving look.

Coco stepped outside the shack, but then stopped and turned around once more. "It's not easy for me to do this. I just want to run away and hide right now, honestly, but I need your help." She eyed Mick and Clarissa in turn.

"I'll just be leaving now," Clarissa said, moving to step outside.

"I need your help, too," Coco insisted.

"What for?" Clarissa stopped walking. Mick stood a few steps behind her, hoping the two women weren't about to fight.

"I need to get back down into the hotel. Scuba diving in is the only way. But there's a huge-ass shark in the lagoon. I need a distraction."

Clarissa gave a sarcastic laugh. "Oh, so you want to use me for bait, is that it?"

Coco shook her head. "Not you. Your dolphins."

The trainer's mouth dropped open in disbelief. "My *dolphins*! You mean the ones there are left?"

"Just one of them. People are dying, Clarissa." It irked Coco that Mick's...*girlfriend*, if that's what she was...would place the lives of her dolphins above those of humans, as if they are so much more important....or is it simply that to lose her dolphins is a step closer to losing her job? Either way, Coco didn't like her. As if she needed another reason not to like her, she thought sourly, glancing over at Mick, who was staring back at her intently.

Mick chose this moment to rejoin the conversation. "What would you do with it?"

Coco looked from Mick to Clarissa. "Let it out into the lagoon. Instruct it to swim away from the hotel out to the edge of the reef. Hopefully the megalodon will decide to follow it, but won't be able to catch it. Meanwhile..." She directed her gaze back to Mick.

"...you drive me in the Zodiac, with my dive gear, out to the hotel directly over the airlock, so I can drop over the side and swim down there fast. I'll slip inside before the megalodon knows I'm there."

"And then what?" It was pretty obvious that Mick was glad to have something to focus on other than the interaction between the two women.

"Then I'm going to lead a group of certified divers out of the hotel and back to the beach."

Mick moved closer to Coco. "You're going to go back down there now that you're safe?"

"That's crazy," Clarissa concurred.

"It's my job."

Clarissa laughed. "Hey, I'm a dolphin trainer, you're a marine biologist, you're probably making about what I make, and I know it's not enough to risk our lives for."

"Actually, I got a raise."

Clarissa appeared confused. "I thought raises were only given once a year during the annual evaluations?"

"Let's just say that there were...extenuating circumstances... down there that enabled me to negotiate for more."

Mick nodded. "Like agreeing to risk your life to save people in the tunnel, and now again to lead them out of there past a killer shark?"

Coco nodded. "Seriously you guys, that building is in sketchy shape down there. There's maybe two or three people down there who have the slightest clue about how any of it works. More people are going to die if I don't help out. I just need you two to help me."

"I drive you out there in the Zodiac, and I'll be waiting on the beach in the boat in case you need any help getting back to the beach."

"Thanks, Mick."

Coco and Mick looked to Clarissa. "I still have Tursi, and he's my fastest. I suppose I could have him streak out to the reef." She shot Coco a hard stare. "I just hope you know what you're doing."

#

An hour later Coco sat on the pontoon of the Zodiac inflatable boat that was tied to the pier next to the sub dock. Mick started the engine and let it warm up while he used the boat's radio to call Clarissa over at the dolphin lagoon.

"Clar, we're ready in the boat, what's your status, over?"

Coco raised her eyebrows at him as she tugged on her scuba gear. Normally she'd wait until the boat reached the dive site to actually put the gear on, but in this case she wanted to be able to hit the water immediately, as long as there were no signs of the mega-shark.

"*Clar?*"

Mick cleared his throat. Realizing his mistake, he spoke into the radio again. "*Clarissa, you read me?*"

The dolphin trainer's voice came loud and clear across the radio channel. "I've got Tursi lined up at the gate. Just say the word."

Mick looked at Coco, who gave him a nod. He spoke into the radio. "Word."

"Okay, I don't see any sign of the shark, so I'm just going to send him across the middle of the lagoon. When he reaches the reef he's supposed to skirt the perimeter, and come back through the atoll lagoon to the dolphin lagoon. Releasing in three..."

Coco looked out across the lagoon, but also saw no sign of the prehistoric predator.

"...two...one...lifting the gate...Go Tursi!"

They heard two shrill blasts of a whistle emanate from the radio.

"Hold on!" This from Mick for Coco's benefit, as he gunned the outboard's throttle, sending the Zodiac skimming across the water away from the pier. The surface of the lagoon was almost mirror flat, making for a smooth boat ride. Despite the seemingly tranquil surroundings, Coco's face was grim as she scoured the lagoon for signs of the hyper-predator. After a couple of minutes, Mick slowed the boat as he neared one of the two end-piece towers which supported lamp-tipped spires protruding a few feet above the surface to mark the hotel's position beneath.

"Airlock's right down here," Mick said, holding the boat steady. "Forgive me if I don't want to drop anchor. Might need to leave in a hurry, if you know what I mean, so I'll just keep her in position for you."

Coco was so focused on the moment, so all-business that she didn't even acknowledge Mick's humor. *Or is it because you're pissed at him?* After a quick glance around one more time (no megalodon), she flopped backwards over the side, Jacques Cousteau style, she always joked.

"Be care—"Mick called, trailing off when he saw that she was already underwater. "—ful."

He watched her descend toward the reef in a trail of bubbles. When he was sure she was underway without problems and clear of the boat, he put the motor into gear and raced back to the beach, double-checking that his radio was standing by on the designated channel.

Underwater, Coco heard the thrumming of the outboard motor grow more distant. She looked up and toward the beach in time to see the bottom of the Zodiac leaving a trail of white water on the surface of the lagoon. Head on a swivel, Coco descended the rest of the way to the reef floor. The hotel loomed before her, the airlock door protruding like a bump on a log just a few feet to her right. Even though she didn't see the shark, she wasted no time finning over to the hotel's underwater entrance. The megalodon was capable of scary-fast speeds, and of course made no noise if it stayed completely submerged. She would not take her safety for granted down here.

Reaching the airlock, Coco hit the switch to open the outer door. It slid open, and she kicked her way inside.

Chapter 26

Coco opened the inner airlock door, and stepped into the hotel. While resealing the airlock she heard voices coming from the dive shop inside. She grabbed her gear, and walked into the shop. There, a half a dozen people, one of them calling out, "Hello, Coco, you here?" walked around the shop.

Among them, apparently pretending he was oblivious to where she should most likely be—dead inside the Wet Bar, now having lived up to its name entirely—was James White. Coco was not at all surprised. In fact, instead of confronting him and creating a scene, she decided it was time to mess with his head a little. Still wearing her scuba gear and holding her fins in one hand, she stepped out into view of the shop visitors.

"Hi, Mr. White! Hello, everyone, are you ready for your afternoon dive?" *Might as well make it fun*, Coco thought. *It's just one short, shallow reef dive. You can do it. Then it's over.*

White looked like he'd seen a ghost, his face paling, lips trembling.

"C—Coco?"

"Hi there, Mr. White! As you can see I'm just back from a dive. I thought I'd test the waters in preparation for the group dive. Everything looks fins out there, people—I mean fine, everything looks fine!" She paused for a second with the group's laughter. "So don't worry, just relax, come with me, and we'll get you all geared up."

"All right!"

"Always wanted to get my shark diver certification," one of the men said.

Coco's approach had worked. In general, the tone of the group was upbeat and positive, all things considered. White, though, while not about to say anything, was having trouble processing the situation. Coco took great pleasure in watching his baffled expression out of the corner of her eye as she ignored him. She could practically read his brainwaves as his mind screamed, *How in the Hell did she get out of there?* She would never tell.

Coco went about the business of getting her divers together and checking their certifications. One of them said he was certified, but didn't have his card to prove it, so she grilled him with a pop quiz only certified divers would know, and pronounced him fit to dive. All told she had six scuba divers to take with her to the safety of the beach. Then she set about assisting the group as they tried on gear, making sure it fit properly, making sure it worked. She was extra careful, taking longer than usual on this process since she absolutely did not want any gear-related issues on this dive above all others. The dive should only last about ten or fifteen minutes if everything went well, much shorter than a standard dive, but the overriding sense of danger was palpable.

As she was nearing the end of the setup, screwing her own regulator onto a fresh tank, White came up to her and knelt down, looking around briefly to make sure no one was within earshot. He spoke to her in a low voice with a smile on his face.

"Coco, I was very concerned when I found out the restaurant flooded, and the pressure door was sealed off. I was worried that you..." He paused, hoping she would pick up the sentence and fill in the blanks for him, but she only continued adjusting her equipment. "I was worried that you might not have made it out of there," he finished, staring her in the eyes.

Coco shrugged as she pressed the purge button on her regulator, testing the airflow and enjoying seeing White jump at the sharp hiss of air it produced. "It was no big deal. I did a sweep of the area, found no one in there, and then squeezed out quick before the door shut." She gave him a big, fake smile.

"I—" he started, clearly confused as hell, but then a diver approached Coco holding a spear gun in one hand, and White stood with an "All right, then, glad to hear it, Coco!" and left.

"This is for sale in the shop," the man, an Egyptian telecommunications magnate by the name of Hatem Safar said. "I will purchase it from you."

Coco shot him a doubting look. "No spearfishing on this dive, Sir. We're just going to swim over to the beach so you can exit the hotel safely. That's the only purpose for this dive."

"In case the shark..." he began...but Coco waved him down. The last thing she wanted was to have to worry about nervous neophytes going off half-cocked underwater on what could be an extremely dangerous dive. No need to make it even more so.

"Absolutely not, Sir. You're welcome to go on your own, if you prefer..." she waved an arm toward the airlock while adding extra conviction to her voice. "But no one diving with my group will be carrying spears of any kind." Then she thought, but did not say, *As if that little toothpick would have any effect on the megalodon, anyway. Well, maybe if it was right in the eye...*

But the man set the spear gun down, acquiescing. "Very well. I trust you to lead us safely." Coco nodded at him, and he left to see to his wife. She straightened up and looked around, judging the state of readiness of her divers. They looked about as ready as one could be to attempt to swim underwater past a living dinosaur. It was time.

"Listen up, everyone!" she called. "Please gather all of your gear, and follow me to the airlock entrance, this way."

Wearing her scuba gear, Coco led the group to the inner airlock. She pointed to the activation button on the wall next to the door. "When I press this button—" she began, but never finished her sentence. At that moment they heard a destructive crunching sound, a heavy impact of some sort that sounded like it came from outside the hotel.

"What was that?" everyone immediately started asking.

Coco stepped back from the door. "Sounded like something hit the outer airlock door." She held a hand up for silence, listening to see if there would be more noise. Again came another wrenching impact—the creaking and twisting of metal. Coco quickly pictured the hotel's construction from the outside. Most of the hotel's "walls" were acrylic, but the airlock doors were metal, as were the internal failsafe pressure doors. Something...*don't kid yourself, you know what it is*...was colliding with the outer airlock door, with great force.

When they heard—and felt, Coco noticed as she sensed a vibration beneath her feet—yet another battering, Coco waved the group away from the door. "Back up, back away!" She led by example, backpedaling several feet from the inner airlock door.

Coco stared at the inner door, dreading seeing it bulge and buckle. The megalodon had to be responsible for this. What else could cause such underwater destruction? Why, she had no idea.

"It's the shark, isn't it?" the Egyptian man asked. Everyone looked at Coco, expecting an answer. She was their guide. She knew this place much better than they did. But the truth was that, although it must be the shark, she had no idea *why*, and that bothered the scientist in her.

"I think so."

"Why is it doing this?" a woman asked. "Are they chumming the waters?"

Coco shook her head emphatically. "No chumming or commercial fishing activities of any kind on this island. Subsistence fishing by the native villagers only."

"Then why is this shark doing this?" someone else wanted to know.

"Look, now is really not the time and place to worry about that, okay? I don't have the answer to that, and I don't want to waste everybody's time speculating right now."

"Why not, we can't exactly do our dive now, can we?" the Hatem pointed out. Coco had to admit that he had a point, but then she was distracted by the airlock door button on the wall. It was blinking red. She'd never seen it do that before. Usually it was unlit when on standby and then green when pressed to either open or close the door. She looked closely at the seal where the door met the floor and saw moisture seeping in. Also unusual; usually it was bone dry, even after wet divers traipsed through it back into the hotel.

"I'm willing to bet," Coco said, shrugging her scuba tank off and setting it on the floor—a signal to the others that they would not be doing the dive—"that the airlock no longer works."

She pointed to the blinking red button, then to the wetness on the floor.

"You think it's flooded in there?" a man asked.

"It's always flooded in there," Coco explained, "until that button is pressed. When that happens the water in the airlock is forced out by pressurization. But if the outer door was banged up, the system would no longer be air- and water-tight, and so wouldn't be able to work right."

Coco walked up to the button, and pressed it before anyone could protest. Instead of the usual whirring and humming sounds, there was nothing. Silence. The door didn't budge.

"See, it's broken," she said, removing her hand from the button, which still blinked red.

"So now we can't dive?" a woman asked. "I'm getting hot in this wetsuit." She tugged at the collar of her neoprene suit, largely unnecessary in the tropics, but she had insisted on wearing it, so Coco had obliged her. "Better warm than sorry," she'd said. But now it looked like she was sorry she was so warm. She began stripping off the wetsuit as Coco shook her head in reply.

"Is there another airlock in the hotel?" Hatem, the would-be spearfisher asked.

Again, Coco shook her head.

Chapter 27

Mick Wright was tense, on edge, as he waited in the Zodiac, idling in shallow water by the beach. Moments before he'd seen the towering dorsal fin of the megalodon plying the waters above the airlock. He shaded his eyes with a hand as he continued to scathe water over the hotel, but noticed the sun was sinking lower in the sky. He was glad Coco was going to be out of there before nightfall.

His boat radio crackled with Clarissa's panicky voice. "Mick, Tursi's not responding to my whistle signals. She was acting weird the last I saw her."

"Megalodon is in the lagoon, by the hotel west tower. Must be spooking her."

"Can you take me out there so we can give her an escort, Mick? Please?"

Mick pondered this while he stared at the ocean over the hotel. No signs of divers. Coco had apparently made it inside, but had not yet come back out, or at least had not yet surfaced with her dive group. He snagged a pair of binoculars, and focused on the surface of the water, searching for scuba bubbles, but he couldn't see any. He wasn't looking forward to giving her his reply, but he didn't see any way out.

"Clarissa, I can't leave my post here. I told Coco I'd be on standby in case she and her dive group need a lift on their way back in. I'm sorry, but I've got to put humans before dolphins."

There was a beat too lengthy for ordinary radio chat pause, followed by: "You sure it's not that you put certain humans before other humans, Mick? Forget it. Let my dolphin get mauled."

Mick exhaled heavily. About what he expected, but it stung all the same. He'd lose her over this, though, he knew that. And Coco...well, let's just say they weren't there yet. He'd like them to be, but they weren't. She was a little wilder, independent. He supposed he could keep an eye on the lagoon for divers while he escorted the dolphin. If he saw any sign of Coco and her party, he'd abandon the dolphin to shoot over to them...

"Okay, Clarissa, listen up. Be ready in front of the dolphin lagoon. I'll pick you up. On my way."

He put the motor in gear, and accelerated the small craft out in an arc away from the beach and toward Clarissa's dolphin lagoon. He kept glancing out toward the hotel as he went, watching for diver's heads, watching for the megalodon, watching for anything that confirmed what he was thinking: *you shouldn't be distracting yourself with the dolphin when people's lives are at stake. Thinking with the wrong head again.*

Then he was coasting up to Clarissa, who stood with a stern look on her face in the shallow water in front of a closed dolphin gate.

#

"So we're all stuck in here now?" The wife of Egyptian diver Hatem Safar harangued Coco with the same question for the fifth time. She felt like the pied piper as she exited the dive shop out into the hotel's main corridor, a procession of divers trailing behind her.

"When we get to the main lobby, I should be able to get more information for you. We're doing everything we can, trust me."

At least I'm doing everything I can. I'm not really sure about the management.

The group cast nervous glances through the glass out onto the reef, which was now a shade darker as the afternoon wore on.

"Can it bash in the regular glass here, like it did the train tunnel and the airlock?" one of them asked.

"Highly unlikely," Coco returned, although she meant unlikely it would want to do that, not unlikely that it could do it. They'd already seen what it could do after all. She wasn't even sure how unlikely it was that it would want to do it, though, seeing as it had already struck twice. *Why are you doing this, shark? Your whole life you spent in darkness in the canyon, and now you come up to the reef...what for?*

They heard voices ahead, and soon the hallway opened into the main lobby, a cavernous room with a domed, clear ceiling above which fish usually swam, but not now. It was hot in here despite the large size of the room. James White was talking animatedly to a small group of employees, while another group of guests milled about further away, some checking their cell-phones, even though they were told before checking in that there was no cell service on the remote island, and even if there was, the signal would not be able to get out through the underwater hotel. The hotel itself had hard wired lines running over the reef to a land-based terminal, and short-distance, higher frequency two-way radio signals were effective, but that was it.

White saw Coco and the divers enter the room, and immediately excused himself from his conversation to approach them. His fake smile threatened to tear off his face as he neared.

"Coco, I thought you'd be on the beach by now—did everyone decide they'd like to stay down here a little longer?"

No one laughed or even smiled. The intensity of White's smile fell back a notch. He eyed Coco, who broke the news to him, explaining that something—presumably the megalodon—had destroyed the airlock.

"So you're positive the airlock is not working? I could have Caesar look at it. He's—"

Coco and several of the divers all shook their heads at White. Coco spoke for them all. "It's completely flooded behind the first door, and the button to drain and pressurize it has no effect. I'm pretty sure the outer door is totally crumpled."

"Water was flooding into the dive shop when we left," Hatem added.

White's eyes bugged out as he turned to Coco. "Is this true?"

Coco shrugged. "Maybe *flooding* is too strong a word, but there was definitely water seeping in from under the inner airlock door when we left, yeah."

White raised a hand in the air, and waved for Caesar to step over. The man excused himself and joined White, who asked him if any alarms in the dive shop had been reported.

The Indian man shook his head as he lifted a mobile device, and glanced at its screen. "Not so far, it's been—"

Suddenly the gadget in his hand emitted a high-pitched siren noise, which Caesar silenced by swiping the screen. He held the phone farther from his eyes, as if straining to adjust his vision to small fonts.

"Well, speak of the devil," he said without looking up from the device.

"What happened?" White leaned in over the small screen.

"The emergency pressure door was just activated at the dive shop. The whole dive area has now been sealed off from the rest of the hotel." He directed his gaze at Coco.

"Was anyone else in there?"

Coco and a couple of the other divers shook their heads. "We were the last ones out," Coco said.

"You're positive?"

Coco nodded. The engineer breathed a sigh of relief that made a few of the guests wonder how well he and White really understood their own systems. Then White changed the subject.

"We're ready to give the emergency escape pod system a try."

He looked at Caesar, as if challenging him to say otherwise, but the man remained silent, neither agreeing nor disagreeing. White prompted him for a response.

"What do you think?"

This time, the engineer nodded, albeit with what looked to Coco like reluctance. "It is ready to test, sir, but it may be best to test the unit without humans inside first. That's what we would normally do."

"Well, is it ready or isn't it?" White's voice raised a notch.

"It is ready, sir, as far as I know, but there are many variables."

"Which pod should we try first?"

"Any of the guest suites."

"The suites are all emergency pods?" one of the divers asked, his tone incredulous. White nodded.

"They are indeed. They're designed to break away and float to the surface in an emergency."

"I'd say this qualifies," one of them said. White agreed with him. He pointed to the group of divers.

"This group here is the adventuresome one, right? You guys were ready to swim out of here, so, what do you think? Want to give the escape pod a try?"

The divers looked around at each other, and at Coco. A couple of them nodded, one shook her head, and the others, including Coco, remained unreadable.

"Those of you who want to go would be placed into a suite—with complimentary food and beverages of your choice, naturally—and then the pod would be jettisoned from the hotel structure."

"What does 'jettisoned' mean?" the Hatem's wife asked politely.

White gave her a smile brimming with bogus understanding. "It means that the individual suite will pop off from the rest of the hotel—with you in it—and float to the surface of the lagoon, where you can be pulled to shore by boat."

"Can't we just open the pod once we're on the surface and swim to shore?" one of them asked. White deferred to his engineer, who appeared less than thrilled at the prospect.

"Yes, there is a ceiling hatch—a trap-door in the ceiling—that you can climb out of. Then you will need to slide off the top of the pod into the water."

He glanced at Coco and saw her shaking her head, and so continued quickly. "However, it would be best to allow the entire pod to be towed to shore by small boat, and then you can exit directly onto the island."

"Yes," White agreed, "that certainly sounds like the most practical way to do it. We can have Mick pull the pod to the beach in the Zodiac, don't you think?" He eyed Coco and Caesar in turn.

"Even a small boat like that can pull it," the Indian confirmed. Coco was about to mention how Mick was already patrolling the lagoon in the inflatable boat, but checked herself. She didn't want to let on that she'd already been to the island and back.

"Make it happen," White told Caesar, who picked up a radio, presumably to contact Mick.

"Which pod should we use?" Coco asked, looking toward the row of suites.

White shouted over to the engineer, now speaking into his radio. "Moon Jelly suite, is it?" The Indian man nodded in return, and resumed his radio conversation.

"Moon Jelly suite," White confirmed for Coco. "The entire suite will detach, and float to the surface."

A man and his wife standing nearby, not part of the dive group, took off running out of the lobby. "Moon Jelly suite, let's go, honey," the man said to his wife.

"Hold up, please!" White called out. The couple stopped and turned.

White waved for them to come back. "We need to do this in an orderly fashion. We'd like to have the dive group go first. If anything goes wrong, after all, at least they'll be able to breathe underwater."

The face of the man reddened with pre-rage. "Nonsense! Whoever gets there first should be able to go."

"How many people can fit?" the wife asked.

White looked to the engineer who held up some fingers in White's direction.

"Six," White returned. "But this is only one suite. Each suite can carry six, so there's more than enough capacity for everyone. This isn't the Titanic."

"They said it was unsinkable, though," the irate man said. "And look what happened. This place is already sunk, though."

"Sir," White pleaded, "please just allow us to conduct our test run of the pods with this first group of scuba divers, and then you and your lovely wife can be on the very next pod to go, I promise."

The man was not placated. He walked closer to White, breaking from his wife's grasp in order to do so. "If I say I want to be in that first pod, I'm going to be in that first pod! It's fucking hot in here! My wife is feeling faint! We are getting on that goddamned pod!"

The man's wife called after him, "Steven, please, it's all right." He whirled around to confront his wife. "No, it's not all right! If there's a way out of this trumped up hell-hole, we're going to be there."

White made eye contact with Coco, and cocked his head toward the hallway, his message clear: *Get going.* She nodded in response, and quietly rounded up her charges, the six divers, indicating for them to follow her with the same hand signals they used underwater. The angry man saw them leaving and spun around, calling to his wife.

"C'mon Alice, we're going with them."

Coco kept her group moving forward, not wanting to confront the man. If White wanted to put the pod to use, he'd have to run security. She heard a scuffle behind her, and turned in time to see White and Aiden, who had some experience with nightclub security at least, subdue the man in a bear hug and wrestle him to the floor.

Quickly she turned back around, pushing her divers forward, hissing, "Let's go!" They didn't need to wait around until more people decided they were willing to fight for the right to be in the first pod. As she led the group toward the suite section of the hotel, she reflected on how bad things had gotten for people to be so vehement about their desire to be first to try an experimental underwater technology.

Considering the failure rate of the rest of the hotel, Coco questioned whether she herself even wanted to be in the first group to try one of the escape pods. Not really, she thought. Why did she really need to go now, anyway? They won't be diving, except in the most extreme case of things gone wrong. Once she left the hotel, now that the airlock and tunnel were damaged, there was no getting back in. White (he was still her employer, after all) would want her here. If this first pod evacuation was successful, there would be others, too. She would lead them to the pod, but stay behind in the hotel. Plus, Caesar had said the capacity of the pods was six people, and she would make seven, so that settled it.

Coco glanced to her left through the clear wall that looked out on the reef. Definitely darker now. The sun was setting. She picked up her pace a little as they neared the suites. It would be nice to spend the night on land, she had to admit, but she had a job to do down here. And with Mick involved with Clarissa, spending the night on land was less attractive. It was hot and stuffy down here, though, and the people were testy. Understandably so, but still. *Get these people on this pod.*

They reached the suites wing, and Coco found the Moon Jelly suite, the medusa form of a jellyfish etched into the door. As promised, the door was unlocked. She opened it, and held it open for the six divers who filed into the luxury suite with their scuba gear. Coco stood there for a moment before entering, listening down the long hallway for the sound of approaching footsteps. If there was an angry throng coming to demand entry to the pod, she'd rather know about it now.

Her ears were greeted with only silence, however, so she stepped into the suite, closed, locked, and double-checked the door. She took a deep breath, facing the closed door in case anyone was watching. *Stay calm. Be a leader. Be strong.* She wasn't sure why she had to remind herself of that, but for whatever reason it made her feel better, so she did it. *It's up to you to keep these people safe. Do it.*

The divers were standing against the scenic window, looking out on the reef, where the exterior lights had just come on with the onset of evening. "Looks nice enough out there," one of them remarked. Coco thought, but did not say: *Most sharks are nocturnal, and become more active at night.* Another answered how she was looking forward to staying in a regular hotel, and just scuba dive on the reef when she wanted to see it. "Amen to that," another replied.

An intercom set into the wall near the door crackled with James White's voice. Are you ready? Coco walked to the LED touchscreen, clicked an icon, and spoke into the microphone.

"All seven of us now inside the Moon Jelly suite—escape pod, that is—myself, and the six scuba divers."

"Coco, I need you to stay behind in the hotel, if that's all right with you. We're short-staffed down here since we can't do any shift changes, and people have to sleep some time."

"No problem, Mr., White. I understand."

"Caesar is going to come on now and explain to everyone what to expect, so be sure to gather them around the intercom, and turn up the volume, okay?"

"Will do."

"When he's done, let them know you'll be staying in the hotel, and let yourself out."

"Copy that." Coco waved everyone over, and told them to listen to the instructions.

The Indian engineer's voice came over the intercom. "None of you need to do anything, but I just want to tell you what to expect. Ideally, all of you should be in a sitting position. It should be a smooth ascent to the surface, but in case you encounter...turbulence...it is safer to be lower to the floor, okay? The pod is designed to float ceiling up, in the same orientation as it is now, but it..."

"But it's untested," Coco completed the sentence for him.

"Right."

Coco looked back, and was glad to see the divers all taking seats of their own accord.

"It should be a slow but steady rise to the surface. When you reach the surface, one of our boat operators will be standing by in a small boat to tow the entire pod to the beach. Do not open the door yourself, wait for instructions. Coco, you have the walkie talkie?"

Coco felt along her belt. "Yes."

"Please give it to someone in the pod so that they can communicate if necessary with Mick in the boat." Coco designated Hatem as the one in charge of the radio. She briefly showed him how to use it, and then handed it to him.

She told the engineer over the intercom that they were ready.

"Great. Then take a seat please. Let's try to get you off the bottom while it's still light out."

Coco opened the suite door, and stepped into the hallway.

"See you on the island a little later!" she called out before shutting the door.

Chapter 28

Coco stood outside the short vestibule to the suite—the escape pod—and listened to the sound of activating levers and machinery from behind a steel pressure shield that had dropped not long after she had exited the unit. The suite was disengaging from the main hotel. After a couple of minutes she heard one more loud clunking sound, and then nothing. The entire suite pod was separated from the hotel.

She took off down the main hallway at a trot toward the main lobby. As she ran, she looked up through the transparent ceiling, hoping to catch a glimpse of the pod on its way to the surface. She couldn't see it, however, so kept on moving.

When she got the lobby everyone—White, Caesar, and a couple of staff along with a dozen or so trapped guests—were lined up against the far viewing wall. They peered out onto the reef, some pointing and shouting. Coco ran up to them, wondering if the megalodon had shown up again, attracted by the exterior lights.

As she found a place within the crowd and stepped up to the window, though, it immediately became apparent that there was no sea life causing the ruckus. Something artificial was out there—something lit up. At first she thought it might be Mick with the sub, but then the logical side of her brain took over, and she knew it was much too large to be the sub.

"...thought it floated?" she heard a woman ask.

Then it hit her. *Thought it floated...* She ran to White's side. He was busy arguing, albeit in hushed tones, as usual, with the engineer, who shot a slightly annoyed glance at Coco as she walked up. Coco didn't care.

"Is that the pod?" she said pressing in next to White as she stared out at the thing.

"Yes," he returned before resuming his intense conversation with the Indian man.

Apparently something had gone wrong. The entire pod—one of the hotel suites—now lay on the coral reef, upright, as if it were a designed outbuilding of the hotel. But Coco knew it wasn't. It lay just beyond the main swath of light from the hotel's exterior bulbs, but the pod still had its own interior and exterior lighting, and Coco realized with a start that she could see into the pod—she could see the people inside pressing their faces against the wall, and looking back at them across the reef!

"What happened?" Coco tried a more direct approach to get information. White disagreed with something the engineer said, and turned away from him in frustration, now ready to talk to Coco.

"Apparently our *crack engineering team*," White emphasized the words with sarcasm as he turned quickly to the Indian, and then back to Coco, "forgot that there would be furnishings and people inside the pod when it would be used in a real escape scenario, and so that extra weight was not in the original buoyancy calculations."

The gravity of the situation took root for Coco as she gawked at the sunken hotel room. It had detached from the main building, but it didn't float like they said it would! It was not a sub, it had no means of propulsion, and therefore was little more than a rock on the bottom. A hollow ball filled with air and people, and when that air ran out...

She watched the divers—there was the wife of the Egyptian man—waving at them through the window. Not waving like, *oh, hi, over there, isn't this fun?* But waving in a panic state to try to get people's attention for help. Coco was reminded of Hatem, the one to whom she had given the radio. She snatched the unit from her belt and checked to make sure it was on and set to the same channel she told him to use. All good.

She held up the radio and waved it above her head, hoping they could see it, and would get the idea that she wanted them to establish communications. She didn't know if White and his engineer did or not—surely they knew they had a radio—but she didn't much care, either. She had personally walked them into that pod, and told them everything would be okay. She was the last person from the hotel they had contact with.

Coco's radio came to life in her hand. It was the Egyptian.

"Coco, this is Hatem, do you read me, over?"

White and the engineer glanced at the radio in Coco's hand. Coco keyed the transmitter, and talked into it.

"Read you loud and clear, Hatem. It looks like there's been a problem with the buoyancy system in the escape pod. I'm giving you to Mr. White for an update."

She handed him the radio. *Deal with it, bastard. Confront the people whose lives you are affecting with your stupid decisions.* She was tired of cleaning up after his messes. It was obvious he didn't want to talk to the pod, but with several of the guests watching him to see how he would respond, he had no choice. He stared at the radio for a second as if it was a foreign instrument to him, and then took it from Coco's hand. Caesar said something softly to him, inaudible even to Coco, who was standing right next to them.

White looked out into the stationery escape pod while he spoke into the radio. "Hatem, I can confirm that there is indeed a buoyancy problem with the pod. I can assure you that my engineers are addressing the problem as we speak."

To everyone's surprise, the Egyptian man's response was calm and collected, although they could hear many other people asking questions in the background of the transmission.

"Copy that, Mr. White. Standing by for further news, enjoying the view, over." He waved at them across the reef.

Coco turned to White and the engineer. "How long will the air supply last in the pod?"

White deferred to the engineer, who gave a doubting look and a shrug as if to indicate that his response was only a guesstimate. "Six people inside...maybe four-to-six hours."

"Can they open the hatch and scuba out?" Coco looked out to the pod, where it was getting difficult to see the shape of the actual pod except for the lights on the outside.

The engineer again appeared doubtful. "Perhaps they could open the hatch against the water pressure, but I'm not sure. We never tested that. But even if they could, water would immediately rush in with great force. I suppose it is possible, if they knew to wait out of the way of the main force of the water with their gear already on, but..." He shook his head as he stared out at the pod.

No one said anything for a moment as they stared at the pod, until the engineer broke the silence. "I think the best bet is to have divers from Topside scuba down and rig a lot of lift bags to the pod, it will rise to the surface where—"

The guests around them started to shout and point. Coco followed their fingers out to the left of the pod, where a mammoth, dark shape moved up on the reef.

Chapter 29

Mick closed his hand around the warm rubber of the Zodiac's throttle as he revved the engine. In his other hand he held the boat's radio transmitter. He had the volume cranked all the way up, and could just barely hear Coco's stressed-out voice above the whine of his outboard.

"...not coming up, Mick. Pod sunk to the bottom...see something...worried."

Mick yelled into the mic. "I'm almost to the hotel. I'll give it a look, over!"

He dropped the transmitter, and focused on driving the boat. He needed to keep a sharp eye out for...for a lot of things, he realized. The pod...the divers from the pod in case they swam out somehow...the megalodon. Clarissa's dolphin....He had told her he was jetting off to look for it, but Coco was right. He had to put human life first. The dolphin was like Clarissa's pet, of course she wanted it looked after, but—

Mick slowed the boat as he eyed a darkish object bobbing in the waves about halfway between the hotel and the reef line. He'd just told Coco that he'd be coming to the hotel to look for the pod, but what if this object was somehow related to the pod? It wasn't all that far away. Then he remembered what he had in the console, and slowed the boat to idle. He reached down and rummaged through the cluttered space beneath the steering wheel until he found what he was looking for: a pair of old marine binoculars.

He focused the glasses on the object he saw on the water. Focused some more, compensating for the bouncing boat....there! Mick recoiled as his brain processed the imagery his eyes conveyed to it.

A bloody dolphin—or half of one, to be more specific—rode the waves. Ragged meat bulged from the lower half of the dolphin, its head completely missing. Mick had seen dolphins that had been attacked by sharks before, and while it could be gruesome, he'd never seen anything like this. Usually there would be multiple smaller chunks removed from the body...but the entire upper torso and head? Unheard of.

Megalodon...

He thought of Coco and immediately picked up his radio.

#

Down in the hotel lobby, Coco pointed to the megalodon as it swept its colossal body across the reef toward the sunken escape pod. Looking up, she saw the outline of Mick's Zodiac limned against the evening sky. She brought the radio to her lips.

"See your boat, Mick. You're over the pod—and the megalodon—be careful!"

"Copy that. Thought that big-ass shark would be down here. I found half of Clarissa's dolphin up here, too, over."

No sooner had he completed his sentence than Clarissa followed the points of several shouting guests. A dolphin's severed head drifted near the lobby window.

"Which half did you see up there?"

"The tail."

"We just found the head down here."

"Odd he didn't actually eat it, isn't it?"

Coco was thinking about this—it *was* odd—when the megalodon swooped into view in front of the lobby. Terrified screams filled the air as the guests ran herd-like away from the window. Coco was too riveted by the view to move. White and the engineer backed up a few steps, but also remained close to the window as the megalodon closed in.

Never had Coco seen firsthand such a massive, all-encompassing predatory maw. The jaws gaped wide, and she swore a small house could fit inside the beast's mouth. It swam low and fast toward the hotel, giving them a perfect view of it head-on, the kind of view one can never forget. The kind of view Coco would never forget. Ragged rips of flesh trailed from several of the giant's six-inch long teeth on the left side of its oral cavity, remnants of Clarissa's dolphin.

Just as Coco was preparing to turn and run, expecting the prehistoric marauder to smash into the acrylic wall right in front of her, the oversized cartilaginous fish veered sharply to the right, a swirl of sediment billowing from the reef as its tail swiped past the viewing window.

"That was close," White remarked.

"It didn't miss, if that's what you mean." Coco still watched the fish's progress with rapt attention as it hurtled out across the reef toward the pod, where the would-be escapees were plastered against the suite's window, watching the apex predator with expressions of horror that reminded Coco of the faces she had witnessed in the tram tunnel—shortly before most of them died.

Coco's radio crackled once again with Mick's voice. "Coco, I think I see the pod, it's down on the reef in front of the lobby main window, lights on, right?"

"That's right. And—"

"And the shark is heading for it?"

"Yes, you can see that?"

"Yeah. Not sure what I can do for them, any ideas?"

Coco looked at White and the engineer who had also heard Mick. White looked at Caesar, who slowly shook his head, and stared out the window. "I'm sure they know not to try to open the hatch and scuba out of there now," was all he said.

Coco raised the radio to her mouth. "Mick, maybe just zoom around up there, make some engine noise, draw it off of them?"

There was a pause while the shark closed the distance to the escape pod before Mick's voice came back. "Copy that, Coco, I'll give it a go." They saw the plume of whitewater from the boat's wake grow larger as Mick throttled up the engine, heading toward the edge of the reef, away from the pod's position on the bottom.

Meanwhile, the shark accelerated as it approached the pod.

Chapter 30

"It's charging the pod!" one of the guests shouted. Coco yelled into her radio.

"Hatem, brace yourselves, shark is ramming the pod! Get your scuba gear ready in case it breaches it!" Looking across the reef, it was mostly dark, and the colossal body of the great shark blocked the view into the escape pod window, so she couldn't see what the people inside were doing, but then the Egyptian's voice came back over the radio.

"Coco, we see it! It's so big! Oh my..."

Whatever was happening, Hatem must have kept the transmitter keyed because Coco could hear the crunching impact when the shark collided with the escape pod's outer window, followed quickly by the rising shouts of those inside.

Somehow cutting through the cacophony was Caesar's voice, which was calm and matter-of-fact as it delivered bad news. "It moved the pod. Pushed it back."

As Coco continued to watch, she verified that, indeed, the pod was now canted over onto one side as the rear portion of it rested on a coral outcropping. The humongous shark backed up, and moved into a forward turn, its two-story high tail moving almost the entire water column in the lagoon, top to bottom. It circled back toward the hotel lobby, where Coco, White, and the engineer were now the only three anywhere near the main window. Several of the other guests had left the lobby altogether, seeking safer ground, while those who remained hung back near the entrance, ready to turn tail if the shark got too aggressive.

The megalodon swept right past the lobby window, one of its serving plate sized eyes gazing vacantly into the hotel. White and the engineer unconsciously took a step back as it passed, but Coco stood her ground, fascinated and terrified at the same time. She pounded a fist on the glass as the mega-predator's eye passed by her at her own eye level. She wasn't sure why she did it—an act of frustration, maybe, or just to gauge the reaction of the animal—to see if a small gesture like that would have any effect on it.

It had an effect on the people in the room, but not the shark. "Stop, you'll turn it on us!" White pleaded. A couple of the other guests agreed with him from their safe distance away. The megalodon, for its part, did not alter its course or behavior in any way, but continued swimming along the lobby window until it reached the end of it, and then turned out toward the escape pod once more.

"Coming at you again, Hatem," Coco transmitted, before adding, "Faster this time!"

Undeniably, the megalodon called on a burst of acceleration she hadn't seen before as it approached the wayward pod with its contingent of shell-shocked would-be escapees. Coco saw Mick's Zodiac leave a soundless wake above as he traversed the area at high speed, hoping to distract the shark and draw it off. The animal continued its bull-rush unabated, however. Whether it knew boats weren't a threat, or didn't recognize them as anything whatsoever, Coco didn't know, but at the moment it was fixated only on the pod. Even the hotel itself seemed to hold no interest for it. It was as if all of its primal instincts were homed in on the isolated, and therefore, vulnerable, oddity that had invaded the reef.

Coco brought a hand to her mouth in a gesture of nervous anticipation. Any hope she had that the rampaging oceanic mega-beast might choose not to hit the pod this time was quickly dispelled. This time when the megalodon crashed into the escape pod, the entire spherical structure was lifted off of the reef as if it were a football punted in slow motion. Coco watched as it tilted up on its side before hanging there over the coral. Inside she could see the six divers being tossed about like ragdolls. She radioed the Egyptian, but received no reply. She could only imagine that the radio must have been flung from his hand.

Even as the pod sat on its end, the megalodon showed no signs of letting up on its attack. It swam a tight circle, this time only traversing half the distance back to the hotel, and then immediately set back on another beeline to its target, the loose pod. The guests behind Coco screamed again as the shark prepared to swim fast into the pod.

The fish came up at its target at an angle, its gargantuan snout hammering the top of the end-up pod, sending it toppling over like a domino so that it landed on its back, with the ceiling lying on the reef. Coco could see that the lights were still on inside the former suite—a good sign that the integrity of the walls hadn't yet been breached—but the pod was farther away now, and difficult to look inside.

Farther away now... As she watched the pod drift and bounce across the reef away from the hotel, and the megalodon circle back around yet again, Coco felt a chill overcome her unlike any she'd ever experienced before. The shark was pushing the pod into the deeper water at the edge of the lagoon...toward the reef.

She watched as the pod took another hit from the living fossil, which sent it skidding across a contingent of brain corals at a random angle.

Toward the submarine canyon...

Coco tried radioing the pod again, without a reply. Again she saw Mick's boat pass overhead, again without effect.

"What can we do? What can we *do?*" she implored White and the engineer, but they merely stood there, mouths agape, shaking their heads. There was nothing any of them could do except to watch, watch as the monstrous fish steamrolled into the pod over and over again, pushing it inexorably toward the edge of the reef.

"Why is it doing this?" someone cried.

"Is it...is it playing with that pod, like a cat with a toy?" White sputtered. They watched in horror as the predator battered the pod out to the very edge of the reef. It was visible to Coco now only as a dark object being jostled about the outer reef. Getting farther and farther away.

She felt helpless just standing there, unable to do anything but watch as the six people she was supposed to lead to safety went through absolute Hell on Earth. How frightening it must be for them, she considered, being tumbled about in a small enclosure underwater by a gigantic shark. Just like a hamster trapped in one of those plastic balls being batted about the floor by a housecat, Coco thought. *Just like that.* But sharks didn't do that kind of thing for fun. *Did they?* Not as far as she knew. But then again, how much did anybody really know about megalodons?

Then she was broken out of her thoughts by her radio bleating frantically with the sound of the Egyptian diver's voice as the pod reached the edge of the canyon, the entrance to the true deep. "...Coco....happening...moving too much...open...."

She gripped the talk button on her handset. "Hatem, listen to me: the shark is pushing the pod off the reef and down the canyon. Get out! Get out and scuba if you can now before you get too deep!" She released the talk button, and heard only a tapestry of commotion—clicking noises, static, a grunt? a scream?—before the transmission ceased. The megalodon was moving the pod faster now, too; making tighter turns to circle back and ram it, sending it longer distances across the reef.

Then the pod wedged into the narrow entrance to the canyon and stuck there, its long axis contacting the reef on either side. Coco didn't know if the Egyptian could hear her any longer, but she shouted into her radio anyway: "Go now if you can, Hatem. It's coming around again!"

The megalodon looped back, very hard to see from this distance, but its large size made it possible. Then it thrust its enormous bulk into the pod once more...

...and the structure tumbled down the incline into the submarine canyon.

Chapter 31

"They're gone!" Coco, leaned her forehead into the lobby window as a tear rolled down her cheek. Neither James White nor her engineer offered anything to contradict her. They *were* gone. Swept off the reef into the abyss by the mega-predator. In full view of the clientele, no less, some of whom approached White now.

"Excuse us, Mr. White?" The Japanese couple who White had seen eating in the restaurant earlier approached cautiously, aware they had all just witnessed a traumatic event. White turned and looked at them without saying anything. Several of the other guests were huddled near the lobby entrance, watching the interaction.

The man spoke after it was clear White was not going to. "A group of us were talking over there, and we decided we don't want to try to evacuate in one of the escape pods."

White nodded curtly. "Understandable, naturally. Let us focus on the situation here for the time being, Mr. Takamoto, and I can assure you that you, your wife, and everyone else here will be well taken care of." At this Takamoto frowned slightly but said nothing, and retreated with his wife back to his group, who appeared eager to hear what had transpired.

White addressed Coco. "You know the edge of the reef better than anyone else here. What's it like? How steep is it where they went over?"

Coco stared out onto the darkening reef as she reflected on this, mentally recalling images from her sub dive yesterday to practice her tour of the drop-off area. She laughed sarcastically to herself at how naive she had been yesterday, how she thought she would be cracking jokes to the guests in the sub during her suave presentation at the edge of the reef. And now look at what had happened. She forced herself to stay focused.

"It's a steep incline, kind of a sandy path sandwiched between two coral walls that slopes down for maybe...fifty feet or so, and then..." She trailed off as she considered the fate of those in the escape pod should that pod tumble past the edge of the sandy trail into the abyss.

"The drop-off?" White prompted.

She nodded wordlessly. If the pod went over that, there was nothing anyone on Earth would be able to do for them in time.

"The crush depth for the pods is only about 1,000 feet," the engineer said dryly. "More than enough considering they were intended to be deployed in forty feet of water."

"But if they roll off that shelf at the end of the slope, they'll go to...I don't know what—10,000 feet?" White said, looking at Coco.

"Twelve," she returned.

"Jesus."

"The pod is pretty big," Coco went on. "I'm hoping it got wedged between the coral shelves on the sandy slope. It hasn't popped up to the surface yet or Mick would have said something."

Her eyes brightened at the mention of his name. "That gives me an idea." She raised her radio and spoke into it.

"Mick, Coco here—you copy?"

They heard the roar of a boat motor accompany his reply. "I copy you, Coco. No sign of anything up here now—no pod, no shark, no people, over!"

"I saw the shark bump the pod off the reef, down the slope!"

They heard the sound of the motor diminish as Mick slowed his craft, probably in order to better hear the radio. "Say what?"

Coco repeated herself. Mick replied, "Jesus! I won't be able to see down there now, though, it's too dark."

"Can you take the sub down, and have a look-see?"

White and the engineer exchanged glances, but neither said a word. Coco broke the ensuing silence where no doubt all of them considered how dangerous that might be for Mick. The megalodon could swallow the mini-sub whole. Yet half a dozen lives were at stake, and only a quick look down the slope would be required to at least find out if the pod was still there. Coco said as much and Mick replied.

"Sure, I'll drop down in the sub and have a look. But listen, just looking at them isn't going to help them you know? And even if it's there sitting on the slope, it might be too wedged in to use lift bags on it."

"So what's' your point?" Coco grew more exasperated by the minute. People were dying out there, and everyone seemed impotent to help.

"You said they have scuba gear in there with them, right?"

"That's right, all of them. If they could only use it."

"I might have a way. Earlier today in the sub shack..." Mick paused for a moment, and Coco wondered if he realized how awkward referencing the sub shack was given what Coco had found him doing there earlier. He continued after a beat. "Earlier I worked on fitting an acetylene torch to the sub's grab arm, because after our dive on the intake pipe it hit me how much that would have come in handy."

"Yeah?" Coco felt a faint swelling of hope stir within her.

"Yeah, and I got it working. Haven't tested it yet, but I guess there's no time for that. But what I was saying is, I can take the sub down, and if it's there and there's some reason they're stuck inside still, like the hatch won't open or it's pressed up against something, then I can cut a new hatch through the wall of the pod for them."

White looked to the engineer who shrugged, and then nodded. "It could work," he said, but didn't sound all that convinced.

Coco was quick to reply. "Okay, Mick, sounds great. Why don't you head back to the sub dock and try it?"

They heard the sound of an outboard motor decelerating. "Been heading back during our whole chat. I'm at the pier now. I'll radio back when I'm in the sub, out."

Chapter 32

The radio call that came in from Mick was a crushing blow to everyone within earshot of Coco's radio.

"*Triton-1* to Coco, *Triton-1* to Coco, I am over the slope and report that there is no pod here. I repeat—the pod is not here, over."

Coco choked back a sob. "It's been swept over?"

Mick's voice came back trying to sound strong, but with a detectable waver to it nonetheless. "I see a lot of broken off chunks of coral like there was a struggle here, and the water is still a little cloudy from where the sand was stirred up, but there's definitely no pod anywhere on the slope, Coco. I snapped a few pics, too."

Coco switched channels to the one Hatem used from the pod, and tried hailing him. Nothing came back. She switched back over to Mick's channel.

"I did a sweep of the reef edge, too, just in case they ended up not down the slope, but along the reef somewhere else, but it's not there, Coco. That pod is too big not to see. I'm sorry, but it looks like it went over the wall into the deep."

A weighty silence followed during which Coco tried not to visualize the final moments of those people as the pod passed its crush depth, and water pulverized them in complete darkness. Even with scuba gear on, the sudden pressure and incoming force of the water would kill them. She placated herself with the knowledge that it must have been a swift death, preferable to being torn apart like a random prey item in the jaws of the prehistoric monster.

"Thanks for trying, Mick. Bring it back in, might as well—"

The suddenness with which the megalodon appeared in front of the lobby window was something that unnerved Coco more than anything she could remember. One second there was only the reef and empty water illuminated by the hotel's exterior underwater lights, and the next an enormous set of jaws occupied most of the acrylic wall.

Then came the impact.

Immediately the plastic glass cracked and water came running in from where the window met the ceiling, which was also an acrylic panel. The guests near the entrance withdrew into the main hallway. White lifted his own radio, and shouted into it to a technician in another part of the hotel.

"Turn off the exterior lights. They're attracting the shark!"

Coco had her doubts as to whether that was true, but now was not the time to argue about it, for the ginormous fish was already arcing around.

"It's coming back again," Caesar said. "Back up."

The monster shark rammed into the window again, its cavernous maw seeming to swallow the entire room as it approached. Then it hit, and Coco swore that she saw one of its teeth actually poke through the inches-thick acrylic before the material gave way and a torrent of ocean cascaded into the lobby. Coco felt the spray of water on her face as she, White, and the engineer turned and ran to follow the guests out of the lobby.

"Hurry, before the pressure door closes!" the engineer warned. The lead doors were designed to drop with the introduction of significant moisture, and the raging flood now entering through the shattered window was definitely going to trigger it.

Coco heard the sound of broken window pieces hitting the floor as the transparent wall fell apart. The three of them ran out into the hall, White radioing that they were clear. Then something disturbing happened, or didn't happen. The water followed them into the hallway, swiftly rising to around their ankles.

White barked into his radio. "Pressure door's not activating. Water's breaching the main thoroughfare off the lobby."

"That's not all that's breaching," Coco announced, pointing at the giant head of the megalodon. It now stuck into the lobby, mostly submerged in water, thrashing side to side in violent, exploratory motions.

White's radio blared a response from the technician. "Pressure door is not releasing. Looks like we may have a short in the circuit related to an overload from working on the train tunnel. I'm sorry."

Coco glanced at White's face, his carotids bulging in his neck, face beet red as he replied into the radio. "Don't be sorry, just fix it, damn you! We've got the whole lagoon pouring in here through the lobby. We *need* that pressure door to work. Do something!"

Coco wasn't about to wait around and hope the tech could get it resolved. "We better move!" But then, ironically, she froze, looking both ways down the spacious hallway. Which way to go? The guests had gone right, toward the now defunct train station, but she also had the option of going left, back toward the pods and eventually the dive shop, which was already sealed off. White was still arguing with his tech on the radio while the engineer waited for him, but glanced longingly toward the right. Coco had an idea, and addressed him.

"Where's the next closest pressure door besides this one?" she asked, looking back at the lobby to see if it might have activated. No such luck, and the water level was filling at an alarming rate, she noticed. The water was up to her knees here in the hallway. Her nerve endings tingled as she imagined the megalodon somehow squeezing its way all the way to her here in the hallway. *It couldn't, could it?*

"It's this way." Caesar pointed to the direction in which he was already looking. He tapped White on the shoulder. "Tell him to prepare to activate Door 4."

White changed the radio conversation with the tech accordingly, and waited for a few seconds while he said to hold on. When he came back, it was not with good news.

"Real sorry, James, but that door has already been sealed. Not sure why. Looks like the short in the system caused some to remain open, but others to shut. Board's lit up all crazy in here. It'll take some time for me to wrap my head around this. I better get working on it. You should go, hold on...*left*, from your location, to Door 6, over."

Coco wondered if the guests from the lobby had made it past Door 4 before the pressure door had experienced the wonky activation. She figured they'd have turned back by now if they'd met a wall, and would at least be able to hear them.

"You're positive?" White shot back.

"Don't go right, James."

He looked at Coco and Caesar, and the three of them took off at a run toward Door 6.

Chapter 33

Not long after they started for Door 6, Coco heard a ruckus somewhere behind them. The trammel of footsteps, shouting, people calling out. Coco stopped running, and held out a hand.

"Wait, you hear that?"

White and Caesar slowed, but did not stop walking toward the next pressure door. White spoke into his radio.

"Dan, what's going on with the doors?" No reply came from the marine technician.

They heard the crowd drawing near while waiting for a reply. Looking outside the hotel, the reef was lit below, but above, the sky was dark.

"Mr. Wang?" White prompted.

"Here they come," Coco said as the people ran into view.

Then White's radio blared with Wang's voice. An Asian-American who dropped out of engineering school to become a technician because he claimed he wanted to make money instead of owe it, Wang had a solid reputation at Triton for getting things done, though White knew he was relatively inexperienced.

"James, we've got a problem with the pressure door system. Number Four shut early on us, and we can't get it to open again, over."

White's fingers gripped the radio hard, like he wanted to crush it, while he shook his head. The guests were calling out to them now, "We couldn't get through! There's a wall!"

"I show that Six is still open, James, you should get through now before—"

"Water's coming in," Coco declared, splashing her foot.

"—the water from the lobby breach is redirected your way when it bounces off Door 4."

White's eyes looked as though they were about to bug out of his head. "You mean to say we're about to flooded here, in the main hallway, right now?"

The radio reply was quick. "Water will be coming that way James, and a lot of it, if the flow meter accuracy is anything like it should be. You should get you and your party on the other side of Six, and then I'll seal it off, over!"

"Copy that, I've got a big party crossing over Door 6 now, Dan. *Don't let it close yet*, over."

Coco was the first of them to greet the panic-stricken faces that ran their way. She calmed them down enough to be heard over their worrying. "Follow us this way, they're going to close a pressure door after we pass through it.'

"Is that what happened back there?" John Rudd, the NFL player asked. His girlfriend, the model, shivered in his arms while he spoke. "They closed it before we got to it? Isn't there some kind of communication?" He directed this latter question right to White, who merely waved an arm for him to follow, and started down the hallway.

"Water's coming! Water's coming at us!" a child of about ten shouted. Coco asked her father to carry her until they passed through Door 6, and then told the group to follow her.

"We've just got a little ways to go, people, then we'll be in a dry area of the hotel. Stay with me, and let's go."

Coco turned to move out in the opposite direction toward Door 6, and immediately slipped on the slick floor, landing hard on a knee. She winced in pain while she felt water flow over the hand on the floor supporting her weight. She felt a hand grip her arm, pulling her up, and turned to see a well-known Internet entrepreneur help her to her feet.

She told him thanks, and he said, "No problem. When we get out of here, though, I'd like to discuss some automation software that would help out a lot around here."

She didn't mention that that was the last thing she was going to care about after she got out of here, but instead said "Good idea," and proceeded to jog with the group toward White and Caesar, a few paces ahead of them.

It soon became clear that the water was entering faster than they had anticipated. Like a swift-flowing river, it was only up to their knees, but moving so quickly that it constantly knocked over the guests. With the lobby window caved, the hotel was truly flooding now. Coco could hear White up ahead yelling into his radio, but the oncoming water noise, along with the loud voices of the guests, made it too hard to hear what was being said. She hoped it wasn't something about how Door 6 wasn't working and wouldn't be able to close, or even worse—that it was already closed, and they'd be trapped in here with the rising water...

Coco snapped out of it when she saw White and the engineer stop running on the other side of the track where Door 6 would come down. At least it hadn't closed already. Yet the incoming water seemed to rise faster still, and with more intensity than before. Coco looked out the window to the reef, hoping she'd see the megalodon out there, because for some reason she found it disturbing to think of the extinct mega-fish swimming around the hotel lobby. *Could it fit in the hallway?* She glanced back down the hall, took in the domed ceiling, gauged the width...it seemed high enough but perhaps—hopefully—a little too narrow. Nevertheless, the young marine biologist couldn't keep from imagining that powerful set of jaws inside that yawning, gaping maw barreling down the hall, scooping all of them into its mouth, and washing them down its black, raspy gullet.

She heard words coming out of White's mouth into his radio that she could understand now, and that jarred her back to the moment.

"...on the other side now. Go ahead."

White saw Coco, and waved an arm to get her attention. She walked up to him. He continued to wave an arm at the guests, ushering them onto the other side of the door track.

"Dan says they initiated the door close procedure."

"Shouldn't we keep going farther down the hall, away from the water?" a woman asked. Clearly frightened, she hugged herself as though cold while she stared down at the seawater rising past her knees.

"Don't worry, a steel pressure door will be sealing us off from the other side momentarily." White beckoned for the woman to take a few more steps on the other side of the door track. She did, but had a sour look on her face.

"You keep saying not to worry, but things keep getting worse and worse!" Clearly the sentiment was shared by at least a few in the group, as several of them nodded. White appeared to be composing a response when he was saved by the bell—his radio erupted with Dan's voice.

"Okay, here we go—you have your people ready now, James?"

White looked away from the woman, and focused intently on his radio as he spoke into it.

"Copy that, Dan. We are ready here on the west side of Door 6, over."

He looked back up at the crowd gathered before him with a smile oozing with false confidence, as if to say, *See, I told you I have this all under control!*

More water rushed in, and as Coco looked back toward the lobby, she saw full-on explosions of whitewater jostling and bouncing down the hallway as the water levels grew higher still. She made eye contact with White. *This thing's gonna close, right?* Just as she began to doubt that it would, she felt and heard the now familiar rumble of the door mechanism unlatching, and preparing to drop.

Then the steel barrier slammed into place, and they heard the drumming of torrents of water beating on the other side of it.

"It worked!" White beamed, but the fact he seemed so surprised that it did was more worrisome than uplifting. Everyone looked around at the floor and at the bottom of the pressure door to see if water would seep through, if they were in fact on dry territory. But the door was watertight, and looking further down the hallway, it was all dry.

"Where to?" Coco asked White.

White appeared to think about this for a moment, scratching at the stubble on his chin while he stared out at the artificially lit part of the reef. When he spoke, he addressed only Coco and Caesar. "Let's head for the MCC, and have a little chat with Dan and see if we can't get things properly sorted, shall we?"

The Master Control Complex housed the technical nerve center of the underwater hotel, with the exception of the now flooded train station controls. It occupied the second floor of the other cylindrical tower, opposite the one that housed the formerly grand lobby.

"Is that far from the water damage?" the woman who'd slipped in the water asked.

White nodded. "As far as you can get and still be inside the hotel."

"Then let's go!"

The soggy group trod down the hall toward the far end of the hotel, passing the row of suites on the way. A blank wall faced them where an entrance vestibule used to be, like a gap-toothed smile, a sobering reminder of the lost escape pod and the fact that they were now in a very deadly situation.

Coco's radio sounded with Mick's relatively stress-free voice. "At the sub now, firing her up. How's things in there, over?"

Coco looked back at the sealed pressure door, at the wet pant legs and footwear of the guests, out at the dark reef, at White's eyes challenging her to tell Mick how bad things really were down here. "Lobby window collapsed after the shark hit it, we made past a pressure door, dry for now."

"God damn it, stay focused!" White moved with alacrity, his hand swiping out and grabbing Coco's radio.

"What are you doing?"

He opened the battery compartment and removed the battery. Just before he did they heard Mick's voice: "Coco, you need to—" "before it went dead.

White handed Coco back the now useless radio, pocketing its battery. "I'll handle Topside Communications from this point forward, okay?"

Clearly the display of power made the rest of the guests uncomfortable, but none of them said anything. White was the boss, and Coco was the employee, after all. Coco was about to throw the radio onto the floor, to shatter it in a display of disgust and anger, to let White know how fed up she was with his bullshit, but as she started to raise her arm, she checked the motion and merely clipped the radio to her belt instead. She remembered that she'd put on a pair of jeans after the aborted dive, and in those jeans she'd gotten into the habit of keeping a spare, charged battery for the radio. She got used to yapping on the thing all day long, admittedly for some chats with Mick on a privacy coded channel, as well as a lot of official business, but still, after the battery had ran out on her a couple of times before the day was up, she'd procured another one, and started carrying two. It was a habit she was glad for now, although she didn't want White to know that she still had comm. She'd have to wait to put the new battery in the radio when he wasn't looking.

She looked at White and nodded. They continued on toward the other end of the hotel in silence, past the pods. Coco made up her mind then and there to get the heck out of here and report this White guy to someone. He was a loose cannon. There's no way his investors would approve of his behavior. Once she got out of here, she'd quit once and for all.

But how to get out? She was locked inside a Plexiglas prison with a megalodon guard and a psycho for a warden. What's more, she thought, looking straight up as she walked at the moon now visible through the clear ceiling and the water above, she now had no way to contact Mick—no way to contact anyone on shore for that matter.

Step up your game, girl. James White is just as bad, if not worse, than the megalodon. She mentally kicked herself down the hall for allowing him to sweet-talk her back on the job, and not leaving when she could have. That reminded her: where was Aiden now? He was trapped down here somewhere, too, and he was an ally. Last she saw him he was in the lobby. Had he made it to safety? He was a big guy, strong, too, and if it came down to having to physically overpower White, she would definitely want him on her side. She wondered if there was anyone still in the suites they were passing, possibly sleeping through the chaos, or just hunkered down, afraid of it all. There must be a few, since the group they had with them didn't nearly account for everyone left in the hotel. A few employees were no doubt scattered about, but there had to be a few more guests somewhere, too.

Up ahead the hallway opened into an oval-shaped area with wide passages leading off in three directions. Coco knew that they had reached the giant cylindrical building at the other end of the hotel, and that each passage led to a different section of it. She was also tired of White's bullshit the more she listened to his voice. As he bellowed at the group to follow him, Coco hung back, allowing the guests to pass her as she smiled agreeably at them. They filed up the middle passage—more like a tunnel really, with the lighted reef visible beneath their feet, and open water on the sides and above.

Coco, White, Caesar, and the guests trooped along the middle tunnel as a great shape shadowed them just outside the cone of light from the hotel's exterior lights.

Chapter 34

The megalodon swam slow circles around the hotel's tower. Her nostrils flared as her Ampullae of Lorenzini detected myriad strange electronic impulses. After so long in the deep sea, the lights of the hotel were blinding; maddening almost. But the unknown intrusion onto the reef compelled her to investigate. She had found prey here. Not the fish of the reef. Those were too small to satisfy her. But the warm-blooded creatures were something to which she was almost completely unaccustomed, save for the occasional sperm whale. She would find more of them. Millions of years of evolutionary drive, locked away deep in her genes, was awakening and telling her to improvise, to adapt, to find a way.

#

Mick sat in the sub's cockpit, frowning as he eyed his radio. Coco had been out of touch for longer than usual. It wasn't like her to ignore his calls. What was going on down there? Earlier she had expressed concern that White was going off the rails, unstable. It sounded like she'd been cut off mid-transmission. Now, he reflected while he stared at the instrument panel without seeing it, that could be due to any number of reasons. But it also could be due to an action from White, deliberate or otherwise.

He stared at the transmitter, contemplating whether he should use it again to call Coco. She, and therefore White—who had been standing right next to her, and as her boss must have sanctioned the request—had asked him to take the sub down to look at the pod. He had done that. The pod, and all souls aboard, were lost, but the capability he had been hoping to use on it—the acetylene torch jerry-rigged onto the sub's grab arm—was still potentially useful. Potentially *very* useful, he corrected himself, for there was now no way in or out of the hotel. No tunnel, no airlock, and although there were other escape pods, he doubted anyone was willing to use them after the fate that had befallen the first. And the pressure doors were further dividing the place, sectioning it off like a warren of locked rooms.

But he had at his disposal a tool capable of cutting right through the hotel's walls—metal or acrylic, although he actually had no experience trying to cut through acrylic with a torch. Still, he was good with cutting steel, and he figured he could cut acrylic if he had to. One way or another, he could open an entrance into the place...

But that would flood it... Coco had SCUBA gear down there, though, or at least she did at one point. He sure as Hell hoped she still had access to it...

Mick drummed his fingers on the sub's dashboard, lost in thought. He wished he could consult with someone on this—maybe the topside engineering team, but they were super-busy carrying out orders to fix the tunnel and other systems, and would not want to give him the time of day. Not only that, but he didn't fully trust them. If he asked them to devise the best way to cut into the place with a torch, they'd tell White, and then White would know what he was up to, and would then have the chance to deny the plan or just plain screw it up somehow.

No, he thought, brushing the hair off his face, he had to take this on himself. Something did not feel right about the situation downstairs, as he liked to refer to the hotel. Not right at all. He would take matters into his own hands; he had the luxury of being able to say he would have asked permission first, but he lost radio contact.

That settled, Mick eyeballed the acetylene torch on the end of his grab arm, appraising it. It had worked great today in the lab and in the quick test he'd done right here at the dock. Should work. Key word, *should*. But there was only one way to find out.

#

They had almost reached the end of the tunnel where it joined the cylindrical tower, when Coco felt the floor move. It reminded her of an earthquake—she'd experienced several growing up in the Hawaiian Islands—but she knew these vibrations were not attributable to any geologic process. She heard a guest call out ahead of her, "Did you feel that?"

Coco looked down through the clear floor into the dark water below. There were underwater lights at the tower, but none here, which meant she could see nothing below them, and only a grayish shade above. Like a chain reaction, first one guest, then, and another began to run for the entrance to the tower. Even White was helpless to stop it, flapping his arms wildly to the non-caring group.

Then she looked down, and this time Coco could make out a shape, only because it was so close and moving fast. Somehow the light caught it just right, and she saw a glint of white, and then the next thing she knew she was watching the megalodon's mouth open wide as its head collided with the bottom of the tunnel, knocking her to her feet.

She felt the lagoon water coursing over her leg, galvanizing her to action. The big shark had broken through! Coco felt a jagged Plexiglas shard rip through her ankle as she got up, her blood mixing with the saltwater as she ran for the entrance to the tower. If it were a race with the rest of her group, she'd be in last place, all of them either already inside the tower, or just now entering. A glance to her left showed her an outsized black orb, unblinking, uncaring, unreal, un-everything. The shark nuzzled along the side of the short tunnel, almost as if in a playful mood. Suddenly, though, the unpredictable fish nose-dived, and came up beneath the tunnel right where it joined the main tower itself.

Coco saw the lights of the tower's interior beckoning, the outstretched arms of two of the guests, White's impassive stare as he stood back from the group at the door, having been the first one inside. Caesar was there, too, actually walking back toward her, saying something into a radio as he stared down, not at the shark, but at some structural feature of the hotel.

This time the impact Coco felt was no mere bump in the night, but more of a full-on explosion. Coco was flung forward and upward in a shower of acrylic shards, water, and megalodon teeth. Even as she flew through the air, the marine biologist flashed on the fact that the horror on the faces of the people watching her was even greater than if she had been flung by a mere explosion of some kind.

The deep sea dweller visiting the shallows wrenched open its cavernous maw even wider as it lunged for Coco, pushing a wave ahead of its snout that would probably be surfable if not for all of the wreckage being flung out with it. The Hawaiian was shoved into the tower, knocking over a couple of guests in the process. She eyeballed the doorway as she rolled on the floor, hoping against hope that the colossal meat-eater wouldn't be able to fit its industrial-sized mouth through the doorway.

Then she was skidding to a stop on a carpeted floor, jabbing one elbow painfully into the hard surface as she came to a stop. This tower was one of the few areas of the hotel that had carpet. Since it blocked the view of the reef below, most areas consisted of bare acrylic floors. Her instinct was to look down to see if the megalodon was coming for her, but she couldn't see through the floor covering, and then, after thinking about it for a moment, it dawned on her that even if she could, she would only be looking down at the first level of the west tower. The tunnel they had taken slanted up to the tower's second floor, the Main Control Room. To access the lower floor that was directly over the reef, it was necessary to go down within the structure. That floor was the now flooded dive shop, though, already sealed behind a pressure door. A third level waited in the opposite direction, up, and it, too, had a non-see-through floor.

She looked back out into the tunnel, and at first thought that another pressure door had dropped, this one of a different color than the rest. But then it moved, and she realized what it was: the megalodon was actually moving through the tunnel, perpendicular to it. It sawed crosswise through a ruptured section.

Then she watched a hand reach up out of the water, about ten feet in front of the shark. A dark-skinned hand.

Ohmygod. Caesar!

The engineer had gone back into the tunnel to look at something and was now trapped in there, engulfed in rushing water, the effect of which was exacerbated by the huge shark's thrashing movements. He gripped a protruding support strut, and struggled to pull himself to his feet. Coco sprinted out of the tower again. She could pull the man to safety. He was only a few feet away from the tower door. Just take a couple big steps out into the tunnel, grab the guy, and pull him back in. That's all she had to do to save his life. White's lackey or no, she would never be able to live with herself if she did not at least try.

She felt the water wash against her, and waded out toward the downed man, and toward the megalodon which now slinked backwards, back through the tunnel the way it had come. Its head stuck out into the ocean, as well as most of the rear portion of its body. Coco took a couple of more steps toward Caesar, who had slipped while getting up, and went under again.

"Caesar, here!" She steadied herself by kneeling to lower her center of gravity as she reached a hand out to the fallen engineer. It was only when the megalodon's wide head backed into the space between the fragmented tunnel walls that Coco understood the only thing keeping the chamber from really flooding had been the giant shark's body itself. The massive head had been acting like a plug, the proverbial finger in the dike. Now that it was free, water raged inside the tunnel unadulterated.

Coco saw Caesar's hand reach up, and she grasped his wet fingers before losing them to the slippery, weak grip. The body of the megalodon was a dangerously heavy object to contend with now, rolling manically to and fro. Caesar disappeared beneath the roiling water. Coco tracked his position. The megalodon swung its jaws her way, and she jumped back, falling on her backside, and then being pulled toward the predatory fish by hectic currents. The shark's head beat back and forth in a true frenzy now, seeking a way out of the small area.

She saw Caesar's shoulders hunched over in the middle of the tunnel, and made a move to grab him before he drifted away again. The shark was too close, though, and the body disappeared once again beneath the maelstrom. Then, after a few seconds, the megalodon lunged backwards, sliding out into the sea.

She saw Caesar's dark hair on the surface, the top of his head. *Now!*

Coco made her move for the engineer. She took two powerful strides forward into deeper water that was rapidly rising as the shark evacuated, and yanked him up by the hair—the only part of him she could reach. His head pulled toward her with surprising ease, and with a sickening realization Coco knew that something had gone horrifically, irrevocably wrong.

Caesar was much too light...*so light*...it should have been a huge effort for Coco's 115 pounds to wrest the man's body out of the water.

She pulled hard with one last burst of energy in case she was about to encounter resistance. Caesar came free of the water...

...but it wasn't really Caesar...it was just his head. She was holding it clenched in one hand by the hair, like a terrorist in a beheading video. A cornucopia of fluids drained from the open neck into the surrounding water.

Coco made eye contact with Caesar's head, and he blinked at her once.

She screamed, a guttural, feral cry that would haunt those who heard it for the rest of their lives, which in some cases would not be long. Coco let herself fall backwards, toward the tower entrance. Anything to be moving away from this horror.

The megalodon had worked itself into a frenzy with the introduction of Caesar's entire blood volume into the water. She shoved herself backwards on elbows and heels, mind whitewashed with abject terror. She saw the megalodon's throat muscles expanding and contracting. It was eating...swallowing Caesar's headless body as it retreated outside the tunnel onto the reef.

Then hands were pulling Coco to her feet, voices shouting but still indistinct. She was in a disorienting haze of adrenaline, fear, and revulsion. The sheer force the shark was capable of stunned her to the very core of her being. That a mere fish could possess such raw power, such overpowering muscle, was not something she had even come close to comprehending prior to this experience. Sure, she'd read the textbooks, done the lab work, seen normal sharks firsthand many, many times. But none of that stood as any kind of realistic reference point for what she had just witnessed. It both frightened and motivated her; lives were very much in danger including her own, yet at the same time she knew she was witnessing something nature had never intended for human eyes. This fish was a dinosaur, and it killed like one.

White's take-charge voice broke Coco out of her shark-induced reverie.

"Nothing we can do for him now. You tried. Control Room's in here. Let's go."

Coco collected her wits about her by taking a couple of full breaths and examining her surroundings. While it was true the shark couldn't reach them right here inside the tower, when she looked back at the entrance to the tunnel she'd been tossed through by the creature, she saw one of the steel pressure doors slam shut, walling them off inside the vertically oriented structure.

Their available space had been reduced yet again by the simple-minded predator—a dumb yet finely tuned beast honed over eons' worth of evolutionary processes to kill whatever it had to in order to survive, to keep swimming, keep eating, keep reproducing. To a megalodon, Coco knew, everything looked like a nail from the point of view of a hammer.

And right now...she was one of those nails.

Coco fell into line once again with the group as they filed through a narrow hallway with plastic strip doors at both ends. Realizing she was bringing up the rear while White was at the head of the line as usual, and that the going was slower than usual after what they'd been through, Coco picked up the radio from her belt, hoping its claim of "water resistant" by the manufacturer would hold true.

She quickly removed the battery compartment cover, exposing the missing battery White had taken from her. Then she plucked the spare battery from her pocket and inserted it into the radio. By the time she reached the end of the hallway, she had put the cover back on and clipped the unit back to her belt, exactly as it had been before. Only now it had power.

She just had to find the right time to use it.

Chapter 35

It was easy for Mick to identify the sections of the hotel that had been flooded or destroyed. They were blacked out. Not only were there no exterior reef lights on in these sections, but the interior was darkened as well. As he skirted the hotel's ruined lobby tower, it became clear to him just how severe the damage to the underwater facility was. He mentally chided himself for not noticing it on the way out to the pod, even though he'd been singularly focused on that objective, and hadn't looked closely at the hotel.

But now...Mick shook his head in awe of the transformation the luxury attraction had undergone in such a short time. The once grand lobby, decimated...just a water-filled space, open to the ocean with a steel pressure door walling off the rest of the hotel. He watched as a stingray swam over a plush red couch as if seeking a good spot to settle down. Then he saw something that had the impact of an unexpected punch to the gut: a body floating in mid-water beneath a chandelier. He didn't recognize the woman, but she had obviously been a guest, her long hair splayed out in the currents, designer dress doing the same. The expression on her face was one of horror frozen in time—eyes wide open, mouth pulled back in a painful grimace.

Mick gripped the steering joystick, and brought the sub in a wide arc around the lobby. He was not as skilled at Coco at driving the vehicle—his job was to fix and maintain them, not to operate them—and so he kept a wide, safe berth from the structure. He knew, though, that when it came to burning a hole through this place, he was going to have to perform maneuvers that required some real finesse. He could only hope he was up to the task when the time came.

He continued to trace the contour of the underwater structure while casting his gaze inside for signs of activity. He skirted along the straightaway where the pods were housed, clenching his teeth as he passed the empty space where the jettisoned pod had been, now being claimed by the sea. A parade of four lobsters walked head-to-tail across the sandy seafloor where the pod had been, as if reasserting dominance over their domain.

He continued on, casting nervous glances off to his left and the edge of the reef, wary that the megalodon would choose to make itself known now that he was down here alone. After passing the remainder of the row of pods, he reached a dark section and double-checked that all of the sub's external lights were on. He found one that hadn't been activated, and flipped it on. Then he worried that maybe all these lights would attract the big shark and reached out to turn it off again, but stopped himself. He told himself he was being silly, and focused on his piloting, taking the sub past the end of the row of suites to where the tunnel branched out into three short tunnels that ran into the tower, one to each of its three floors.

The sub's spotlights illuminated a scene of devastation Mick was not prepared for. At first the tubes looked normal—clear tubes, clear water...but it was the steel plate in front of the middle tunnel that alerted him to the problem. Another pressure door had been activated. He looked back to the tunnels, and then he noticed it: there were particles floating through the tubes—nothing really unusual, just the same debris and particulate matter that floated in the seawater all around him—but that was just it. There was water flowing through the connecting tunnels!

A chill ran through him as he processed the destruction. Somehow the tunnel had been broken. Not somehow, he corrected himself, for there was only one thing around here that could do that kind of damage. The megalodon had smashed through the tunnel. He twisted his body in the seat to get a good look all around the sub, as if the patrolling dino-shark would pop out of the darkness and suck the entire mini-sub down its ravenous gullet at any moment. But there was only the mute testimony to the megalodon's passing: the ruined hotel. He traced along the tunnel with his gaze, and saw another pressure door at the end of the room suites. The gravity of what this meant hit him hard.

Whoever was in that surviving tower now was stuck in there. Panic gripped him as he realized something else—what if someone had been trapped in the tunnel when it flooded, like the train tunnel? He shone the spotlight slowly along its length, half-expecting to recoil in horror at any second with the sighting of a body, but by the time his light beam played on the pressure door guarding the pod suites, he had still found no bodies floating in the tube.

He willed himself to stick to the job at hand. What was he looking for?

Need a contained area, flooded or unflooded, but near to a working pressure door if it's unflooded, so that Coco can scuba dive out of it and get to land. It occurred to him that he was only going to be able to save one person using the sub in that manner, since the other six divers had already been killed in the pod. But if he could only save one person, he was glad it would be Coco, and at least land-based divers would then be able to penetrate the hotel in order to effect a rescue.

Now that he'd traversed the length of the hotel, he felt like he'd seen enough to call it an assessment, and was now ready for the next phase of his plan. Time to make contact with Coco. Since so many parts of the hotel were now sectioned off and compartmentalized, he couldn't just drill a hole anywhere and tell her to come meet him there. She might not be able to reach it. He had to make contact with her and find out her location.

Mick picked up the sub's radio transmitter, and called Coco's name into it.

#

"Where's Michaelson?" White demanded of Dan Wang, the only technician apparently manning a massive circular array of controls. With Caesar gone, White feared that Wang might be the only technical person in here with them.

"He's not in here," Wang said. White was painfully aware that although competent, Wang had not been involved in the design of the hotel as Michaelson had, but was brought on to operate it after it was built because he had experience with commercial diving systems as well as a small, single-room underwater hotel in Key Largo, Florida.

"So where *is* he?"

"On dry land. He took the last train out—the last working train," he corrected himself, before adding, "Not because he was scared or anything, just because that's when his sleep shift is."

White gave an exasperated gesture. "So he's still asleep in his *bure*, right when we need him most?" It did seem impossible anyone could sleep through so much commotion and chaos.

Wang shrugged. "I haven't needed to contact him. Handling things on my own so far, but—"

At that moment, White's radio crackled with Mick's voice, a static-ridden, underwater-to-underwater connection traveling from sub to hotel. "*Triton-1* to Coco, *Triton-1* to Coco, do you read, over?"

White snatched up his comm unit from his belt, and barked into it. "This is James, Mick. What are you doing?"

There was a slight hesitation, one which Coco thought—or liked to think, at any rate— was due to his surprise at White answering the radio call instead of Coco. Would be he pick up on the fact that something was amiss in the group dynamic? She wasn't about to bet her life on it. Mick worked for White, after all, and it wasn't that unusual for someone other than the person called to respond to a radio call. The normal channels were open.

Mick came back, "On my way out there, passing the hotel now, just checking in, over."

"We've got a situation here, Mick," White returned. "But it's nothing you can help with at the moment, so—"

The technician interrupted White, tapping his shoulder. "There is something he can do," Wang said, pointing over to his console. "I've lost intercom link with Topside. You could get him to go back to the island and wake Michaelson's ass up, and tell him to work on the comm problem."

White nodded to his tech and responded, "I'll tell him."

He told Mick to go rouse Michaelson, or find him wherever he was, then signed off, and turned to look at the rest of the group.

Most of them were gazing uneasily out the windows, looking for stirrings of the megalodon. Coco met his gaze, and then looked away. White then stepped over to Wang, and the two huddled in quiet conference, no doubt discussing the unpleasant cost of failure for various scenarios.

Coco walked slowly around the edge of the room, ostensibly to survey the reef outside, checking for the megalodon in a more professional and thorough fashion than the guests, but in actuality pursuing quite a different purpose.

#

Mick eyeballed the sub's instrument console. Battery power, oxygen level, everything looked A-okay. Then his radio squawked, and he felt his pulse quicken as Coco's voice filled the cabin of her submersible. Her words were quiet, and he had to turn the volume up high to make them out clearly.

"...got my own radio. Can you hear me, Mick?"

Mick gripped the transmitter while he held the craft in a hover just outside the reach of the hotel's reef lights. "I hear you Coco!" Then he noticed that she was coming through on a different channel than the standard one. The sub radio had scanned the available frequencies, and detected a transmission. He wondered if she was worried about White hearing what she said. Mick knew that the walkie-talkies like the one he carried when topside would not be set to scan.

"I hear you, Coco. What's the situation?" Mick figured that was ambivalent enough of a question, and if there was someone listening in, Coco would let him know.

She replied once again with a lowered voice. "*Mick*, Mr. White took the battery out of my radio—said he didn't want me calling Topside anymore—but I found a spare. I can only talk a few seconds more without him seeing. We are trapped in the west tower, Main Control Room, *over*."

Mick replied immediately, understanding there was no time to squander. "Copy that. I came back down in the sub to see if I can get you out of there."

"Get me out of here? How the Hell are you going to do that?"

"Do you have access to scuba gear?"

"Negative. It's in the lobby, which is now flooded and behind a pressure door. Or floating out along the reef somewhere. Let me know if you come across it."

Mick's fist pounded the sub's console in frustration as he watched a small school of baitfish pass close by outside. Coco continued before he could formulate a response.

"Doesn't matter anyway, because the airlock is sealed off, even the escape pods—if I were crazy enough to try using one of those after what happened— are sealed off. We're trapped in the west tower, Mick. But at least we have air...for now. The megalodon's been on a rampage."

Mick shook his head even though the fishes outside his window were the only ones who could see the gesture. "It *would* matter if you had access to your gear, because I fitted an acetylene torch to the grab-arm today, and I'm pretty sure I could use it to burn a hole through the hotel."

This time when Coco transmitted he heard White's voice calling her name in the background, sounding angry. "Burn a hole through and then what—flood the last remaining place in the hotel with air we can get to?!"

Mick exhaled heavily, swinging the fist holding the transmitter in mid-air, like he was punching an invisible opponent. She was right. What in the Hell *was* he thinking? Punch through the hotel like John fucking Wayne and the cavalry coming to the rescue? Ridiculous. And yet, what other choice did she have? He talked into the transmitter again.

"I was thinking that I meet you in a small area that's easily sealed off, maybe by a pressure door after you leave, or just a small little room, and then you have your scuba gear on when I cut the hole. When the place floods, you swim out, hold onto the sub like a remora, and I tow you back to the beach."

In spite of the situation, Coco's laughter bubbled through his radio speaker. It was music to his ears. "Remora, ha! Don't I wish? I've got no scuba stuff, though, Mick. Maybe—gotta go!" He heard White's voice permeating the connection again.

"I'll stick around. Call me when safe, out!"

He listened for a response, but none came. Mick put the transmitter down, and surveyed his surroundings outside the sub.

He looked up at the tower, all three stories of it, and mostly still lit, with the exception of the dive shop on the bottom floor. He had to scout it out in more detail, find a suitable site to burn through it.

His course of action decided, Mick activated the sub's thrusters, and banked into a turn around the tower.

Chapter 36

The Saudi sheik, a composed man of fifty-some-odd years of age decked out in full robes and headgear, had up until now remained quiet, his wife by his side even more so. Now, however, standing in the tower's control room while James White conferred with his lone surviving technician, the guests' legs sopping wet, with even the knowledgeable marine biologist standing around wondering what to do, he decided to make his voice heard. The billionaire cleared his throat forcefully and turned to White, interrupting his conversation.

"Excuse me, Mr, White."

White continued speaking to the tech in hushed tones. "Mr. White! You will answer me when I speak to you!" The sheik raised his voice to a near yell that startled the property developer and the technician, both of whom bumped heads when they turned to look up at the angry Arab. White rubbed his temple while glaring at the tech for a second before addressing his irate client.

"Forgive me for not hearing you sooner, Abdullah bin Antoun, but I am in the middle of discussing possible solutions to our problems. Is there something I can do for you?"

The Saudi's gaze was stern as his wife stood by his side. "Yes, Mr. White, there is. I have been most patient with you and your staff up to now, and that patience has not been rewarded. Things continue to worsen as time goes by. I demand that you tell me right now what you are doing to get us out of this hotel. When can we leave?"

A rumbling of agreement rippled through the room as the other guests crowded in to hear the exchange.

White snorted derisively, and swept a hand toward the dark sea beyond the tower glass. "If you've figured out how to walk through walls and breathe underwater, Abdullah, by all means, let us know. In the meantime, I'm working on a solution that actually obeys the known laws of physics, if that's okay with Your Highness."

White assumed a look of smug satisfaction as he looked over at the guests in turn, but none of them looked happy or impressed. In fact, they were beginning to look downright hostile toward White. But compared to the Sheik, they were compliant.

The Arab took a step closer to White, leaning down to put his face closer. "What exactly is the solution you are working on, Mr. White?"

"Right now, we're attempting to reestablish communications with our Topside support."

The Sheik made an expression that conveyed he was unimpressed. "That is all? Trying to reach other people to say 'please help us'? There is nothing you yourself can do to get us out of here?" He shot White an accusatory stare.

White stood up, and looked the Arab in the eyes. "I'm open to suggestions. I'm not standing around in here for fun, if that's what you're getting at."

"You have no radio link to the outside?" What is that? He nodded to the walkie-talkie clipped to White's belt. As the sheik became more accusatory, more direct, some of the other guests became uncomfortable. In the group of them ringed around the control station, a husband gently moved his wife back. Coco stood at the perimeter of the group as well, monitoring the situation carefully, one hand moving to her radio to make sure the volume was turned down lest Mick contact her and White hears it.

"This is a radio, it does have sporadic, limited contact with the outside, but is nowhere near as good as the hardwired intercom system we have with our Topside Engineering team on the island. We're trying to get that working again so we can regain conferencing abilities and do some real brainstorming on our situation here."

"Give me the radio." The Arab extended his left hand.

"Pardon me?"

"You heard me, Mr. White. I said, Give. Me. The. Radio." He over-enunciated each word for dramatic effect, then added, "I will not repeat myself again."

White's features took on a confused look. Dan Wang squinted briefly, and then buried his nose in his controls. Whether he was merely pretending to look busy in order to stay out of the fray, or was actually working on something, Coco didn't know.

"I will not. I remind you, Mr. bin Antoun, that regardless of your stature in your home country, that while you are in this hotel or on this island you are a guest on my property."

The sheik's face cycled through several shades of red, settling on a beet color. "*Guest*? Is this how you treat your so-called guests? Look around. All of these people are suffering. And we are the ones who are still alive, Mr. White. It seems you fail to comprehend the gravity of our situation. Now, I will not repeat myself again! Give me the radio."

"I will not. If you have a request, you may relay it to me and I will—"

White broke off mid-sentence as he laid eyes on the pistol that had materialized in the Arab's hand. Pointed at his chest.

"I am at my wit's end, Mr. White. You leave me no choice but to resort to the use of force. Hand over the radio to my wife." He nudged his wife forward. She took a step toward White and extended a hand, her expression unreadable.

"What? Are you crazy? Put that thing down this instant!"

"You are the one who is crazy, Mr. White, if you think we will stand for your ineptitude any longer. I want that radio."

"Who else in here is armed?" White yelled. He swiveled his head as he looked at his technician, at the guests, at Coco, not that he expected her to be armed, except for perhaps a dive knife. Nobody moved or spoke. The Arab's gun remained trained on White's heart.

"The radio, Mr., White. Please, let's make this easy on everyone, shall we? Hand it to my wife, please."

With obvious reluctance in the face of no other recourse, White very slowly handed the walkie-talkie to the Arab's wife while the gun was trained on him.

"How did you get that thing here, anyway?" White wasn't talking about the hotel itself. There were no security checks, an oversight he now regretted. He was referring to the fact that the sheik had flown internationally. He must have either checked his weapon disassembled the entire way, or else have purchased it upon arrival to Fiji's main island, in the capital city. But it was no matter, since he had it, and it was aimed right at White. The sheik also seemed to recognize that it didn't matter how he had got it here, for he ignored the question.

"What channel should I use to contact someone from...Topside," the sheik said, recalling the term White had used. Then he seemed to have second thoughts because he started fiddling with the radio's controls without waiting for an answer, looking up every couple of seconds through his gun sights.

"Channel 3," White intoned. But the sheik waved his gun at him.

"Never you mind. I do not trust you to tell me the correct channel. I will scan them all."

Coco raised an eyebrow in the Arab's direction. He was an astute observer indeed. She wondered if he happened to be a naturally good judge of character, or if he knew something about White that she did not. Either way, she agreed with him.

Suddenly Mick's voice burst into the room through the radio in the Arab's hands. Coco was stunned for a moment, scared that somehow her radio volume had been turned up, but as she fumbled for and found the knob, she realized that it came from the radio in the sheik's hand.

"...read me, over?" Mick finished.

The Arab raised the gun to White's head. "You see. This is not channel 3, it is channel 8. You lied."

"No, you're not on a Topside channel. Mick is in the submersible now, so that's an underwater channel."

"Whatever, he is outside of this hellish fishbowl, that is good enough for me."

Coco started to slink to the back of the gathering, wanting to take advantage of the argument to respond to Mick on her radio. Then she stopped herself. Why take any more time? She could lose him if she waited too long, and what did it matter anyway? White had a freaking gun trained on him. There was nothing he could do! Screw him, Coco thought, unclipping the radio from her belt, and turning it on.

She had just brought it to her mouth and pressed the transmitter button, when a mammoth form struck the floor-to-ceiling acrylic wall of the tower on their level.

Chapter 37

The megalodon slammed its gargantuan bulk into the side of the tower's second floor. The guests screamed as water poured into the hotel along with big sections of plastic glass. A guest standing near his wife looked up too late, and was sliced across the neck by a lance-like shard. Blood ran from his open throat as he dropped to his knees. His wife was at his side, screaming for help, but now there was water pouring into the hotel, the shark was still just outside the window, and people were looking out for themselves.

Including White, who seized the opportunity to charge bin Antoun like a bull, lowering his head, and plowing into his gut while using his arm to fling the man's gun hand up and away. The gun flew from his grasp, and clattered to the floor ten feet from White and the sheik.

Coco, who had never taken her eyes off White despite the crash, ran for the gun. She figured that as a staff member, she had more right than the guests to grab it. Better keep everyone safe by making sure it doesn't fall into the wrong hands, right? She thought it would be an easy grab, what with the megalodon causing a major leak into the place, and breach alarms going off, but at least two other people in addition to White and the sheik were attempting to gain control of the firearm as well.

One of them was Wang. Coco didn't think he was particularly sympathetic to White—not enough to want to give the gun back to him, anyway; he probably just wanted to get control of it to avoid a shootout between the two fighting men, the same as Coco did. But she wasn't one hundred percent sure. Maybe he would give it back to White. Or maybe he'd keep it for himself, but end up being just as much of a loose cannon as White? The safest thing for her was to be the one controlling the gun.

And then she experienced the underlying current of fear that swept through her consciousness as she dove headlong for the fallen firearm—that possession of the gun would matter not at all compared to the destruction and mayhem that the megalodon would continue to bring down upon them. She was tired of feeling out of control, though, and with the megalodon she had no control. With this gun, on the other hand, she at least had the chance to gain a small measure of influence over the people around her.

Coco felt the arm of a hotel guest—a woman, she registered with surprise—brush across the side of her face as both of them dove for the pistol. Coco extended her arm as far as it would go, and felt her fingertips brush against the metal.

She heard Mick's voice shouting into his radio. She was in too much of a situation to focus on his words, but by the general urgency of his voice, she guessed that he'd seen what the megalodon had done to the tower. Coco pushed forward on the floor by digging her shoes into the carpet until she was able to close her hand around the weapon. She quickly slid it beneath her body, shielding it from would-be grabbers. The situation in the hotel was precarious, and there was no telling what a person might do to defend themselves and their family against threats real or perceived. Coco had enough to worry about with just the prehistoric predator and the hotel systems failures it caused, without having to add gun-toting psycho to the list.

She slithered away from the female guest, protecting the gun flat against her belly with both hands while she looked for the technician. Was Wang about to spring on her? No. There he was, jumping onto White and the sheik, trying to separate them. So he must be okay that I have the gun, Coco thought. He wasn't trying to get it for himself, he just didn't want White or the Arab to have it. The guest likewise seemed comfortable backing off once it was clear Coco had control of the weapon.

Coco felt something cold and wet on her head, and realized she'd moved under to where water poured in from high up on the broken wall. With a start, she saw the belly of the massive beast, its body so long that its head was somewhere out in the blackness beyond the reach of the exterior lights, some of which had been blacked out by the shark.

Piercing it all was Mick's voice, still raging into the microphone of the sub's radio, and coming out of the one the Arab had taken from White. Coco looked, and incredibly, that unit was still attached to the sheik's belt. She didn't need it, though, since she had her own. Mick's voice was actually reaching her ears in a weird kind of stereo sound from close on her hip, to over on the floor of the wrestling Arab. She snagged the radio from her belt, and started transmitting while she watched Wang try to break up the fight, which was still on the floor.

"Mick, it's me."

"Coco! Get upstairs! I can get you out. Upstairs now!"

She looked to the middle of the room where a spiral staircase ran both up and down. The one that ran down, however, met with a steel plate—a horizontal pressure door—that sealed off the flooded dive locker. Up was the only way to go, and she was dismayed to see that some of the others also followed her gaze, and had, in fact, heard Mick's directive. Nothing she could do about that, and now the megalodon was back for another pass, this time attacking the opposite side of the tower's second level. The screaming began anew.

Coco moved past the fighting men and the control console, and made her way to the stairs. "On my way," she said into the radio as she went. When she got to the stairway she had to walk around the circular ladder-like structure to gain the entrance point. She was startled to see about half a dozen people following her, zombie-like, fixing her with vacant-eyed stares and a hunger to trail anyone who might know something they didn't; that would allow them to live a little longer.

"Be right back—going to check out the situation up top." Coco jumped onto the stairs, and began taking them up without waiting for more questions. "Why? What's up there? Can we come?" all echoed off her back as she ascended. The metal stairs were slick with seawater and she slipped and fell halfway up, saving herself from falling back the entire distance by grabbing the rail.

She got her first view of the third floor while still a few stairs up. It was dry. That was the main thing. The other thing was that she saw a pair of piercingly bright spotlights from outside shining in, and it dawned on her what they were.

"I see you, Mick! I'm in here!" She jumped from the stairs onto the flooring, and ran across the open floor to the window in front of the sub. She couldn't see Mick inside the machine; the spots were like car high beams on steroids, blinding her when she looked at them.

"Your lights are too much, Mick, can you take it down a notch?"

In response the two halogen spotlights winked out, leaving only a weaker floodlight for Mick to navigate by.

"Much better, thanks." Coco immediately directed her gaze upward. Mick was out there with the megalodon! Sure, he was in a submersible, but still—she recalled with a shiver how easily the brute of a fish had knocked her around while she piloted the machine on the coral slope. And this was at night, with the sub's lights to attract it.

Now that she could see, Coco got her first look around the room. She'd actually never been to this part of the hotel, though she was well aware of its existence. She was standing in the hotel's Fitness Complex, a grandiose term for a combination gym and tiki-themed juice bar. All around her stood state-of-the-art workout machines—free weights, elliptical trainers, stationary bikes, treadmills, rowing machines, and a few she wasn't even familiar with. Above her the ceiling was acrylic, affording a view of the water above, and even the moon, casting its pale white light down to the reef.

"Coco, on the opposite side of the gym, next to the juice bar, is a restroom. Get to it, I'll follow you there from outside, over."

She wasn't sure why he wanted her to go there, but with water now trickling down the stairs into the second level, and the sounds of pandemonium coming from down there, Coco didn't ask questions. She threaded her way between the exercise machines until she reached the other side of the round room, where a wooden bar decked out with palm fronds to give it a tiki feel followed the curvature of the wall. Now silent juice machines lined the counter behind the bar, piles of lush fruits stacked for maximum presentation between them.

To the right, a closed door featuring unisex bathroom signage opened into a small alcove, the walls, floor, and ceiling of which were not made of clear material. Coco ran inside. Two stalls occupied the bathroom, with a pair of sinks opposite. She found the room to be oddly claustrophobic after the fishbowl experience the rest of the hotel offered.

She wasn't here to use the facilities, though, so she cut her thoughts from wandering, and raised the radio. "Okay, Mick, I'm in the ladies room."

"Copy that, I'm almost there. I—"He broke off the transmission.

Coco stared at a sign on the wall reading, ALL OF OUR WATER IS RECYCLED—PLEASE DON'T WASTE IT—while she replied, "What is it, Mick—what's happening?"

"Our friend the dino-shark is bashing into the third floor windows now. Place is really flooding, second and third floors."

Coco looked at the closed door separating her from the rest of the tower's third floor. She willed her voice not to crack as she replied. "Is that why you wanted me to come in here, Mick? Because I don't know if this little bathroom door will stand up to that kind of flood."

"I'm hoping it will withstand the incoming water pressure long enough to equalize the force of the water coming in after I drill a hole into the bathroom."

"Say again?"

"Coco. I don't want to scare you. But unless you know of another way out, I think this is your best chance."

"I don't have a way out. What is my best chance?" Coco could hear the sound of water raining into the room outside the bathroom, cascading down the juice bar's false tiki roof.

"I can—I *think* I can, anyway—burn a hole through the bathroom wall large enough for you to fit through."

Coco thought about this for a couple of seconds, her blood quickly growing colder than that of the megalodon. "I see two huge problems with that, even if you can burn through. One: I don't have any scuba stuff with me, Mick. Dive shop is flooded and behind pressure doors, and the one rig I did have with me outside of that was in the lobby, which is also long gone."

"Copy that, Coco. You're just going to have to hold your breath, swim out, and grab onto the sub, like a remora, remember? Then I can escort you to the surface. At least you'll be starting from the high point on the third floor instead of the bottom."

"I can swim to the surface faster than the sub can go."

"Agreed, but the sub will give you some cover from Mr. Megalodon. Won't be so exposed, swimming straight up through the water column."

"True, I can see that. May as well hold on to the sub as long as I can, anyway, and bolt for the surface only if I run out of breath, right?"

"You got it."

"Then there's that pesky second problem I was thinking about."

"Always thinking. That's what I like about you."

"Yeah, I can see you're into the thinking type. The type who think about dolphins anyway."

A beat, followed by, "Stay focused, Coco. We'll talk about that, but right now we need to earn the chance. Get back to the problem."

"You're right. Okay, so the problem is that when you cut the hole and the seawater starts pouring in here, obviously I won't be able to fight that incoming water, Mick."

"Of course not."

"I'll have to dodge the incoming fire hose stream, and then wait until the entire bathroom fills with water above the level of the hole..."

"...which will equalize the pressure between inside the bathroom and outside in the lagoon, in theory allowing you to swim out."

"Exactly, but only *if* this bathroom door holds." She rapped on the wooden door with her knuckles. "If the door breaks off the hinges with the force of the water, then I won't be able to get out through the hole. The ocean will just pour in until..." She couldn't bring herself to say it.

"Right, well it's already pouring in like that from the floor below you, so..."

Coco cradled her head in her hands with the understanding that her life—what was left of it, anyway— had, somehow, some way, taken a very drastic turn for the worse. Here she was, practically trapped in a bathroom on the bottom of a reef at night, with a *Carcharadon megalodon* circling the hotel and destroying it by the minute, and her only option to escape was to risk drowning or being instantly crushed by millions of gallons of water. How she regretted voluntarily coming back into the hotel after she had gotten back to the island. *Shouldn't that whole train tunnel thing have been warning enough for you, stupid girl? You just had to come back for more, didn't you?*

She knocked her forehead against the wall a couple of times in complete frustration, not believing that her best shot at survival had come down to this. But as the cascade of water onto the floor in the gym outside the door reminded her, to simply remain inside the hotel was almost certain death. She couldn't imagine drowning with that group of perfect strangers down there; no doubt all of them would be fighting and clawing each other tooth and nail until the very bitter end. She couldn't help anyone stuck in here, either. That much was obvious.

"Coco? What's it going to be? The shark is hanging out up above on my side now. If I'm going to try, I'd better get started."

Coco raised her head straight, took a deep breath while looking at the radio (*How much battery is left in this thing, anyway? That's another reason to get on with it...*). "Okay, okay. I'm ready. Let's try it. And Mick?"

"Yeah?"

"Thanks for doing this."

"No worries."

Coco heard the sound of an acetylene torch searing the outside of the bathroom wall.

Chapter 38

Ten minutes later, while Mick was still working away with the torch, Coco saw water seeping under the bathroom door from the gym. She clutched her radio, the only link now between herself and Mick, between herself and possible survival.

"How's it going out there?"

His instant reply and unwavering voice gave her confidence even more than the actual words he spoke. "If only I were half as good at piloting this thing as you, I'd have been done already. I keep having to back off and come back in, usually too low. But even so, the torch seems to be working, and I don't think it'll be long now."

"Try just bumping that thruster control. Don't hold it down at all. Just tap it when you're moving in close."

"Thanks for the tip. Back to work. Standby..."

Oddly, with nothing else to do, and forced to stare at a toilet for so long, Coco felt the urge to use it. *Might as well. Going to want to be as comfortable as possible for this stunt, no need to feel the urge to pee while I'm dodging megalodons or even worse, actually pee and give off a chemical scent for it to home in on.* Although she was mostly joking with herself to lighten her dark mood, as a marine biologist she knew it to be true that sharks could pinpoint and zero in on not only blood, but just about any kind of bodily fluid, even when present in very miniscule amounts.

She finished her business, and then her radio crackled again with Mick's voice. *Can't a girl get any privacy around here?* And she actually managed a smile as she exited the stall—laughing at herself when she went to flush (*what the hell difference does it make now*)—but Mick's words wiped the smile off her face real quick.

"Megalodon's coming down to have a look."

"Are you almost through?" Never in a million years would she have imagined that she would be looking forward to having the only air source available to her flooded in the presence of a monster predator, but here she was, practically begging for it. Because a chance at life was still a chance. Staying in here...she forced herself not to dwell on it.

"Looks like it. You should be able to see the flame pretty soon through the wall, can you—"

"I see it!" As Coco stared at the wall she watched the orange flame—dull through the material, but in actuality a bright, sun-like orange—as it crept along the wall in a rough oval shape.

"Hey, am I going to be able to fit through that? I'm flattered you think so much of my figure but really..." The shape the torch was describing looked mighty small indeed. She understood that time was of the essence, and it was quicker to cut a small shape than a large one, but still, she had to be able to fit through it. She doubted there would be enough time to expand the hole if she found out the hard way that this one was too tight.

"Funny girl. You'll fit. Might have to swim sideways or something, but you'll fit. Almost there; stand clear, and brace yourself."

Stand clear, and brace yourself...

The words both frightened and galvanized her. She did as he directed, moving to one side of the cut area. She began to hyperventilate to saturate her lungs with oxygen, again visualizing freediving in her home waters of Hawaii, where the most dangerous shark she had ever seen was a tiger shark. *That thing out there would chomp the biggest tiger you've ever seen down like a snack.*

But first things first. Forgetting for a moment about the megalodon, Coco reminded herself that untold tons of ocean were about to come waterfalling into the bathroom, and when it did, she was going to drown if she couldn't stay conscious and swim through the hole in the wall Mick was making...and then find her way to the surface after that.

Piece of cake...

"Okay Coco...get ready for—"

She never heard the rest of his sentence, because at that moment the wall burst apart. She was not at all prepared for the violence of the liquid incursion. The portion of the wall Mick had been cutting suddenly flapped open like a door, pushed by tons of seawater. The loose wall piece smacked the radio out of Coco's hand.

She hyperventilated one final time, knowing she had to hold this last breath, that she had to fill her lungs with air in order to have sufficient oxygen in her system to make it to the surface alive. She felt her lungs stretch to the bursting point, and then that was it—the water was rising startlingly fast—already up to her chest. She eyed the opening Mick had cut for her, and rejoiced in the sight of the sub's external lights flicking on. Mick showing her the way.

Quickly she placed her hands on the ragged edge of the burned aperture. She could not afford to lose track of where it was, and could picture herself tumbling around in here like a surfer wiping out and going through the "spin cycle," as her friends back at home on the North Shore called it. She did not have the air for, and had no desire to be found dead in the shitter of all places.

Gripping the ragged edge just as her head was submerged, Coco pushed off the floor and tried to angle through the opening. Her first attempt was way off. The top of her head bumped hard into the still-intact wall above the cut opening. Knocking herself out would be one hundred percent fatal in this situation, she knew. But the water was starting to swirl inside the bathroom now, and pretty soon she'd be in that spin cycle. She had to get through that hole. Now.

She pulled with one hand still on the edge of the opening, slicing her palm deeply in the process. But it worked. She swam through a small cloud of her own blood out of the hotel and into the lagoon, where the submersible was visible to her as a blurry yellow blob a few feet away.

Chapter 39

She was free! Despite the critical nature of her current situation, Coco felt a brief flare of relief at being outside of the hotel. She didn't allow herself to look up, but instead made a beeline for the sub, to Mick, her ticket to the surface. She swam a sort of combination scissor kick and breaststroke that propelled her quickly through the water toward the sub's halogens.

Leave the lights on for me, Mick.

Coco reached the sub, and rejoiced in the feel of the smooth metal beneath her hand. She could see into the bubble sphere, lit by the cockpit instrumentation, and there was Mick's blurry form, waving frantically for her to come on. There was no way for them to communicate any longer except for these blurry visual signals, not that she needed to communicate much. When one had only one breath of air in their lungs, it was clear what one needed to do.

Coco gripped onto the sub's metal rail, thankful that she was so intimately familiar with the craft that she knew it like the back of her hand, and didn't need to be able to see it clearly to orient herself. She hoped Mick would hurry up—she would have to abandon the shield of the sub to bolt for the surface if he didn't—but thankfully, before she even completed the thought, she heard and felt the sub's twin thrusters revving hard.

She felt her legs flailing behind her as the underwater craft took off at a steep angle for the surface of the lagoon.

Yes—go, Mick!

From her position on the right side of the sub just behind the cabin, she had a decent, though blurred, view of the hotel off to her right. She could make out the lights of the second floor as she rose, and she wondered if they could see her out here, trailing off the sub like a remora on a shark.

*On a shark...*that reminded her of the reason she was in this predicament in the first place. In the gym she had thought she'd be terrified not being able to see the megalodon, but now that she was here, she found that not being able to see lulled her into a kind of just-go-for-it, you're-almost-there trance. *Hang on!*

She did, and Mick pulled her up and toward the beach. Just when she allowed herself the faintest glimmer of hope that she might make it, that she would at least live long enough to experience another breath of air, the submersible was slammed hard from the opposite side she was on. The impact was terrible— like a medium speed car accident—and she felt one of her ribs crack as the metal strut she'd been hanging onto rolled into her side.

Even worse for Coco, the blunt contact forced most of the remaining air from her lungs in a sudden and very much unwanted exhalation. Questions swam through her mind like a school of fish darting to evade a predator. How deep were they now? What had caused the accident—did Mick run into the hotel? She wasn't sure which way the hotel even was anymore after tumbling around through the water. Worse, she was no longer attached to the sub.

She could see it, though, a few feet higher up than she was. Fortunately the moon was high up in the sky. If not for that, she would have been totally disoriented, not even sure of which way was up.

Coco was out of oxygen. Her lungs burned with a painful want for air. She had no idea how long she'd been holding her breath already, but it had to be at least a minute, maybe two. Her documented record, verified with a dive watch, was ninety seconds. But that had been a few years ago already, and in much calmer and more controlled conditions than these. Anything would be calmer and more controlled than this. Anything.

She saw no point in trying to stick by the sub at this point. If she wanted to live she needed air, and she needed it right now. Mick had at least brought her what looked like most of the way to the surface. She kicked toward the world of air, longing for it intensely.

And then out of the blurred peripheral vision her naked eyes afforded her underwater, Coco saw a shape so unmistakable, so unreal in its proportions, that even without a dive mask she knew that the megalodon was coming for her. She felt her sliced palm erupt in pain when she flexed her hand and it dawned on her: she was bleeding!

Great...not only am I about to pass out in the water at night with a prehistoric dinosaur predator, but I have to be bleeding at the same time. Wonderful. Coco did not dwell on these type of thoughts; they were but a mere reflex, an impulse riding through her brain that she knew how to override. But there was no way she could override the 100 tons of fishy muscle tormenting her now. The megalodon's snout nosed against the sub, and sent it streaming off with a powerful head shake.

She could no longer worry about the sub or about Mick. She was about to drown, to simply inhale water against her wishes due to involuntary muscle contractions. She knew panic was the enemy, but she was losing the battle with it, and fast. Her legs kicked in a flurry, arms too. At any second she expected to be scooped up into the mouth of the megalodon, sliced apart on its field of teeth like an unprocessed animal through a meat grinder. After a while her mind dropped all processing of any thoughts— only supporting the neural functions necessary to propel her limbs in order to obtain oxygen.

She was moving, not thinking, when she broke the surface, and felt the sensation of cool air wash over her skin. Rapid gulps of air took precedence over all else. Never in her life had she needed air so badly. The purple spots faded from her vision as she inhaled maniacally.

The surface! She had made it. Even with a prehistoric shark lurking beneath her, she was unable to suppress a joyous surge of triumph—of being alive when perhaps she shouldn't. She would not ever want to try that Houdini-like escape again—she didn't put her odds of making it very high, and yet here she was, glimpsing the carpet of stars over the South Pacific that was so thick it was hard to believe they were natural, and so very far away.

A big splash broke her from her reverie. Not ten yards from her, the transparent dome of the submersible gleamed in the moonlight as it broke through into the atmosphere. Something was obviously wrong, since the sub was canted at a weird angle, totally off-kilter. Inside the cockpit, she caught a fleeting glimpse of Mick's inert form—slumped over the cockpit—before an even larger splash diverted her attention.

The truck-sized fish writhed and thrashed at the surface, having chased the sub up and out of the water. Coco watched, stunned, as it nudged the sub with its snout, attempting to flip it back into the air like it was playing with a seal. For a megalodon, a seal would be a small snack, but the sub, although it wasn't food, was the right size for a good megalodon meal. Coco wondered if it was possible the shark was mistaking the sub for food.

Then abruptly the great predator changed course, submerging while it swam toward the beach. Coco decided not to swim in that direction just yet. The shark would have no trouble plucking her from the water like a juicy morsel. The dorsal sliced the water like a scythe, now heading toward Coco.

In a full-fledged panic now, she swam for the sub with loud, splashy strokes, speed important above all else. The megalodon already knew she was here, so stealth was out. She was moving too fast and chaotically to tell whether Mick was doing anything inside the cockpit. She didn't care, though, because one way or another, she was boarding that underwater boat.

Coco knew the shark was closing the gap between her and it, but she maintained her focus on the sub with laser-like intensity that did not waver. At the back of her mind was the nagging thought that the sub might not even do her any good, but she was all out of options. She reached the underwater vehicle which now lay disturbingly on its side, even though it appeared to be watertight.

Instinctively and by rote, Coco placed her feet on parts of the sub she knew she could reach and that would support her weight. She scrambled atop the vehicle's metal frame, just behind the acrylic dome, which was higher up than the frame, but much slipperier. She was sure she would slide off of it into the sea—into the megalodon's waiting mouth.

Indeed, the giant shark pushed a wake in front of it that rocked the little sub, almost knocking Coco off the steel structure on which she now stood. But she held on and stayed with her perch, eyeing the monster as it slid into a circular holding pattern around the sub.

She peered into the dome where Mick was clearly slumped over the dashboard, unresponsive. She couldn't even tell if he was breathing. She rapped on the dome with her knuckles, hard, trying to get his attention. Blood from her sliced palm sluiced over the dome.

Still Mick remained inert. She didn't know if he had somehow run out of oxygen in there, and then the shark had prevented him from getting to the surface in time, or if he had experienced some kind of blunt force trauma when the shark had rammed the little sub. Either way, it meant that both his and her situations were dire.

Looking to the beach to see if possibly there might be help available from that direction, she saw only empty sand and gently swaying palm trees. She would have preferred some sort of human presence, even reporters, who would at least document the tragic events unfolding here at this distant island. But she was on her own. No doubt White or his backers had instructed the staff not to do anything that would draw attention to what was transpiring in the hotel.

None of those thoughts mattered anymore, though, because here came the megalodon, its sail-like dorsal appendage parting the water with a small wake as it charged the sub like an orca hoping to knock a seal from an ice floe. Coco now had a newfound appreciation for the fear felt by the seals she'd seen on nature shows, being flopped off of their little piece of ice directly into the shark's mouth. She did not want to die like that.

Yet, the megalodon was very near now, its monstrous head rising up out of the water, seeking her cowering form atop the effectively pilotless submersible. This was it. She would not be able to withstand the onslaught of this, nature's perfect predator. Then a burst of last-minute inspiration hit her, and she reached into her pants pocket.

Her fingers swept across an object. Hard. Metal. Something with substance.

The gun.

She quickly pulled it from her pocket, and took aim at the rampaging mega-predator. The big fish was almost upon her, its massive, monstrous maw beginning to crank open in anticipation of an exploratory bite. Coco had no idea if the gun was even loaded or what—she had almost zero experience with firearms—but still she raised it and pointed it at the oncoming aquatic assailant.

She aimed for one of the eyes, since she figured this little gun was but a mere peashooter for an animal the size of the megalodon. Steadying herself as best she could on the rocking craft, she watched the shark's black eye grow larger and larger as it neared.

When its jaws gaped open even wider, she pulled the trigger.

Chapter 40

The first shot didn't seem to do anything. Coco couldn't even tell if it had hit the shark, but it didn't hit the eye, or she would have seen a reaction. She hadn't been expecting the recoil, either, which most likely ruined her aim. As it was, the shark continued to extend its prodigious bulk up and out of the water toward Coco, perched on the sub.

She fired again, this time prepared for the gun to jump in her hand as she pulled the trigger. She saw the megalodon's flesh pucker just beneath the eyeball, but the great fish did not alter its prey assault. Suddenly the submersible shifted in the water, and she had to regain her balance and take aim again. Another shot, another miss, or at least another ineffective hit.

She had to hit the eye, but a moving target the size of a dinner plate, at night from a moving platform, was not an easy proposition even for an experienced shooter, which Coco was not. She was going to have get lucky, she knew, but she told herself she could do it nonetheless.

She recalled her father's words, long ago in Hawaii: "You create your own luck. Luck favors the prepared..." silly things like that. I sure created my own luck this time, Dad, she thought. But she did have knowledge. She did have skills. She wouldn't have made it this far if it weren't for that. She willed herself to calm down, take a deep breath, and focus. She would be able to get off one more shot before the beast-monster was upon her.

Suddenly the sub's external floodlights activated, bathing the shark in high intensity light. Ah, much better, Coco thought. She could see the target that much easier now. She didn't dare take her eyes off the incoming shark to glance into the cabin to see what Mick was doing, but he must have woken up enough to flip on the lights, knowing it would help her. He could probably hear the muffled sound of the shots from inside. Looking at the shark, she could now see a bullet hole oozing a trickle of blood between the eye and the nostril. So one of her shots had at least hit the animal.

But none of that changed the fact that the megalodon was upon her now, its monolithic head rising above the sub, above Coco, a primeval force lit by the moon and driven by raw instincts alone. She tracked the eye with the gun barrel, actually waiting for the eye to drop lower before taking her shot. She had no idea how many rounds were in the gun, either, but she hoped with everything she had for just one more, because that was all she would have time to get off, anyway.

Coco cursed her active mind, for somewhere in the back of it a pessimistic voice nagged, *Even if you do hit the eye, it might not stop it. Even blind in one eye it might continue to charge, and it's not like it could all of a sudden stop its forward momentum anyway, even if it wanted to.*

She would have to banish the voice with the sound of a bullet firing. The megalodon was at the apex of its leap now, hanging there suspended for an ephemeral instant in which the beauty and rawness of the South Pacific volcanic islands served as a backdrop for all of the shark's primordial glory.

Falling   back   down...falling   back   down....falling... back...down....

Coco was ready for the shark's drop, at once tracking its gravity-driven movement with the gun, and balancing herself on the upturned submersible as it rocked in the swells. Then the saucer-sized eye presented itself as a viable target. When it was perhaps six feet above Coco's head, she knew all of the variables had aligned in such a way that it was now or never—this was it. The opportunity for a shot at the eyeball would not get better than this.

She squeezed the trigger and delighted in the resulting pulpy explosion of black, fishy retinal matter, some of which splattered her in the face, while more of it splashed over the sub's bubble dome. The megalodon fell onto part of the sub itself, canting it precipitously to the right, causing Coco to have to drop the gun in order to hold on and save herself from being pitched into the water. Then the marauding leviathan snapped its gargantuan jaws in her direction, ragged bits of flesh—some of it no doubt human—hanging from its putrid oral cavity. She kicked off a support strut with one leg, raising herself out of the water.

Fortunately enough, the shark's thrashing had this time righted the sub, putting it back on an even keel and making it that much easier for her to hold on behind the bubble dome. *Luck favors the prepared...*

The gigantic shark, now undoubtedly blind in one eye, rolled away on the surface, at least temporarily abandoning its pursuit of prey. Coco would like to think permanently, but she couldn't count on that, would not count on it. And then she heard what to her was the most beautiful sound in the world—the mechanical hum of the sub's thrusters activating.

She shot a glance into the cabin, and saw Mick looking back at her, mouthing the words "Hold on!" while his right hand worked the thruster control joystick. The sub began to move toward the beach, at an angle at first, but then more directly as it gathered momentum and Mick guided it into a turn toward the island.

Coco solidified her hold atop the sub. No way was she going to fall off now. *C'mon, Mick, beach this puppy!* She looked back, and saw the shark still rolling about on the surface, churning the water like a naval warfare submarine. The submersible, a slow, clunky boat on the surface, churned its way toward the tropical beach.

The huge shark was gaining and gaining fast. Mick kept the sub aimed for the island at full speed, but it wasn't remotely enough. The megalodon was simply too fast. Coco watched in terror as the cave-like mouth raised once again from the water and drew nearer. She was calculating which side to jump off to give her the best chance at survival, when suddenly the shark fell back. She waited for it to barrel ahead, but farther back it stayed. She swiveled around, saw the progress they had made toward the beach, and then understood.

The water became shallower the closer to the beach they came. The megalodon was unable to come any closer to land without risk of beaching itself. Coco held a fleeting hope that it had in fact done just that—gotten stuck on the shallow reef, unable to move back into water deep enough for it to swim in—but as she watched, it wrenched its massively proportioned frame off of the coral and into some decent water once again. *No such luck.*

But the little submersible could still operate, and Mick continued to propel it toward the beach. To Coco the soft hiss of the craft's steel runners scraping over the wet sand as it skidded up onto the beach was the sweetest sound she had ever heard.

Chapter 41

Coco and Mick embraced by the side of the sub. Then they stood there on the beach, staring out at the lagoon. The *Carcharadon megalodon* had disappeared from sight once again. Nevertheless, a most disturbing sight greeted them in the water. A glowing haze of orange was clearly visible beneath the water's surface, and it took Coco a few moments to realize that it was not some exotic algal bloom or animal spawning event...it was the hotel.

On fire.

Underwater.

"Mick, all those people are still trapped in the tower. We have to do something."

"What can we do?"

At that moment they heard the rustle of leaves as someone came running down the path leading to the beach. A pair of engineers ran out onto the sand, one of them yelling into a radio as he went, "It *is* a fire. There's a fire down there!"

Coco approached them. Their eyes grew wide as they realized who she was, standing there dripping water onto the sand. How did you get out?" they asked her. She told them about Mick using the torch from the sub and her swimming out of the flooded fitness center.

"What's happening there—in the tower? Our sensors showed that the fire suppression system—ceiling sprinklers—has been activated, but doesn't seem to have pressure. That probably means that the main water pipe has been ruptured."

Coco nodded. "Listen. Everyone still alive down there was in the second floor of the tower when I left. What can we do to get them out of there?"

Albert Johnson looked at them with a look of grave seriousness. "We've been working on the escape pod system. The entire third floor of the west tower is an escape pod. If they could get up there, I'd say their best shot at survival, with a fire down there, is to let us activate it."

"And hope it works this time?" Mick shot back.

"What else can we do?" the other engineer said defensively.

"He's right," Coco said. "They can't have more than a few minutes—maybe thirty at most—left down there, even without the fire. We have to do something right now."

The engineers' radio crackled, and they heard some technical information delivered in a frantic tone. Coco watched as both of the men's faces fell with the news.

"What is it?" she prompted as they looked out at the dull orange glow beneath the lagoon's surface, shaking their heads.

"Good news is that the escape pod appears to be one hundred percent operational after our quick-fix earlier this evening. Bad news is we just confirmed via radio report from Mr. White that they just started taking hits again from that shark. He said it stopped for a while, but just now started again."

Coco and Mick exchanged glances. Coco said, "We drew it off when we escaped in the sub. It followed us almost all the way in to the beach, until it was too shallow for it to swim anymore."

"It must have gone back to the hotel after it couldn't get us," Mick added.

One of the engineers looked like he was about to literally tear his hair out. He shook his head back and forth rapidly while he pulled at it. "If we put people in that pod, and the shark rams it..." He shook his head, leaving the sentence unfinished.

"It's already in pretty precarious shape as it is," Al said. "We managed to patch it together, but it *still* needs one more fix applied, *and* it can't take *any* more damage. We won't be able to fix it in time if we have to start over."

Coco was staring at the beached sub, its dome hatch still open from when Mick had popped it and stepped out. When she spoke, her words were so quiet the men almost didn't hear her.

"I'll draw it off in the sub."

Mick and the two engineers looked at Coco like she had a death wish.

"I can do it," she reiterated. "I'll need full batteries and fresh oxygen cylinders, though." She looked at Mick.

"How soon can we turn her around for another dive, a deep one?"

Chapter 42

Coco slid into the sub's pilot seat, taking comfort in the cozy confines with which she was so familiar. Mick untethered the sub from the dock, and she guided the craft out into the lagoon. She wasn't looking forward to the solo night dive, but she was the last hope of those innocent—and not so innocent—people still trapped in the hotel.

She knew what must be done. The geeks had worked out some iffy techno-fix that nonetheless represented the best hope to get the tower escape pod working. All they needed was for Coco to draw off the megalodon.

She took the sub into a dive as soon as it was deep enough, not wanting the shark to be able to hit her from below and behind, as an apex predator like the megalodon preferred. She checked the compass. Not being able to see beyond the cones of light the sub provided meant that she would use navigational aids to keep her on course. She would need all of the sub's precious power and air reserves to pull off her planned objective.

It terrified Coco to look for the shark like this. With the sub's light field representing the extent of her field of vision, by the time she saw the megalodon it would be mere feet away from the sub. Then there was the hotel. Even when knowing its location and expecting to see it coming up, she had to be careful about the building itself appearing suddenly in front of her fragile craft.

The tower lobby appeared in the halogen lights as a water-filled greenhouse, with sections of the glass still intact, but the entire structure flooded within.

She knew she would find the dinosaur-shark close by somewhere on the hotel's perimeter. All she had to do was follow the hotel around, and she would encounter it. She began tracing the structure's contours with the sub, working her way from the destroyed lobby tower to the compromised, but still standing tower on the opposite end.

Occasionally she glanced inside the hotel—really looked in there, carefully—searching for people who may still be imprisoned in this part of the hotel rather than in the remaining tower. She didn't think the hotel staff, including herself, would be able to deal with it if she did sight someone still stranded in one of the few remaining air pockets in this part of the complex, but thankfully she didn't see anyone.

Including the shark. So far the megalodon had either been staying out of reach of the sub's halogens, or else was still on the other side of the hotel. She would find out soon enough, for up ahead, according to her compass reading and the way the hotel structure angled out, was the west tower. The tower that right now contained a drama playing out inside as that scoundrel James White attempted to channel whatever valuable resources still remained in his favor.

#

Inside the tower, White had finally gotten the upper hand on the Arab while half of this floor burned, a couple of the men battling it with a single fire extinguisher grabbed off a wall, and rerouted water from a burst pipe dangling overhead. The floor was wet everywhere, pooling over the first level which was already flooded and pressure sealed off. Now the second floor was filling. Most of the other guests were still trying to figure out a way out for themselves, while White and the sheik had reignited their fight after Coco had absconded with the gun. White was about to try and land a right hook to the Arab's jaw, when his radio blared with his engineer's voice topside.

"James, James—this is Al, do you read me?"

Both fighters silently agreed to a break between rounds in order for White to answer the radio. They all wanted out of here now, and hearing someone from Topside was a welcome intrusion.

Out of breath, he held down the Talk button and replied, "I copy, Al. I know you guys have been working on it, and now tell me you've got a solution? We've got a big fire in here, and lots of flooding, over."

"I know. James, tell me about the tower...first floor flooded and sealed, right?"

"Right."

"Is the third floor also on fire?"

White looked toward the spiral staircase in the center of the room that led both up and down. It spewed orange flame. "Can't really tell, because the stairwell is on fire. Could be just the stairs; could be flame shooting down from the whole third floor on fire, I don't know."

"Okay, we need you to confirm for us if you can get up there."

"To three?" White's face screwed up into an angry red ball.

"Yes, to the fitness complex on three. That whole floor makes up one large escape pod."

"I thought those were—"

"We've been working on it all afternoon, and think we have a fix."

"You *think* you have a fix?"

An exasperated sigh shot from the radio's speaker. "Mr., White, work with me here. You're on fire down there. This is the only way we can think of to get you out right now. If you know of any other ways let me know."

The ensuing silence told him that he did not. The engineer continued.

"There's no fire suppression sprinklers in the stairwell itself, but we'll activate the ones on three right now, okay? Are you ready to get a man up there?"

"I'll go," White said, seeing that the Arab was already eyeing the stairs. "Go ahead, activate them."

"Some of them may be on already, but this will be forcing them all on in every area. Start running. Sprinklers on in three...two..."

White made a dash for the two guys battling the fire on their floor. He yelled to the one with the extinguisher to follow him, and together they ran to the stairwell, some of the other tourists looking on with curiosity born of fear.

When they reached the opening through which the stairway ran floor-to-ceiling, they saw a spot fire burning about four steps up. It appeared to be contained, and not tongues of flame shooting down from the floor above. White directed the guy with the extinguisher to smother it out. He doused it, and then the two men stood and watched the smoke dissipate.

White had just stepped onto the spiral stairwell when he heard cries of terror from the second floor.

"It's coming back!"

The man with the fire extinguisher dropped the now empty red cylinder, and looked back to the source of the yelling.

"Screw it, come on!" White took off up the steps, leaving the amateur firefighter on the second floor. He wound around the steps as fast as he could while still maintaining the ability to stop on a dime should he be confronted with a wall of flame. But, although warmer and smokier, there were no actual flames on this floor.

White shook his head at the ridiculousness of this area: the Fitness Complex and Tiki Juice Bar. That's what his investors had wanted him to do with this section. It was nothing but a tiki-themed health bar overlooking the coral reef from thirty feet, the lagoon's surface only a few feet up. Workout while you look down on the reef. A massive tribal tiki statue, carved from a single, massive log, stared down at White with a menacing grin from the ceiling. Plush couches, bean bags, and throw pillows, now soaked, randomly encircled the room.

Now what the hell is everybody screaming about... White walked toward the west edge of the circular room, straining to see outside into the dark water. Most of the tower's external lights had stopped working or had been ripped away altogether. But then he saw one—or a set of them, it looked like—stabbing through the gloomy 3D inner space. Moving, so they couldn't be part of the hotel. He watched as it drew nearer the complex, down one level, but already angled up in a shallow ascent.

The sub. What the Hell was it doing here? Must be that Mick dork who banged every woman on the island looking for Coco, like she was the special one for him or something. Made him want to puke. That reminded him. He scooped up his walkie, and yapped into it for Al.

"Okay, I'm on Floor Three. No fire in here, was just a spot fire on the stairs that we put out. But all the smoke from Floor 2 is rising up here."

His employee's voice came back fast and furious. "Okay, get everybody up there now, James, you got that? Now! We'll start the procedure. It takes a few minutes."

White was about to give a reply when he saw a shape materialize behind the sub that dwarfed the underwater vehicle. Gliding. Menacing.

#

Coco rounded the west tower, cringing as she saw the orange glow still burning in the middle of it. It was still on fire. She looked around for the megalodon, but apparently it was keeping its distance, nowhere to be seen.

Were the people inside on the third floor yet, in the escape pod?

Coco decided that she would both get closer to the tower, as well as ascend to the third floor to get a better look at what was happening inside. She maneuvered the sub accordingly, taking care not to come into contact with the tower's glass wall. She looked inside as long as she dared, and saw a hellish scene of destruction, of flame, cascading water, what looked like a fight in progress...she had to turn away in order to keep the sub following the curvature of the tower.

Time to get a look at the third floor. She didn't see how anything in the hotel could possibly function, but that was the engineers' problem, not hers. She would carry out the plan they had worked out.

So where was the shark? Glancing out to her left, to the edge of the sub's spotlights, she saw only an empty dark void. Without the tower's external lights working, the submersible provided the only light. She looked below, too, to see if the enormous creature was prowling the reef floor, but she saw nothing in that direction either.

As she passed the ceiling of the second floor, she turned her attention back to the inside of the tower. No fire up here. That was good. And no major flooding yet, either. It was definitely wet in there, and getting wetter, but the topside geeks might have a chance after all. Everyone was still down on the second floor, though, she thought, wondering what was taking them so long to get up there. Then she saw movement, and realized she was looking at White. She saw him stop and look in her direction, and he froze, seeming to be transfixed with a look of horrified fascination.

The she saw him raise his arm and point her way. Was he pointing her out to someone she hadn't seen yet? *No, he's pointing at you. Pointing* for *you, for you to see something...*Coco whirled around in the pilot seat.

Thar she blows.

Behind her, level with her at the same depth, came the megalodon.

Game on.

She flicked the halogens off and on at White to let him know she saw him before turning the sub sharply away from the tower. As soon as she straightened out and verified with the compass that she was on a course out to the edge of the reef, she grabbed the radio transmitter.

"Topside, topside, this is *Triton-1*. Target has been engaged. I repeat: target engaged. Heading for the drop-off now. Oh, and I think I just saw Mr. White on the third floor; looks like he's the only one up there so far, looks bad on the second, over."

The reply was immediate. "Copy, that Coco. Good work. The rest of them are trooping up into the pod now. We'll let you know when we launch it, then again when it's been recovered. Good luck down there. Out."

Coco looked back and saw the megalodon trailing the sub, very close behind, almost nose to tail. Good. She hadn't been sure what she would do if it stayed by the hotel. Aggravate it into a chase, she guessed, but it decided to give chase on its own. So far, anyway. It wasn't what she would call an aggressive chase, for a predatory fish. It swam almost lazily. Coco realized that the little sub is so slow and cumbersome in the water compared to a shark, that the megalodon might even find it difficult or uncomfortable to maintain such a slow speed. Perhaps it would become irritated, and swallow her entire sub whole at any moment?

Coco eased the thrusters up to top speed, and left the hotel behind, shooting across the reef to the drop-off.

Chapter 43

Faster. That's what Coco willed the sub to do. When she had to slow down to navigate around a coral formation or stay within a particularly windy stretch of sandy path, the megalodon became more agitated. Once it even nudged the sub, eliciting a yelp from her in the pilot's seat, but then it hung back once she hit a straightaway through the coral and got up to cruising speed again. *This shark wants me to keep moving. It's like it's escorting* me *away from the hotel instead of the other way around.*

Then as she saw the coral growth thin out ever so slightly, and the ocean floor begin to slope downward, another thought struck her. *What if it's just toying with me (with the sub), like a cat with a mouse before going in for the kill?* To her it seemed a very un-shark-like thing to do, but the very existence of this particular shark was unlikely, was it not? It shouldn't even be here at all, much less let her lead it away from the hotel which had captured its interest, and back out to sea.

Every minute that passed by was a minute for the guests to be safely evacuated from the hotel, though, so she kept driving toward the drop-off, a megalodon on her tail. She remembered the GoPro camera she'd mounted behind her seat, facing backwards. Perfect! She'd bought it to mount from the top of the dome, and one of the managers had the idea to sell guests high definition movies of their sub dives, but in the end they decided the camera both invaded privacy and blocked the upward view somewhat, so they had nixed the idea. Not wanting to waste a perfectly good setup, however, Coco had mounted it discreetly behind the pilot seat facing backwards, so that at least it could be used for taking video behind the sub.

She reached back with one arm, and felt for the button she knew powered on the unit. Found it. "Smile Miss Megalodon, get ready to be the next viral video star!"

Then in the radio she heard the engineer's voice at the same time as she saw the sandy cut that dropped off between the two coral shelves up ahead.

"Topside here—Coco, you read?"

"Copy. Almost to the drop-off. The big girl's on my tail, over."

"Be careful, Coco. We've got everybody into the escape pod now, and we're preparing to jettison."

"Pod gonna float this time, I hope?" Coco whipped her head around for a quick glance at the great shark. Still right there, but it paused to lash out at a small school of fish either not wary, or not caring enough, to have detected its presence. Either way, they paid the price as the monster fish decimated their ranks with a single open mouth gulp before falling in line behind the sub once again.

"It should work this time. I'll be back in touch after we jettison it, over and out."

"Copy. Out." Coco let go of the transmitter with an air of finality that said, this is it.

She glided over the sandy entrance to the drop-off, the sub's lights illuminating tracks in the sand that Coco guessed came from the first escape pod tumbling down the slope as it was pushed by the megalodon.

Pushed by the megalodon!

As soon as she had made the connection between the megalodon pushing the pod down through the drop-off, and the fact that the big shark was now right behind her sub, Coco was jolted in her pilot seat, whiplash style.

The massive megalodon had rammed her sub. It was shoving her down the drop-off the way it had done to the escape pod before her. Would she see it down there, the dead people's faces plastered against the windows, waiting for help that would never come in time?

Her nemesis gave her little time to ponder that unpleasant scenario, though, because she saw the colossal snout nose ahead on her side of the bubble cabin, bashing the sub towards the right.

The sandy trail narrowed considerably at the entrance to the canyon proper. So this is what the megalodon's game was, Coco thought. It chases its prey down here, and then beats it up against the sides of the coral passage on the way down the deep sea canyon...where it did who knows what.

Suddenly Coco didn't want to know. Whatever curiosity she once had had been quelled out of her by all of the deaths she'd witnessed. She couldn't take it anymore. The sub couldn't take much more either, she knew, so she got her mind back on task, and focused on driving the craft down the middle of the passage without hitting anything.

At least it was still following her, and closely, too. The gigantic fish barely fit in this narrow upper part of the canyon, yet it wedged and squirmed and wriggled itself down through it faster than the sub could go, bumping into her more often now, and harder, too. Then Coco flew off the cliff-like section that until now she'd seen, but never reached. A glance at the depth gauge showed her 100 feet. She was leaving the shallows. Below her yawned a serious chasm from which there was no outlet other than to come straight back up.

She squinted at the radio display. *Is this thing working?* What the hell was up with the tower escape pod already? She wanted to test the radio by asking the Topside crew what was going on, but the megalodon had other plans. The great fish suddenly took to the midwater, flying above the sub for a few seconds before launching itself back down on top of it.

Coco screamed in surprise and fright when the prehistoric monster's white belly fell across the top of the dome bubble, its contours conforming to those of the sub. Was it keeping her from returning to the surface? Who was really leading who, here? She was no longer sure, but the longer the shark was away from the hotel, the better chance they would have to evacuate those still trapped inside.

Might as well keep following this down...

Coco followed the sandy shelf that constituted the drop-off, to its end. The depth gauge told her she had reached a depth of 200 feet. It was very dark down here. The glow of the sub's instrument console provided the only light. At night she was totally dependent on the sub's lights and instrumentation in order to navigate. Were she to have any kind of equipment failure down here...Coco forced herself not to think about it. *Just get it done.*

She peered over the edge of the drop-off. Below her was sheer deep ocean; just a black void waiting to swallow her whole. She looked up at the megalodon. It was higher up now, apparently losing interest in her. She didn't want to chase it up and down and all over the reef, but it seemed like its curiosity over the sub might be wearing thin. She wished she knew how much more time they needed, but the shark could reach the hotel from here in about three minutes if it really wanted to, so she thought of how to best keep it here.

She tried flashing the sub's lights off and on in rapid succession. It did draw the mighty beast nearer for perhaps a minute, but then it rose even higher than before. Then she tried something else, something that scared her, but she was willing to do it if it worked. She turned the sub's external lights off and kept them off, plunging her into near darkness. Looking up, she couldn't really see the megalodon, but could tell it was moving by the way it became dark and then light again as it traversed across the available moonlight.

The megalodon was coming back down to investigate.

Then the radio burst with chatter, startling Coco from her fish watching. The voice of the engineer filled the cabin.

"Coco, you copy?"

She picked up the transmitter. "I copy, Topside. I'm over the drop-off now, depth 200 feet, with the megalodon in sight, over."

"Be careful, Coco. Is it attacking you?"

"Not yet. A couple of love taps so far, that's about it, over."

She looked up and around for the shark, but couldn't see it now. Consulting her depth gauge, she noted that she had dropped a little, her depth reading 225 feet.

"Good news is we have jettisoned the escape pod with everyone from the tower inside, and it is floating this time."

Coco breathed a sigh of relief. "Is there bad news to go along with the good?"

"Nothing terrible, but the pod ejected a little more forcefully than we anticipated, and as soon as it hit the surface it was already halfway across the reef. We have two boats chasing it down to tow it to shore, with Mick driving one of them, but the wind picked up, and is pushing it pretty good out toward the edge of the reef, over."

Coco felt a chill creep over her as she contemplated the turn of events. When the pod reached the edge of the reef, the megalodon would swim up to investigate it. Perhaps that's what it had already started doing. She flipped on the sub's external lights again.

Damn. The massive fish was even higher up than before, swimming upward in lazy circles. The megalodon seemed to be attracted to movement, or perhaps to the electrical activity that went along with it. She needed to do something to get the shark interested again. The lights were already on again, and that wasn't cutting it. She looked down into the darkness, and then activated the sub's thrusters on high. The whiny revolutions of the electric motors were easily transmitted through the water to the shark's sensory systems.

She craned her neck around, and watched the marine leviathan spiral into a steep dive. It was coming fast. She could level out, but she feared being rammed by the beastly fish at high speed. If she went straight down she would have more time.

She put the *Triton-1* into a deep dive.

Chapter 44

At around three hundred feet down it dawned on Coco that she was in great danger. By descending in a quirky corkscrew pattern and intermittently flashing the sub's lights, she had been able to keep the megalodon's interest. Perhaps a little too well. It was terrifying her now, staying just beyond the reach of the halogen floodlights, and then darting in to press its raggedy mouth up against the smooth bubble dome. Its jaws worked up and down as it attempted to sink its teeth into the smooth, curved surface, like a toddler trying to bite a whole apple.

It couldn't do it, but that didn't make it any less horrifying, watching those bloody gums wipe the sub's dome from mere feet away. She wasn't sure why it wanted to do it, either. It could probably swallow the sub whole. Perhaps it was used to delivering a crushing bite that sapped the lifeblood from its victims to make it easier to swallow, to go down its gullet without a fight.

And then a thought that was most troubling overtook her: what if she had lost radio contact with Topside? Normally the communication system was used from reef-to-shore; she'd never used it from such a significant depth. Still she descended, she noted with a worried glance at the depth gauge.

340 feet...

She scrambled for the radio, but the shark bumped the sub, hard this time, sending it careening to its port side, causing Coco's hand to flip the switch for the sub's grab-arm instead. She heard the mechanistic whirring noise as the arm moved....and then something most unexpected happened.

The end of the arm—now fitted with the acetylene torch, although it was not activated—grazed the megalodon's skin on the underside of the mouth, or its "chin" if it had one. Coco flashed on the possibility that she could turn the torch on to burn the animal, and then just as quickly dismissed the idea. It would simply pull away when it felt the heat—it was not a way to kill it. It might even drive the shark back up to the reef, exactly where she didn't want it to go.

But as she stared out at the primitive creature, expecting for it to bash the sub at any moment with its great head, Coco paused in wonderment. The megalodon was slowly moving so that the grab arm was rubbing under its mouth, and its movements became slower, more lethargic. Coco expected this to be a momentary fluke, but a minute later the shark was still exhibiting the same behavior.

The *behavior*...

That's when it hit her that she had knowledge about this behavior, that she had seen it before, even if only from videos. *What was it called? Something that certain species of sharks did...makes them all sleepy and slow, like they're doped up on something...*

Coco racked her brain while adjusting the position of the manipulator arm when needed to massage the shark and keep it in its low energy state.

Tonic immobility. That's it! She recalled with stunned realization the information on tonic mobility she'd heard in class and in books. Some sharks, when upside-down and stroked in a certain way, became extremely lethargic and enter a semi-inebriated state. In this state, they do not swim or even move much at all; they float, eyes rolled half back in their heads, fins not moving, just hanging there in some kind of oceanic trance.

Exactly what the megalodon was doing now, Coco thought, watching it loll passively at the end of the sub's remote arm. How long would this behavior last? She had no idea, but she made sure the grab-arm was in contact with the snout area, since that's what seemed to send it into its trance-like state.

While she was doing this, the sub and the shark sank together like two oblivious dancers on a dark floor, spotlights providing the only illumination. She eyed the depth gauge again: now passing 400 feet. The little submersible was not rated for the deep sea, and its oxygen and carbon dioxide scrubbing system would not last that much longer. As if to underscore that fact a battery alarm sounded, a buzzing noise that Coco feared would wake the megalodon from its tonic trance.

But she kept falling while the big predator fell limply with her. She shut off the alarm, knowing it did nothing to fix the serious underlying problem: the sub's batteries were running low, and when they ran out, it's thrusters would no longer work, along with the cabin's air circulation system, and carbon dioxide scrubbers.

She needed to begin the long ascent to the surface, or risk losing all power and sinking forever into the void. Yet the megalodon was still very much alive, just in a comatose condition. Was there a way for her to kill it? She tried to think of one but another alarm went off—low oxygen this time—and the huge shark stirred, momentarily coming out of its tonic immobility to right itself. Quickly Coco nudged it with the sub to return it to its upside-down orientation.

It worked; the creature slipped back into its unaware state, sinking with the sub into the deep ocean. This time, she watched it go while retreating in the opposite direction: up.

Chapter 45

Coco didn't know what fate exactly would befall the hapless fish. Would it sink all the way to the bottom—presumably from whence it came to remain undetected for all these years—or would it snap out of it at some point on the way down? She had no idea, but she knew one thing. The lack of oxygen in the sub's cabin was threatening to send her into her own tonic immobility state—and a permanent one, at that— if she didn't do something about it soon. She had done her job, drawing the shark away from the hotel while they activated the escape pod.

It was time for her to get back to the island.

She jettisoned the last of the submersible's ballast—lead weights to help the craft sink—so that it would rise faster. Still, she was concerned. She had no choice but to surface now if she wanted to live. If the megalodon followed her back up, there would be nothing she could do about it.

She pointed the sub up, and just as she hit the thrusters the batteries died, sending the cabin into darkness. But because she had ditched the ballast, the sub was rising. She leaned back and looked up, wondering if she would pass out before she reached the surface.

#

"Well done, Mick!" Albert Johnson clapped Mick on the back as he coasted his small boat up onto the sand and stood next to the escape pod which he had towed here. The pod was open, and the surviving guests and staff, including a dumbfounded-looking James White, stumbled out of it in a daze onto the moonlit beach.

Mick muttered a quick thanks, and looked back out to sea, his gaze tracing the reef line.

"What's the latest you heard from Coco?" he asked the engineer, eyeing the handheld radio clipped to his belt. His expression softened as he answered.

"Last transmission we received from her was about an hour ago. She said she was a couple of hundred feet down where the drop-off becomes sheer, nose-to-nose with the shark."

"What? That's it? No more contact?"

"No more. If she went deeper than that, though, we'd probably lose radio contact, so I'm hoping that's what happened. Because I keep trying..." He picked up the radio, and uttered quick syllables into it..."Coco, Topside, repeat: Coco this is Topside, do you copy, over?" He stared at the radio for a few seconds, and when no reply was forthcoming, he resumed speaking to Mick.

"The other possibility is that maybe she did surface but drifted with the currents..."

But Mick was already running back over to his boat, no longer listening. He pushed the Zodiac into shallow water, and then jumped in and started the outboard. He called into his radio transmitter as he turned the craft around so that it faced out to the reef.

"Coco, this is Mick. I don't know if you can hear me, but I'm taking the boat out to the reef to look for you." He dropped the transmitter, and threw the boat into high gear, jetting out toward the reef, a single bow-mounted light scanning the water as he went.

He passed the hotel, now marked by bits of flotsam and floating debris—and there—a body floating face down in the water. He slowed the boat and maneuvered to it, in case the person might somehow still be alive. But when he reached the form it was clear that this was now a corpse. He grabbed the lifeless human by one arm and flipped the body over. He stared into the slack-skinned face of the Arab who had fought with White in the tower, Abdullah bin Antoun. Mick let the body go, and started the boat again. It was too late for him to help that man. He just hoped it wasn't too late for Coco.

#

Coco found it hard to think straight through the throbbing headache induced by lack of oxygen and buildup of carbon dioxide. The entire sub was electrically dead—she had no power, was rising only because earlier she'd had the foresight to empty the ballast—there was no radio, no depth gauge, nothing. The only thing that gave her hope was that, even at night, she could see the water growing lighter as the craft buoyed up closer to the surface of the moonlit lagoon. Was she almost there? It was too much effort to raise her head to get a good look around...

She started to nod off. Her thoughts came in an incoherent montage of memories...the megalodon drifting into the abyss in its seemingly blissful state of tonic immobility...Mick and Clarissa making out in the sub shack...the faces of the divers from the first pod who had been tossed into Hell...peering inside the tower at James White standing atop a flaming floor...

Time passed, she didn't know how much, but she was shaken from her trance-like state by a change in motion patterns. Rocking, side-to-side. It was a very different feeling from the steady rise the sub had been doing. She forced her eyelids up, and tried to focus.

Water. Moving. Sloshing over the bubble dome. When her vision resolved, it was on a fine spray pattern of water droplets exploding off of the sub's dome. And then the realization of what that meant hit home.

She was on the surface!

But too weak to deal with opening the hatch.

Where was the megalodon?

And then she heard the sound of a boat engine, muted through the sub hatch. The sound stopped, and she saw the bow of a small boat pull up alongside the sub. An inflatable boat.

Mick!

She saw his strong hands unlatching the catches for the dome, and flipping it open. Gloriously cool night air flooded the cabin where she sat, her lungs working furiously to suck in this new source of energy. She heard a voice, as if in a dream calling her name.

"...me, Coco, Mick...Coco? Coco!"

Then she felt a hand on her face, feeling for breath under her nose, in front of her bluish lips.

"Coco! Wake up!"

She focused on his blue eyes, watching them swirl until they solidified into two distinct orbs. Slowly she lifted her head from the seat.

"Mick?" Her voice was faint, tentative.

"Yes! Coco, it's me. Let me get you into the boat. Do you know where the megalodon is?"

She let her head fall back into the seat. "Down...deep. Deep down..."

"Okay, good. We've got the pod up on the beach. Now we've just got to get you up there, and we can call it a day. You with me?"

"Hell yes."

Mick grinned his million-dollar smile at her. "Excellent. On three, here we go..."

He lifted her from the seat, and Coco felt like she was floating up and out of the sub...into the Zodiac where she was gently placed in a horizontal position on the floor, a pile of life jackets for pillows.

"Get the sub." Coco's voice was still very weak, but must have been stronger than before to carry across the air in the open boat. Mick shot her a disapproving look.

"My, we must be feeling better to worry about that old rust bucket." But deep down he understood her reason for wanting to bring it back. She was a professional sub pilot; to come back without her craft would be to her a shortcoming, having achieved her objective on the dive or not.

Quickly, Mick rigged a tow harness from the sub to the boat. While he did he stared out at the water towards the reef, searching for signs of the megalodon, ready to ditch the sub and hightail it in the Zodiac to shore the second he saw anything. He hoped Coco was right and not in a state of total delirium when she had said the shark was down deep. By the time the sub was secured behind the boat, however, he had still not sighted the prehistoric fish.

"Coast is still clear, Coco! I've got the sub. Let's go home."

Mick put the boat into gear, slowly at first, mindful of the sub in tow, but before long they were making steady progress toward the beach, where a large crowd was gathered around the rescued escape pod and its disheveled, raggedy group of survivors.

Chapter 46

After so much time in the sub, alone in the ocean, the scene on the beach seemed like a madhouse to Coco.

She looked at Mick as he helped her from the boat onto the sand. "Where did all these people come from?"

"Reporters flew in from the main island to be here once word got out that the hotel was in trouble. Then, of course, we've got the whole Topside crew who came out of their holes in the wall to check it out, and last, but not least..." Mick raised his voice when he saw that several reporters were closing in on him and Coco with cameras and microphones extended. "...our survivors from the hotel who have you to thank."

Coco rose unsteadily to her feet, and took her first few exploratory steps while still holding Mick's hand. She couldn't help but notice Clarissa standing nearby, watching them with a scowl on her face. Coco couldn't blame her. Her dolphin program was up in smoke along with the hotel, many of her dolphins either dead or missing, the resort itself in shambles. And here was Coco being carried to the beach by her love interest.

But that wasn't Coco's problem. In fact, like Mick had said, she was ready to go home—only for her she really meant *home*, not just back to her *bure* here on the island. She was ready to go back to Hawaii. Back home for real. This place would never be the same for her again. The hotel was done, and she was done with it.

That went for Mick, too. She liked him, had been with him for a time, but he had feelings for another woman, and coming to her aid would not change her mind about that. Just before the reporters began shouting questions at her, she looked into Mick's eyes, and with all the sincerity she could muster, said "Thank you."

And that was that. She had washed her hands of her island romance; wrapped up that piece of her life.

Coco walked among the crowd, looking for Aiden. She couldn't find him anywhere. She found a somber staff member with a list of missing and dead. "Aiden?" she asked, terrified of the reply. The Indian woman ran her pointer finger along a printed list, then shook her head with a heavy expression.

"I'm sorry. He was last seen in the tunnel leading from the main lobby, he has not yet been found."

"Let me see that." Coco grabbed the clipboard, and scanned down the list of missing and deceased. She was saddened to find Kamal's name under those who had passed. She thought of him taking her side in the train control room against Mr. White, and smiled. She scanned the list a bit longer, heart breaking with each of the names on the list as she placed a face to the name, and recalled a memory she had shared with them. But then she was being assailed with questions she could no longer put off. She handed the clipboard back to the woman.

Now it was time to deal with the reporters.

"How long were you down there in the sub for?"

"What happened to the big shark—what's it called?"

Coco took the softball question first. "*Carcharadon megalodon*. A primitive relative of the Great White. Long thought to be extinct, but apparently not!"

To her surprise this got quite a few laughs from the contingent of reporters. It didn't stop the questions from coming, though.

"How long were you trapped in the hotel for?"

"What exactly happened down there in the hotel?"

"What happened to the megalodon?"

Coco was exhausted, and the first two questions didn't have short answers, so she tackled the third. It was also more familiar ground for the marine biologist, since it concerned sharks.

"I lured the megalodon away from the hotel in the submersible..." she pointed to the yellow sub, now being wrangled up onto the sand by hotel staff ...so that the engineering staff could get the escape pod launched without interference."

"So where is the shark now?"

"I took care of it. It's—"

At that moment James White stepped into the circle of reporters, walking over to Coco, a fake smile perched on his lips.

"That's right, folks, our marine biologist took care of our little shark problem, and the Triton Undersea Resort will rise again. We have already initiated the rebuilding plans."

Most of the reporters had a question on their lips, but it was Coco who was the most vocal. "I certainly hope you're kidding, Mr. White. That would be reckless."

White shot Coco the dirtiest of stares for about a microsecond, about as long as he thought it could go unnoticed. "Pardon me? Didn't you just say you took care of the mega-what's it—the one-in-a-million dinosaur shark? It's dead, right? So we won't have to—"

"No, Mr. White. It's not dead. I said I took care of it, I didn't say I killed it."

The developer stood there with his mouth agape for a second too long, and the reporters jumped at the opportunity.

"Where is the shark now?"

"What did you do to it?"

"Is the shark not real—just a ploy to divert attention from operational problems?"

White looked like he was about to have a heart attack. His outburst of *whoa, whoa, whoa*! was ignored in favor of hearing what Coco had to say.

"The shark is very real," Coco said with White nodding enthusiastically in agreement. "But it is also very alive. I baited it into chasing me in the submersible down the submarine canyon to deep waters. Once there, I used the sub's grab-arm to stimulate the shark in such a way that it entered into a condition known by shark experts as *tonic immobility*. This is where a shark is upside-down in the water and becomes very sleepy, sort of like it's drunk."

Amazingly, this was met with complete silence as everyone tried to make sense of this; a few reporters even took notes. Coco was about to continue when White butted in, attempting to hijack the spotlight, and put his own PR spin on the outgoing information.

"So basically the shark was dead as it sank into the depths, meaning that now we can move forward knowing that our beautiful tropical lagoon is once again safe from any threats."

Coco shook her head emphatically. "No, Mr. White. I stand by my professional assessment that the megalodon shark is not dead."

White's carotid bulged as he replied in fury. "You lie! You're just trying to create a sensational story to get your name out there, get your own reality TV show—*Shark Girl*—or some such nonsense!"

The reporters ate it up, alternately zooming in on the incensed hotel developer, and the irritated but more sedate marine biologist. Coco was about to simply refute her boss's allegation when it occurred to her that she could do better than that.

"Don't believe me? Well then, what's the old saying? A picture is worth a thousand words? Here you go..."

She jogged over to the sub, its dome hatch still open while Mick inspected it for damage. She reached in behind the pilot's seat and unsnapped the GoPro video camera from its mount. She withdrew her arm from the sub, holding the little camera high for the crowd to see. To her great satisfaction, White's face paled visibly when he recognized what it was. Coco addressed the reporters, most of whom now had their own cameras focusing in on the GoPro held in her hand.

"Let's see the footage!" a reporter from a New Zealand newspaper shouted, eliciting a chorus of *yeah*s.

Coco asked for a laptop. One was quickly produced, and she connected the video camera to it, transferring its files. She started the video from the last dive with the megalodon, while the news media people crowded around, filming the laptop screen as the video played. White got into a brief shoving match with a cameraman as he fought for a decent vantage point from which to view the footage.

On screen, the yellow frame of the submersible was visible in the foreground while the background was filled with the toothy visage of the planet's greatest predator of all time. The parts of the submersible visible in the foreground gave some scale to the shark. Gasps of wonder and excitement issued from those watching. The shark's head was positioned upside-down relative to the sub.

"Look at it—it's practically dead!" White shouted joyfully.

Coco calmly shook her head. "No, this is textbook tonic immobility." She pointed to a portion of the screen. "Watch here.

See how it rolls its eyes back when the manipulator arm passes over the skin just below the mouth? Then when I take it away its eyes open—watch."

The events unfolded in the video exactly as Coco described, while the reporters murmured amongst themselves in excited tones. Coco resumed her narration.

"This is where I leave the megalodon behind, and it sinks into the deep ocean while I start back to the surface in the sub." The video depicted the living fossil writhing slowly with its eyes closed as it fell into the black abyss, illuminated only by the sub's floodlights. It would fall still for a moment or two, and then come to life with a small burst of muscle activity, wriggling until it found the upside-down orientation again, and settled into a state of torpor.

"And there it goes, this is it..." They all watched as the truck-sized shark began to sink beneath the cone of light.

"It's on the verge of death right there!" White said. "Its eyes aren't open at all. You probably gave it some sort of electrical shock with that thing on the sub." Coco silently shook her head to refute this, while they continued to watch the video.

Soon only the fish's monumental head was visible at the bottom of the lit zone. Just as the megalodon drifted out of the light, both of its eyes opened wide, and with a powerful swish of its massive caudal fin, it turned and swam straight down into the blackness.

"Didn't look dead to me," one reporter said.

"It was alive, at least at the last we saw it on camera," added another.

"Apologies for being late, but I've just flown in from Singapore after hearing the news. Play the video again for me, would you?" The new voice made heads turn as the tall man it belonged to threaded his way through the crowd until he was standing in front of the laptop. Mr. Frederick Cimmaron, James White's boss and the chief bankroller of the Triton Undersea Resort, watched the portion of the video where the megalodon opened its eyes just before it sank into the abyss. He made a spitting noise, and then turned to address White.

"James, we're done here. That thing—and who knows how many others like it—could very well still be alive down there waiting to cause us more grief. Now *you* might be willing to serve up a buffet for these fish, but I'm not. I'm pulling out of the Triton project, James, effective immediately. I expect we'll have lawsuits to deal with as it is—or settlements, as the case may be—and that's fine. I'm not trying to run from anything here. But the project is over. That's my final word on the subject."

White's face turned purple. "That's preposterous! You're going to base the fate of a billion dollar enterprise on the word of this...this...*girl?*"

White's boss did an about-face, and delivered a challenging stare to White. "Her word, her video..." He paused to wave an arm out toward the reef where so much construction debris now lay on the seafloor. "...the death and destruction that occurred here. Face it, Mr. White. This project was too risky. We gambled and lost. Sometimes it happens. For me it's on to the next. For you..."

He left the sentence unfinished as he worked his way back out through the group, the film teams stepping over one another to video him. White watched expectantly, calling out after him.

"For me, what?"

"For you it's over. You'll never work in this business again, Mr. White. Go home. You'll be hearing from my legal team."

White was left there stammering in the old man's wake, while the reporters moved on, turning their attention back to the hero of the day.

"Miss Keahi, Triton's chief investor just said rebuilding the resort is not an option that's on the table, due in large part to information that you yourself provided. What's next for you?"

Coco looked at the throng of reporters on the beach—at Mick, at Clarissa, at the other hotel staff, and back to Mick. She looked him in the eyes while she answered.

"I'm going home."

Epilogue

For Coco Keahi, stepping inside Fiji's International Airport at Nadi, even though by airport standards it was quaint, was like a return to civilization. The packed commercial airliner with its international cross-section of society was even more so. The only flying she'd done in months was aboard scary-small propeller planes that seated six or eight people.

A flight attendant informed them to stow their belongings, and buckle up for take-off. She had the window seat on the right side of the plane, the two seats beside her occupied by honeymooners reviewing their scuba diving pictures. Coco caught a glimpse of the pink soft corals and rainbow-colored walls, and turned away to look out the window instead. She leaned back in her seat as the plane accelerated down the runway, seeming to defy the laws of physics as tons upon tons of metal and fuel and humans were lifted into the sky.

As soon as it was airborne, the aircraft banked into a turn that took it across the ocean and over a smattering of some of Fiji's hundreds of islands. Coco gazed down at the green, mountainous isles as they passed overhead. She recognized a pattern of islands from flying in, and then counted out one...two...three islands more along a semi-colon shaped chain of them. That was the resort atoll, where she'd spent the last several months of her professional career on a failed project.

Well, not really failed for her, she thought, watching the mountainous high point of the island appear closer beneath her. She had done her job, and done it well, as was reflected by the numerous job offers that came her way following the frenzy of media activity in the wake of the hotel disaster. She now had opportunities far and wide, all of them in her chosen field, a couple of them even in Fiji, and for that she was grateful. But after some reflection, she opted for the job that would keep her very close to her beloved Hawaii for a long time—a position working for the State of Hawaii as a full-time shark scientist. She couldn't be happier.

And yet, looking down as the plane began its climb to the cruising altitude at which it would cross the Pacific, she couldn't help but feel so very humbled. There was still so much about the sea she didn't understand; she wondered if she could ever possibly comprehend a meaningful amount about it.

As the plane passed over the island's highest peak, Coco watched a column of smoke waft into the atmosphere. She just barely had time to catch a wisp of orange from a campfire down in the jungle. She couldn't possibly know it, but on the peak of that mountain next to that fire, five elderly men sat and gazed out over the same sea that she did.

Coco stared into the cobalt blue of the open ocean as the jet left Fiji behind and headed northeast toward Honolulu. She thought about the megalodon, even felt sorry for the creature, which had somehow survived millennia longer than it was supposed to, only to have its environment invaded by things it could not hope to understand. It must be a lonely existence. But it was a thought Coco found even more compelling that would drive her career going forward, a thought that fueled her inner spirit...

What else is down there?

THE END

CHECK OUT OTHER GREAT
DEEP SEA THRILLERS

MEGA
by Jake Bible

There is something in the deep. Something large. Something hungry. Something prehistoric.

And Team Grendel must find it, fight it, and kill it.

Kinsey Thorne, the first female US Navy SEAL candidate has hit rock bottom. Having washed out of the Navy, she turned to every drink and drug she could get her hands on. Until her father and cousins, all ex-Navy SEALS themselves, offer her a way back into the life: as part of a private, elite combat Team being put together to find and hunt down an impossible monster in the Indian Ocean. Kinsey has a second chance, but can she live through it?

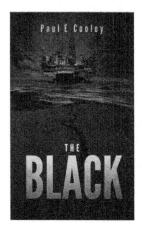

THE BLACK
by Paul E Cooley

Under 30,000 feet of water, the exploration rig Leaguer has discovered an oil field larger than Saudi Arabia, with oil so sweet and pure, nations would go to war for the rights to it. But as the team starts drilling exploration well after exploration well in their race to claim the sweet crude, a deep rumbling beneath the ocean floor shakes them all to their core. Something has been living in the oil and it's about to give birth to the greatest threat humanity has ever seen.

"The Black" is a techno/horror-thriller that puts the horror and action of movies such as Leviathan and The Thing right into readers' hands. Ocean exploration will never be the same."

CHECK OUT OTHER GREAT
DEEP SEA THRILLERS

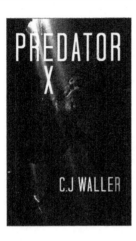

PREDATOR X
by C.J Waller

When deep level oil fracking uncovers a vast subterranean sea, a crack team of cavers and scientists are sent down to investigate. Upon their arrival, they disappear without a trace. A second team, including sedimentologist Dr Megan Stoker, are ordered to seek out Alpha Team and report back their findings. But Alpha team are nowhere to be found – instead, they are faced with something unexpected in the depths. Something ancient. Something huge. Something dangerous. Predator X

DEAD BAIT
by Tim Curran

A husband hell-bent on revenge hunts a Wereshark...A Russian mail order bride with a fishy secret...Crabs with a collective consciousness...A vampire who transforms into a Candiru...Zombie piranha...Bait that will have you crawling out of your skin and more. Drawing on horror, humor with a helping of dark fantasy and a touch of deviance, these 19 contemporary stories pay homage to the monsters that lurk in the murky waters of our imaginations. If you thought it was safe to go back in the water...Think Again!

CHECK OUT OTHER GREAT
DEEP SEA THRILLERS

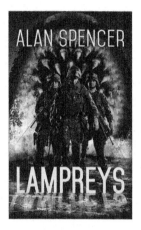

LAMPREYS
by Alan Spencer

A secret government tactical team is sent to perform a clean sweep of a private research installation. Horrible atrocities lurk within the abandoned corridors. Mutated sea creatures with insane killing abilities are waiting to suck the blood and meat from their prey.

Unemployed college professor Conrad Garfield is forced to assist and is soon separated from the team. Alone and afraid, Conrad must use his wits to battle mutated lampreys, infected scientists and go head-to-head with the biggest monstrosity of all.

Can Conrad survive, or will the deadly monsters suck the very life from his body?

DEEP DEVOTION
by M.C. Norris

Rising from the depths, a mind-bending monster unleashes a wave of terror across the American heartland. Kate Browning, a Kansas City EMT confronts her paralyzing fear of water when she traces the source of a deadly parasitic affliction to the Gulf of Mexico. Cooperating with a marine biologist, she travels to Florida in an effort to save the life of one very special patient, but the source of the epidemic happens to be the nest of a terrifying monster, one that last rose from the depths to annihilate the lost continent of Atlantis.

Leviathan, destroyer, devoted lifemate and parent, the abomination is not going to take the extermination of its brood well.

CPSIA information can be obtained at www.ICGtesting.com
Printed in the USA
BVOW06s0632291115

428761BV00010B/134/P